Death Reigns

Mortis Series: Book Nine

J.C. DIEM

Titles by J.C. Diem:

Mortis Series

Death Beckons
Death Embraces
Death Deceives
Death Devours
Death Betrays
Death Banishes
Death Returns
Death Conquers
Death Reigns

Shifter Squad Series

Seven Psychics
Zombie King
Dark Coven
Rogue Wolf
Corpse Thieves
Snake Charmer
Vampire Matriarch
Web Master
Hell Spawn

Hellscourge Series

Road To Hell
To Hell And Back
Hell Bound
Hell Bent
Hell To Pay
Hell Freezes Over
Hell Raiser
Hell Hath No Fury
All Hell Breaks Loose

Fate's Warriors Trilogy

God Of Mischief
God Of Mayhem
God Of Malice

Loki's Exile Series

Exiled
Outcast
Forsaken
Destined

Hunter Elite Series

Hunting The Past
Hunting The Truth
Hunting A Master
Hunting For Death
Hunting A Thief
Hunting A Necromancer
Hunting A Relic
Hunting The Dark
Hunting A Dragon

Half Fae Hunter Series

Dark Moon Rising
Deadly Seduction
Dungeon Trials
Dragon Pledge

Unseelie Queen

Dedication

My thanks go to everyone who stuck with me all the way to the end of this series. Dedicated fans truly are an author's greatest inspiration.

Chapter One

Sitting next to Luc on one of Gregor's comfortable leather couches, I listened in as my friends brainstormed for ideas. We were trying to figure out how to identify the next threat that was lurking on the horizon. We didn't know exactly what it was yet. We only knew that it was some kind of undead creatures that we'd never encountered before.

We'd been discussing the topic for a couple of nights now and hadn't made any real progress. The problem was, we didn't even know which country the threat would originate from, which made our job even harder. *Sitting around waiting for the crap to hit the fan isn't exactly a proactive approach,* I complained to myself.

Geordie agreed with my unspoken thought. "Can't you just teleport to the creepy old monastery so we can put an end to all this before it even starts?" he asked me almost crankily. He hated waiting for action almost as much as I did. Maybe we both had an attention deficit disorder. At the very least, we had short attention spans.

"I would, if I had any idea where the monastery was," I replied. I needed at least some idea of where to search and my dreams had given me very little information to go on. Nothing happened when I tried to zap myself to a random monastery that could be almost anywhere in the world. I'd tried more than once and had failed each time.

"I fear we will not be able to act until these creatures make themselves known," Gregor said.

As was usually the case, my close friends, Danton, two of my soldiers and I had gathered in Gregor's library. It was less formal than the elegant sitting room and had the added bonus of having far more comfortable furniture. The delicate couch that usually sat next to the fireplace had been carried over to offer more seating around the large coffee table

Gregor had just finished grilling me on every detail that I could remember about my dreams. Again, I'd described what I remembered about the monastery and the hideous creatures that I'd briefly encountered within the underground area. Sadly, I hadn't been able to tell him much that would help us to narrow down our search.

As the master of the mansion that we were currently residing in, Gregor had graciously allowed my nearly two hundred fledglings to bunk down wherever they could find a space that would hold them. Frankly, it was getting a bit squishy with all of us living in the one house, even one that was three stories high.

Luc almost seemed to pluck the thought from my head. "Until the threat rises, perhaps we should split our forces in two. Natalie and I could utilize Isabella's estate until we are called to action."

Geordie eyed my beloved peevishly. "You two just want somewhere private where you can share your flesh hunger without all of us listening in." His thin arms were crossed over his chest and he was on the verge of pouting. Only fifteen mortal years old when he'd been turned into a vampire, he could still act childishly at times. He was jealous of Luc, but not for the reasons he'd once been. While the teen loved me, he no longer believed that he was in love with me. Now he just craved what Luc and I had, a closeness that would last for eternity and perhaps even beyond.

Luc inclined his head in response. "That is one reason, but we cannot continue to feed so many vampires from one small town each night." Gregor's mansion was in the south of France on a sprawling property that was almost rural. The closest large city was hours away by car. We hadn't strayed very far from the grounds so far, expecting the latest drama to unfold at any moment.

My number one minion spoke up. "Besides, they won't be alone. *We'll* still be able to hear Natalie and Lucentio when they get naked together," Higgins said dryly. Sergeant Wesley smirked slightly and nodded in silent agreement.

Higgins was the first human that I'd turned into one of my undead soldiers. He'd taken it upon himself to always be around just in case I needed his help. Both men were lounging on chairs nearby. They were close enough to leap to our defence, but not close enough to be intrusive.

Sergeant Wesley, my unofficial third in command schooled his face to neutrality when I narrowed my eyes at him. Both soldiers had once been fairly ordinary in looks. They'd become far more handsome with their quasi-deaths and had attained the dark magnetism that drew mortals to our kind so easily. Higgins was medium height and build with brown hair and eyes. Both his and Wesley's pupils were far larger than normal now that they were undead. Wesley was shorter, with wide shoulders and sandy coloured hair.

Both men had once been normal American soldiers before I'd bamboozled them and their comrades into becoming my puppets. They'd aided me to murder not just their president, but also a bunch of officials and diplomats. They'd been incarcerated after that little fiasco and had been destined to rot in prison for the rest of their lives. I'd rescued them from that fate. I'd then offered them a choice of becoming the undead and of joining our team. Most had agreed and they'd been instrumental in helping us deal with the alien octosquids that we'd only recently vanquished.

"I would like to join you at Isabella's estate," Ishida said, drawing me back to the conversation again.

Isabella had died at the hands of my imposter back when Luc and I had discovered that I was the dreaded Mortis. Ishida had hatched a devious plan to eradicate the European Vampire Council by creating a false Mortis. Ishida had chosen a girl when she was barely a toddler and had begun brainwashing her from an early age. Crude crosses had been burned onto her palms and she'd received the finest training in both weapons and hand to hand combat. Her mind had become twisted when she'd been turned by Ishida himself once she'd become an adult.

It had taken decades of training before he'd deemed her to be ready to undertake her mission. She'd genuinely believed that she was Mortis, scourge of the vampire race and doom to our kind by then. He'd sent her after the nine European Council members with the hope that she'd be able to kill them all and to cause disruption within their ranks.

It had been a good plan, but there could be only one Mortis and she was me, or maybe I was her. I often grew confused when I tried to use the correct terminology.

Being confronted by the real Mortis had broken the imposter's already fragile hold on her sanity. I believed she'd actually been glad when I'd killed her and had put her out of her torment. Then again, maybe I was just trying to assuage my guilt. She'd only been following her master's orders, after all.

I hadn't been able to stop the imposter from cutting down several of the more ancient vampires, but I'd saved the Council from certain death. Looking back now, it was fairly ironic that I'd rescued them from the anti-me, since I'd ended up killing most of them anyway. They'd been fated for death from the moment that I'd been turned and nothing could have saved them.

These thoughts flitted through my mind at the speed of light and I didn't give my sense of irony away. "You're welcome to join us, Ishida," I said.

"What about me?" Geordie asked almost belligerently. He'd become more and more petulant the longer we sat around waiting for something to happen. His childish behaviour was beginning to grate on everyone's nerves, including mine.

"I will be staying here," Igor said with a frown at his apprentice's peevish tone. "You may choose whether you wish to go with Natalie and Lucentio, or if you wish to stay here."

The teen was torn between his loyalty to the man who had been his second father for the past two hundred years and his affection for me. I didn't flatter myself that he thought of me as a mother figure. I was more like an annoying big sister that he counted on to protect him from bullies.

"You can always alternate between the two properties," Gregor offered. "I have several cars that you may choose from, if you wish to borrow one."

Nodding his acceptance of the offer, Geordie subsided into a sulky silence. Igor shook his head, baffled by the adolescent's attitude. One of the things I liked the most about Igor was his practicality. Unfortunately, he didn't understand Geordie sometimes and now was one of those times. The kid was lonely and craved companionship of a female nature. Igor had suppressed his needs for so long now that I wasn't sure he even felt them anymore.

Kokoro, Ishida's maker and former oracle of the Japanese vampire nation, was close to dry sobbing at the thought of being separated from the teen. She'd turned Ishida when he'd been twelve and had been dying from a fever. Her visions had told her to save him and she'd become his guardian and secret master. She'd only recently discovered that he'd known that she was his maker all throughout the ten thousand years that he'd ruled their small empire.

Gregor slid his arm around her shoulder and pulled her to his side. The pair had bonded on the alien planet of

Viltar and their love seemed to deepen every day. *Watch over Ishida for me,* Kokoro thought at me and I nodded. I'd grown used to being able to read the minds of pretty well every being on the planet, but I tried not to pry into the thoughts of my close friends and acquaintances on purpose.

"I would also like to accompany you," Danton requested formally. He might be wearing dark brown trousers and a long-sleeved white shirt instead of a tattered robe, but the fringe of white hair that circled his otherwise bald head still gave him a monk-like appearance. Former protector of the Romanian prophet who had foreseen my arrival, he'd taken it upon himself to chronicle my life as Mortis. I still wasn't comfortable with the idea of having my every thought and deed written down, but I'd resigned myself to the inevitability of it.

"Great, that'll give me a chance to read through what you've typed up so far," I said with false enthusiasm. I'd caught a few glimpses of his manuscript and it was written in Latin, which wouldn't be a problem for me to decipher. One of the first talents that had set me apart from the rest of my kin was my ability to understand and read foreign languages. That talent had been boosted somewhere along the way. I could now speak all foreign, and apparently alien, languages.

"It will be dawn soon," Gregor reminded us all, not that we really needed it. As creatures of the night, we were well attuned to the sun. "I suggest you split your men into two teams and transport them to Isabella's estate so they can become familiar with their new home."

It wouldn't really be our home. It would be just another temporary dwelling that we would utilize out of sheer necessity. Shortly before he'd been murdered, the prophet had warned me to be vigilant and to keep a watch over my home. He seemed to imply that if my vigilance slipped, the human race would once again come under the threat of decimation.

Keeping his warning to heart, I periodically swept my senses out worldwide, trying to pick up on any new dangers that might have risen. Apart from the dozen ex-courtiers who were still in China and a few random vampires spread throughout Europe, the planet was devoid of the undead. At least as far as I could tell.

Strangely, I hadn't been able to sense the undead creatures in my dream, not even when one had been towering over me. Not all of my dreams came true down to the finest detail, but I was beginning to worry that this particular detail might be accurate. If these new unliving monsters were undetectable from my supernatural radar, then we would be in serious trouble.

Chapter Two

We were used to facing down one danger after the other by now and it was almost boring waiting for something to happen. Two more weeks went by and there were still no reports of unusual activities anywhere in the world.

Geordie had taken Gregor up on his offer to borrow one of his cars. He alternated between Gregor's and Isabella's estates. He stayed at each mansion for two or three nights before taking the one hour trip back again. I felt a bit like a parent that had joint custody of their unruly child. Usually, the teen was fun to be around, but his surly attitude was becoming harder and harder to put up with.

I'd expected Geordie to show up a couple of nights ago, but he hadn't arrived yet. He'd been increasingly discontent lately and had started an argument with Ishida over a computer game that he was particularly bad at playing. They hadn't resolved their issue yet and I assumed he was sulking. The problem didn't stem from Ishida's far superior gaming skills. Being continually exposed to Luc's and my happiness was like a stick poking Geordie in the eye. Kokoro and Gregor were just as bad to be around for the lonely adolescent.

"You're worried about Geordie, aren't you?" Luc asked. He had an uncanny knack of knowing what was on my mind, which was weird because I was the one who was supposed to be able to read thoughts.

I sat beside him on a rose coloured antique couch, staring blankly at the TV. Isabella's mansion was far more girly than Gregor's and pink tones could be found in every room. We'd chosen to sleep in one of the guest rooms due to the overwhelming pinkness of her bedroom. Besides, the ancient vampire had been murdered in her bed and I just couldn't stand the thought of sleeping in her room. We'd had to replace the mattress and bedding so the room could be used by my soldiers.

At a casual glance, Luc and I appeared to be just a normal couple. On closer inspection, we both had an unnatural beauty. My beloved had short black hair, a perfect face and an equally appealing body. He was six feet tall, which was almost too tall for my average five feet four inches.

I'd been fairly ordinary before I'd become the undead, now I was almost as attractive as Luc. Only my hair had remained the same, dark brown with blonde highlights and a tendency to curl if I didn't blow dry it straight.

Sadly for Geordie, he and I were the same height and roughly the same size. We were both a little too thin, but neither of us would ever be able to put on weight. That was one bonus of being a vampire. I'd never have to worry about aging, catching diseases, or having to watch my weight. Then again, how fat could you get on a steady diet of nothing but blood?

Thinking about how unhappy Geordie had been lately, I belatedly nodded. "I don't know what I can do to help him."

"I don't think you can help him this time. He might be fifteen years old in body, but he is over two centuries old in reality," Luc said. "He is mature enough to make his own decisions."

"You don't think he's going to leave us, do you?" I asked softly. I hated the idea that Geordie might one day want to strike out on his own, even if I did understand his need for independence. I'd lived on my own for a long time before my life had been drained out of me by my maker. After Luc had found me and had taken me under his wing, it had taken me a long time to get used to being around other people again. Now, I couldn't imagine spending my life alone.

Luc smiled and my heart tried to stutter in my chest at his sheer beauty. "I do not think he will be able to leave you forever."

I acknowledged the fact that Geordie loved me more than everyone, except for Igor, with a nod. A second later, I winced as a mental shout from the adolescent almost blasted a hole through my brain. *Speak of the devil.*

Chérie, help! I caught a confusing series of images of Geordie running through some trees while holding onto a struggling form. He whipped his head around to peer over his shoulder and I saw dozens of humans chasing after him. Some carried flaming torches, reminding me of old black and white movies of a crazed mob on the hunt for monsters. Others held pitchforks, machetes and guns to back up the impression. He should have been able to easily outrun the pursuing humans, but was being slowed down by whoever he was holding onto so tightly.

Luc tensed beside me, accurately assuming that all was not well. "What is wrong?"

"Geordie is in trouble." I didn't elaborate because I had a feeling the teen didn't have the time for me to explain the situation. I didn't know what trouble he'd managed to get himself into, but it had looked dire.

Offering me his hand, Luc drew me to my feet. He'd told me on more than one occasion that he would go wherever I did and I didn't leave him behind this time. In the blink of an eye, we left the comfort of the mansion behind and appeared in a clearing in a forest.

Black eyes wide with fright, Geordie almost ran straight into us. His expression of relief was almost comical when he realized that the cavalry had arrived. "Quickly, you have to get us out of here," he said and looked back over his shoulder again. "The townspeople are right behind us."

Fighting to free herself, a young woman was caught in his grip. She was tiny and frail looking. If I wasn't mistaken, she was also a fledgling vampire. The blood on her face and hands was a dead giveaway, no pun intended.

"I am not sure that it was wise to make a servant when we do not yet know how our blood has been altered by the Viltaran nanobots," Luc said gravely.

Easily holding the thrashing girl, Geordie looked unaccustomedly mature as he replied. "I did not have a choice. If I hadn't turned her, she'd be dead."

It was on the tip of my tongue to point out that, technically, she *was* dead now. Sort of, anyway. For once, I resisted the urge to voice my sarcasm. Now wasn't the time for jokes.

Moving far more quickly than I'd expected, the villagers spotted us through the thin screen of trees. "There they are!" a woman screamed. "Kill the monsters who murdered my children!" In her late twenties or early thirties, she was dressed in nightclothes and was barefoot. Her feet were torn and bleeding, yet she didn't seem to feel the pain. Her grief at losing her children had transcended all other sensation.

I whisked us all away before the humans could fire their weapons. With Geordie so rattled, I opted to take him straight to Igor rather than back to Isabela's estate. The Russian would know how to calm the teen down. At least, I hoped he would, because I sure as hell had no idea what to do. I'd been placed in many strange and dangerous situations during my life as the undead, but this was a new one.

Igor started when we appeared right in front of him. He was in the garage working on one of Gregor's cars. The garage was the place where he felt the most comfortable. A man of simple tastes, he actually preferred his bare cell beneath the catacombs of the now demolished Court mansion to living in opulence. Then again, he was old enough to have been a caveman once upon a time. Even a crappy cell probably seemed like luxury to him.

Taking in the struggling fledgling held in his apprentice's arms, he didn't waste time in berating Geordie for the problem that he'd created. "I take it the girl is your servant?" he asked calmly.

"Yes," the teen said bleakly. "I did not expect her to rise so soon. I have only bled her and fed her twice. She should not have turned until tomorrow night."

Luc and I exchanged a glance. That answered the question of whether their blood had changed or not. It seemed that their servants didn't take as long to change as a normal vampire's.

"What happened, Geordie?" I asked. Not wanting to exacerbate the already tense situation, I copied Igor and kept my tone calm. Geordie had a healthy dose of empathic abilities and he'd be able to sense it if we grew angry with him.

"She escaped from the cellar of an abandoned house where I'd locked her and went to the nearest house and drained three children dry. Their mother witnessed her last child's death and called on her neighbours to hunt the girl down." Guilt warred with his worry. He had created the fledgling and he was ultimately responsible for the children's deaths. Being a vampire didn't mean that we lost the ability to care. He felt pity for the humans and would never have purposefully caused the children any harm.

The girl in question moaned pitifully. A true fledgling vampire, she hungered for blood above all else. It was her nature to hunt and feed. I was once again very glad that my own army of soldiers had been spared from this mindless craving. I tried to read her thoughts, but they were a twisted jumble of confusing images.

"Where were you when we rescued you?" Luc asked.

I had the sense that Geordie hadn't gotten very far from the house where his servant had had her first meal before he'd called for me. "We were roughly halfway between the two estates," Geordie replied. He sent a look of compassion and tenderness at the girl when she attempted to tug herself free.

"Do the humans know what she is?" Igor asked.

"They know," his apprentice replied. "There is no way they couldn't know after the mother saw her fangs buried in her child's throat." Geordie's memories told me that he'd arrived in time to witness the death of the youngest child through the bedroom window. His newly made servant had worn an expression of bliss as she'd fed. Two small bodies had been crumpled on the floor at her feet. Hearing the mother arrive, she'd whirled around, still feeding from the child that was little more than a baby.

Geordie had dived through the window to stop his underling from attacking the mother as the first screams had pealed out. She'd bellowed for her neighbours, who had reacted quickly. Geordie had fled, but the humans had been hot on their trail. "I have put us all in danger," he realized and turned a stricken gaze on me.

Chapter Three

I'd promised Geordie that I wouldn't deliberately read his mind, but it was difficult not to give into the temptation to now. He would tell us his story of why he'd turned the girl when we were all gathered together. "We'd better let Gregor know about this," I said and put a hand on the teen's shoulder.

The fledgling turned and snapped her bloody fangs at me. Even with her eyes rolling wildly and her face a mask of fresh blood, she was delicately pretty. Her eyes would eventually turn as black as mine, but for now they retained an edge of light brown that was almost gold.

"What is her name?" Igor asked. As I'd hoped, he was being gentle with Geordie. He knew when to be supportive and when to give the adolescent a well-deserved slap up the back of his head.

"I don't know," Geordie said. "It all happened so fast, we didn't exactly get a chance to talk first."

Reaching out with my mind, I located Gregor and Kokoro and also sought out Ishida and Danton. I snared them all in my mental net and they appeared in the garage at the same time. Each was equally surprised at being suddenly transported to a new location. Gregor and Kokoro were in mid-embrace, but thankfully they were clothed.

Turning, Gregor straightened his tweed jacket, attempting to pretend that he hadn't just been kissing his ladylove passionately. He saw the bloodstained fledgling and came to the correct conclusion that we were in trouble. "Are we in direct danger?" he asked me.

Knowing what he wanted me to do, I sent out my consciousness and honed in on the furious and frightened posse. Insane with sorrow, the mother of the three dead children urged her neighbours to continue the hunt. Their numbers had grown to nearly a hundred now as more of the people in the nearby town were roused from their beds and joined the hunt.

They planned to search every house, barn and building in the area. It would take hours for them to reach Gregor's property on foot, but they'd eventually stumble across us. I wanted to be long gone before that happened.

Casting a look at Geordie, I didn't want to add to his guilt, but honesty was called for. "They're not going to stop until they find us and get their revenge."

It would have been easy enough for me to reach out and wipe their minds of any memory of what had happened. In this instance, it would be a useless venture. The kids would still be dead and any doctor with decent training would recognize what had caused their blood loss. A mature vamp's bite tended to heal quickly, but they still left a small mark behind. A newly risen blood sucker tended to mangle the throats of their victims. Wounds that severe didn't heal if the blood donor became a corpse.

The teen's narrow shoulders slumped and he had to tighten his grip on his minion as she nearly pulled free. "I never meant for my servant to kill anyone and to bring us to the notice of humans. If you wish for me to leave, I will understand." He dropped his eyes to the floor as he waited for Gregor to order him off his property.

"Don't be ridiculous," Gregor said briskly. "You are family, Geordie, and we don't abandon our family."

Gratitude shone from the teen briefly then it was overshadowed by his guilt and worry. I would have hugged him, but I was pretty sure his freshly minted lackey would try to bite my face off. She wouldn't attack me because she was hungry, but because she was demented. From the little that I'd glimpsed inside her mind, she'd been mentally damaged even before she'd become one of us. Under normal circumstances, I'd have put the fledgling down like a rabid dog. Since she was Geordie's first servant, I didn't have it in my heart to kill her. At least not right in front of him.

Igor caught my eye and shook his head slightly. He knew me well enough to know what was on my mind. My purpose was to kill anything that threatened humanity and this girl had already mauled three kids to death.

"I suggest we each pack a few changes of clothes and move to a safer location until the danger dies down," Gregor said.

"Are we going to have to return to the catacombs?" Ishida asked. His distaste at the idea came through loud and clear. Unlike Igor, he was used to opulence and wasn't fond of the idea of slumming it indefinitely.

I couldn't picture the former emperor sleeping on a pallet on the dirt floor of the servants' quarters of the catacombs at all. I'd spent a few months shacked up in a musty old mausoleum and knew first-hand how uncomfortable lying on the ground was. As unpleasant as it was, even my temporary home had been roomier than the cells in the catacombs.

"I know of a place that will be far more comfortable and will be safe for all of us to use as our base," Luc said to the surprise of us all.

Intrigued, I didn't ask questions despite the fact that it would be my job to shift us all to this mysterious new location. Leaving the others behind to pack, I whisked Luc, Ishida and Danton back to Isabella's estate.

Higgins and Wesley were waiting for us in the parlour. I sensed their relief and anxiety when we returned. "Has something happened?" the corporal asked.

Perched on the edge of a delicate rose patterned chair, he looked out of place in the very girly room. A portrait of a beautiful woman hung over the fireplace. Her beauty was spoiled slightly by her stern expression and black hair that had been pulled back into a severe bun.

It was a portrait of Isabella herself and had been painted several hundred years ago, back when stiff, ruffled collars up to the chin had been in fashion. Her dress was dark grey with gold thread and looked about as comfortable as wearing a scratchy potato sack. She seemed to stare down at us with disapproval for invading her home.

"There was an accident," I told my soldier without going into detail. "The humans know we're here and they've formed a posse. Get the men to pack their gear. We're leaving in ten minutes."

That should be more than enough time for them to gather their belongings. My soldiers were nothing if not efficient.

My men had gathered outside well before their time limit was up. Too disciplined to ask questions, they were armed and ready to defend themselves. We'd stolen a plethora of weapons and ammunition from the Brits during our battle with the octosquids. We had no intention of handing them back. I considered the equipment to be payment for saving the entire population of the Earth from being eaten. It was the very least the flesh bags could do for us.

"We're ready, ma'am," Higgins said.

"Let's go," I responded and snared them all in my mental clutches. It was no longer necessary for everyone to be touching for me to teleport us all back to Gregor's estate. Like most of my weird and whacky talents, I'd learned how to teleport more by accident than on purpose.

We arrived just as Gregor was locking the door of his mansion. Knowing him, he'd already arranged for both his and Isabella's properties to be managed by the same business that he'd used when we'd been sent on an unplanned vacation to Viltar. Hopefully, when they didn't find any monsters in either of the estates, the posse would leave without burning the buildings to the ground. We'd left no evidence of our true natures behind to damn us. We preferred fresh blood and there were no bags of the precious liquid stored in the fridge. The fridge and cupboards were bare and the kitchen had never been used. It was just for show, in case humans ever came to call.

Everyone was ready to go, so I cocked an eyebrow at Luc. "Picture where you want me to take us and I'll zap us there."

Visibly bracing himself, a picture flooded into his mind. The image that came to him was a beautiful valley and a sprawling stone manor and barn that looked archaic to me. Unexpectedly, soft afternoon light bathed the grey stone walls of the building. A small vineyard lay to each side of the dwelling. It was a peaceful scene and I knew that it came from Luc's distant past, way back when he'd still been able to walk in the sunlight without bursting into flames.

Keeping the image in my mind, I willed our small army to appear in a field near one of the vineyards. Gone was the ancient stone manor and in its place was a far more modern mansion. Made of brick, it was three-stories high and had a terracotta coloured roof and white render on the walls. I didn't know much about Italian architecture and had no idea if this was a typical dwelling or not. The vineyards had multiplied into over a dozen and were spread out over several acres. New buildings had been erected on the property, including a far larger barn than the rickety old one from Luc's memory.

Beholding a scene that he hadn't laid eyes on in over seven hundred years, Luc struggled to contain his emotions. He'd been something of a wastrel when he'd been a youth and he hadn't exactly been a model son to his parents. Despite that, he'd loved his family dearly and he still missed them after all this time.

"How it has changed," he said softly. I slid my hand into his and he sent me a wistful smile. He wished he could go back in time and see his parents one last time before the Comtesse had stolen him away and had turned him into her sex slave. I squeezed his hand, offering him my silent condolences. *I wish I'd made that bitch suffer more before I'd killed her.* Luc's master hadn't died painlessly, yet I was sure I could have caused her far more agony than she'd felt before I'd ended her lengthy existence.

"Where are we?" Geordie asked. His servant's thirst for blood hadn't slackened at all. Sensing food nearby, she lunged forward, but couldn't break free from her master's grip. His vampirism gave him far greater strength than his slight frame suggested. No mere human would ever be able to beat him in an arm wrestling match, no matter how big their muscles were.

"We're at my ancestral home," my beloved said to the astonishment of everyone, but me. While he was skilled at shielding most of his thoughts from me, some of them still leaked through. Strong emotions were the hardest of all to hide. I was pretty sure this wasn't the first time he'd had to flee from an angry mob of humans, but I doubted he'd ever expected to return to his home under quite these circumstances.

"Why did you bring us here?" Ishida asked as he appraised the vineyards and buildings.

"Because I own this property and the surrounding lands."

I was as surprised as the rest of our group at that. Luc had managed to hide that knowledge from me easily enough. He was used to guarding his expressions, thoughts and emotions from his maker and it was habit by now.

"How long have you owned this place?" My astonishment was reflected in my tone.

"I kept track of my family as the centuries passed. As you can see, they prospered. They bought more land and became very wealthy. Then disaster struck around thirty years ago and they lost everything. I could not bear for the land to pass onto someone else, so I arranged to buy it. I offered to let the owners stay on if they wished. Some accepted my offer." That meant that some of the humans who worked in the vineyards were his flesh and blood kin.

"Did the Comtesse know that you bought this land?" Igor asked.

Luc shook his head. "She did not know that I had slowly amassed a fortune of my own. I hoped to one day distance myself from the Court forever and to move back to the home of my birth." I caught a glimpse of him squirrelling money away and investing it wisely. He owned property all around the world. He clamped down on his thoughts, shutting me out before I could see exactly how much his empire was worth.

"It is a large mansion, but I do not think that there will be enough room to accommodate us all," Gregor said doubtfully as he eyed the main building.

Luc sent Gregor a reassuring smile. "There is suitable accommodation nearby, old friend. If you will wait for a moment, I will advise the staff that we have arrived. We would not want the humans to become alarmed at our sudden appearance and to alert the authorities."

Chapter Four

Luc held his hand out to me and I took it. It was far quicker just to teleport us to the front door of the expansive mansion than to walk the distance. Footsteps hurried towards us when Luc knocked. A woman in her fifties opened the door and stared at us in surprise. Despite the deep lines at the corners of her eyes and the silver streaks in her black hair, she was still quite attractive. I could definitely see something of Luc in her features. He'd been a night person for so long that his naturally olive skin was far paler than hers.

"May I help you?" she asked.

"I am Lucentio Black," Luc told her and her jaw sagged open in shock.

"Mr Black, this is an unexpected surprise!" she sputtered. It took her a few moments to collect herself. "I am Maria, the caretaker of the property." She offered him her hand and her shock became calm acceptance as Luc's hypnotism settled over her.

"My wife and I will be taking up residence in the overseer's house," he told her.

It was lucky he'd bamboozled the human, because I couldn't hide my surprise at the title he'd just lumped on me. A small part of me was thrilled at the thought of being his wife, but a far larger part was terrified at the idea of being married. I'd never been in a relationship that had lasted for more than a few months before I'd met Luc. Somehow, the possibility that I'd ever end up married had seemed very remote even before I'd become the undead.

"We have brought some guests along and they will be residing in the village," Luc continued. "Please ensure that none of us are disturbed. I will advise you if we require any assistance. Oh, I will require the keys to all of the houses," he added almost as an afterthought.

Slightly taken aback by his request even beneath the hypnotism, Maria nodded and motioned for us to wait as she traversed the long hallway. The floors were polished wood that had been stained dark brown. The walls had been painted light green and colourful paintings hung on both sides. Most were of wine bottles, grapes and other vineyard themes. A side table held a bright vase filled with red roses that I could smell from twenty feet away.

Maria returned a few minutes later holding a small wooden box. It looked several decades old and the picture of a vineyard had been hand carved onto the lid. Luc smiled in appreciation of the workmanship and Maria's spirits lifted. She'd had a feeling the boss she'd known about, but had never met would like the box. Her father had made it for her when she'd been a child. None of her children or grandchildren had been interested in taking ownership of it. It seemed fitting for her to hand it over to this man. She'd never know it, but she was one of his relatives who had decided to stay on after he'd bought the property.

"Here are the keys," she said as she handed the box to Luc. "Each one is tagged with the house number. I've arranged for the electricity and water to be turned on and I would just like to welcome you and your beautiful wife to the estate, Mr Black," Maria said formally. "I hope you both enjoy your stay here." Her smile was open and friendly. "May I ask your wife's name?"

"I'm Nat," I said before Luc could respond. She stiffened and gave me a pitying smile. *Oh, Lord, how awful of her parents to name her after an insect,* she thought. "It's short for Natalie," I said sourly and her smile brightened. *Her accent sounds Australian, that would explain the strange nickname, I suppose.*

Luc's shoulders moved in silent mirth as he tried not to laugh out loud. He knew I'd read her mind and had picked up on her incorrect conclusion that my name was Gnat. It was far from the first time that this had happened, but I sincerely hoped that it would be the last.

"What a lovely name for a lovely young woman," she said with a slightly embarrassed smile. She had no way of knowing that I'd plucked her pitying thought from her mind, yet she was mortified anyway. "Please, let me know if you need anything at all."

"We will, Maria. Thank you," Luc offered her a courtly bow and she blushed. She was probably something like his far distant niece, but she was still human and he was a gorgeous man. Who could blame her for getting hot under the collar?

I felt her watching us as we turned to walk away. I waited for the door to close before zapping us back to the others. Most of our team eyed the box in Luc's hand, but I shifted us before anyone could start asking questions. While Luc hadn't seen the village with his own eyes, he'd seen photos of it, so I had something to lock onto.

We appeared in the middle of a dirt street a couple of miles away from the main house. It was lined with around a hundred small, neat wooden two-story houses. They looked roughly the same, with only the colour of the roofs, doors and trim varying. The houses were dark and empty, but looked as though they'd been well maintained. The street sign was rusty and leaned precariously. I read the words 'Ferrenzi Lane' and deduced that that was Luc's real surname.

Opening the box, Luc plucked out a key then offered the container to Gregor. "There should be enough houses for us all, if we pair up." Gregor took a key and the box was quickly handed out to everyone. I made sure to retrieve the box and reminded myself to tell Luc of its significance later.

"What is this place?" Ishida asked curiously.

"This village was built for the staff and their families to live in fifty years ago," Luc replied. "They were responsible for working on over twenty vineyards in the area. When the business went bankrupt, most of the staff was laid off. When I bought the property, I began to re-employ people and to buy back the vineyards and properties that were sold. With modern transportation and a large city less than an hour away, most of my employees preferred to commute to work rather than to live here. I ensured that the village was maintained more out of habit than out of any particular need for it."

"Or because you were directed to by unseen forces," Gregor said shrewdly.

"You mean by Fate," I surmised. Her influence was even more insidious than I'd realized if she'd set all this up decades in advance.

He nodded and glanced at Geordie and the ravenous fledgling held in his grip. "Speaking of Fate, we should discuss this new development."

Luc pointed to the lone house that stood on a small hill nearby. It overlooked the village and must have belonged to the overseer that he'd mentioned to Maria. "Perhaps we should hold our discussion up there."

Turning to my men, I signalled for Higgins and Wesley to accompany us. "The rest of you, make yourselves comfortable in your new homes," I instructed my soldiers.

"Are we going to be able to feed tonight?" Charlie asked. A redhead with bright orange freckles on his less-than-handsome face, he was one of Higgins' close friends. Not all vampires attained good looks upon their creation. Some developed other talents. Whatever Charlie's talent was, it hadn't made itself known yet.

"If we'd brought my car along, they could have taken turns driving into the city," Igor said with a hint of wistfulness. He'd never admit it out loud, but he loved that car. Large and black, it was old, but he kept it in immaculate condition. I wasn't sure what make or model it was, but it was a muscle car and most men seemed to admire it.

Having transportation other than me was a good idea and it was one that I could make possible without too much trouble. Reaching out with my mind, I pictured Igor's car and willed it to appear on the street. Several of my undead soldiers made exclamations of surprise at its sudden arrival. Being able to call inanimate objects to me was a skill that I'd only very recently learned. We were all still getting used to it.

Remaining stoic and unimpressed, Igor held out his hand. "The keys would be useful." A second later, his keys lay on his palm. Tossing them to Charlie, Igor gave the soldier a stern frown. "Make sure that no harm comes to my vehicle."

Charlie snapped the Russian a salute that was only half-mocking. My men all respected the older vampires. The ones who were smart feared them to some extent. "I'll keep her safe, sir," Charlie promised.

"Do you want me to retrieve any of your cars?" I asked Gregor.

"They would probably come in handy," he replied. "Can you bring all eight of them to us?"

It was couched as a question, but he had supreme confidence in my abilities and with good reason. In quick succession, eight cars appeared and eight sets of keys came with them. The last car to appear drew Igor's attention and he crossed to it with a frown. He hunkered down to inspect a large dent in the grill. The hood was also dented and the windscreen had been smashed. Dried blood was smeared on all three of the damaged areas.

Igor stood and turned to his apprentice expectantly. "Isn't this the car that you took to Isabella's estate two nights ago?"

I had my suspicions about what had caused the damage to the car and Geordie's guilt-stricken expression confirmed them. "Geordie didn't arrive at our place two nights ago," I said. "I thought he was still with you guys."

Igor's expression turned even more serious. "I believe it is now time for us to have our discussion."

For a second or two, Geordie looked like he wanted to flee. Proving that he'd matured, he straightened his shoulders and nodded. "I will do my best to explain everything."

I sensed his mental gulp and felt his dread that it was time to confess. He'd hoped to keep his servant a secret for longer out of fear that we would destroy her for killing the three children. From what I'd seen of her mental state so far, it wasn't looking good for the girl.

Chapter Five

As the official chronicler of our group, Danton wasn't about to miss out on hearing the details firsthand. He waved his five guards to remain behind and followed the rest of us up to the house on the hill. A quick dip into his mind told me that he had an excellent memory and that he wouldn't need to take notes. He remembered nearly every conversation he'd ever had in his long, long life.

Luc unlocked the door to the three-story house and we filed inside. It was larger than the others, but not by much. We walked down a short hallway and entered the first room on the right. The walls were a soothing cream and the carpet was a soft, mossy green. The living room was more spacious than I'd expected and a worn couch sat in front of a fireplace. Twin matching chairs in the same dark brown fabric flanked it on each side. A few paintings would liven up the place a bit, but art wasn't exactly something I was an expert in. I'd leave the home decorating up to Luc.

While the house was well kept and had been recently dusted, it was obvious that no one had lived here for a very long time. There was very little furniture and the few pieces that existed were outdated. It was strange to be in a living room that lacked the most important feature of all, a TV.

A door to the right led to a kitchen and another door at the back led to a dining room. The kitchen looked bare without a fridge, kettle, toaster or any of the normal appliances that every modern home should own. Extra chairs were scrounged up from the dining room. Like the table, they were made of plain blond wood. A homey touch of green cushions had been added to soften the hard seats.

Geordie remained standing with his captive held firmly in his hands while the rest of us took a seat. When we were settled, he launched into his explanation. "Two nights ago, I was driving to Isabella's estate when this girl ran out in front of my car. I saw only a flash of white skin before I hit her and she was thrown up onto the windscreen. I hit the brakes and she fell onto the road. Then a car hit me from behind, pushing me forward. I felt the front wheel bump over her body."

It had been a horrible sensation. Unfortunately, I felt and saw it all through Geordie. He remembered the accident so vividly that there was no chance of me not seeing it. Igor hadn't inspected the back of Gregor's car. If he had, he'd have seen the damage that the second car had left.

"I jumped out and found her trapped beneath my vehicle. I dragged her out while the car that hit me fled. The girl was hanging to her life by a thread." He sent a stricken look at me, hoping for forgiveness. "I couldn't just let her die, *chérie*. She'd lost a lot of blood and her injuries were terrible."

The images that had been seared into his mind were now also imprinted in mine. I saw her lying on the road, gasping for air through her caved in lungs. Her torso had been crushed and it was a miracle that she'd still been alive at all. Naked, her arms, legs and body were covered in barely healed scars and fresh cuts that weren't consistent with being hit by a car. I was more puzzled about that than Geordie was. He was just concerned that I was going to kill her.

"So, you drank from her, then fed her your blood in the hope that she would turn," Igor said far more gently than I'd expected him to. His expression was stern, yet it contained a hint of compassion. I wasn't sure if it was for his apprentice or for the girl.

Geordie nodded miserably. "She went so still and quiet that I didn't think it had worked. I hid Gregor's car in some trees, then carried her to an abandoned farmhouse. The next night, I fed from her again and gave her more of my blood, but she still didn't rouse. I left her for only a short time while I found her some clothes, but she was gone when I returned."

His anguish at what had come next was palpable. "I heard screams from the neighbouring property when I returned and I ran there as fast as I could. I was too late to stop her from slaughtering the children." His shoulders heaved in a soundless sob. "The mother knew that my servant was a vampire and screamed for help from her neighbours. I fled, stopping only long enough to clothe the girl. It was a stupid move, because the humans almost caught up to us. I called Natalie for help when I realized they would catch us eventually."

Snarling, snapping her fangs at us and rolling her eyes wildly, the fledgling seemed more animal than human. "Are they usually this wild when they rise?" I asked Gregor. I had little experience with normal newly made vampires. I'd been far from normal when I'd turned and so had my own servants.

Gregor seemed as disturbed as I felt at the crazed behaviour of Geordie's minion. "Not usually, no. The only times I've ever seen a fledgling act this way was when they were already insane before being turned."

"Do the deranged ever regain their sanity?" Kokoro asked. While she seemed serene on the outside, I sensed her deep concern. She was hiding it for Geordie's sake, which I was grateful for. He was already suffering and didn't need anyone to add to it.

Gregor hesitated before replying, knowing that his words would cause the teen more pain. "I am afraid not."

Geordie's shoulders slumped in utter dejection. "I did not know that she was mentally damaged," he said softly and came to the only conclusion that he could. "I shall put her out of her misery."

I was on my feet before I'd even intended to move. "Wait!" Geordie looked at me with hope shining from his dark eyes. "Maybe I can do something for her."

I hated to see him destroy the one and only servant that he'd ever made. The thought of killing any of my soldiers was abhorrent to me. Only a heartless monster would feel no remorse at dispatching their fledglings. My maker had gone through his servants regularly, which just proved that Silvius had been an evil bastard.

"What do you think you can do for her?" Igor asked me almost sourly. He was hurting as much as I was at seeing Geordie's anguish. "Insanity cannot be cured."

"I managed to fix a human whose mind had almost been obliterated by the Comtesse once," I told him almost absently as I closed in on the girl. Nicholas, the traitorous overly muscled courtier, had witnessed that particular episode. He'd hardly been able to believe that I'd restored the human's mind either.

"That should not have been possible," Gregor said. For the first time, I sensed fright from him. He'd grown used to the strange things that I could do, but he hadn't expected me to possess the ability to mess with people's minds to that extent. I'd warned them all that I was pretty sure my hypnotism could last forever now if I willed it to. I had the distinct impression that no one had really believed me.

Geordie wrapped his arms around his servant's chest to hold her still. She whipped her head from side to side, seeking escape. I captured her face in my hands and held her easily. "Please do not hurt her," the teen whispered.

"I'll try not to," I replied then stared deep into the girl's eyes as I delved into her mind.

Chapter Six

I was instantly sucked into a whirling maelstrom of horror that I could barely make sense of. I sent a calming thought at her and the images slowed down, then her mind stilled. Her body went limp and now Geordie was holding her up rather than holding her still.

What is your name and how old are you, I asked her.

My name is Gabrielle and I am sixteen, she replied. Her mental voice was as small and timid as her fragile body.

Why do you have scars all over your body?

Shying away from the question, she pelted me with images of being tortured by several men. They didn't just cut and beat her, they also used her as their sex slave. She'd been kept in a dank, dark cell for months. The faces of her captors were clear in her mind. All five ranged from their late-thirties to their mid-forties and they looked similar enough to be brothers.

While her ordeal was horrible to witness, it grew worse when I realized she hadn't been the only captive in the dungeon. More women or young girls were being held by these monsters. Gabrielle had found a small crack in her cell wall and had dug her way out where the bricks had crumbled. Out of her mind from the constant barrage of torture, she'd tried to commit suicide by throwing herself in front of Geordie's car.

You're safe now, I told her. *Those men won't ever hurt you again.*

While Gabrielle had managed to escape, they would continue to hurt the other girls that were still penned in the dungeon. She hated them not just for what they'd done to her, but for the torture they'd put the other girls through as well. *I want them to pay,* she said vehemently. *They stole my innocence and my life. They deserve to die!*

I closed my eyes at the thought of an innocent young girl being abused by these monsters. She'd never recover from the pain and degradation that she'd suffered, not unless I took steps. *I promise you they'll pay for what they did to you,* I vowed. There was zero possibility that I would allow them to live now that I was aware of their depraved acts. *I will give you a choice, Gabrielle. I can take these memories away from you forever, but I am afraid that you will never be able to return to your old life.*

Puzzlement clouded her eyes. *What do you mean? Why can't I return to my normal life?*

She'd been so close to death after being run over that she had no idea what Geordie had done to her. I hated to break the news to her, but she had to know what she was. *The guy who ran over you isn't human. He's a vampire. He didn't want you to die, so he turned you into one of us.* I had to elaborate further when she remained clueless. *You're a vampire as well now.*

The news hit her hard and she blanched. *Is that why I taste blood? Have I killed someone?* A vague memory of biting into the neck of a small child rose and so did her dread. *Did I murder a child?*

I'd been keeping her calm so far, but hysteria rose and I sent out another soothing thought. She didn't need to know all the details about the three small children that she'd eaten, so I just nodded. *I can take that memory away from you, too, and I can also stop you from killing anyone else.*

Thinking it over, Gabrielle turned her head to examine Geordie. She was startled to discover that he was roughly her age. He wasn't much bigger than her and his thin frame wasn't exactly threatening. He offered her a strained smile, but his eyes reflected his misery. She turned back to me. *What will happen to me if I choose to become a vampire?* I didn't correct her assumption that she had a choice about that. Gabrielle was already undead and nothing could change that. I didn't say it outright, but I was giving her a choice between unlife or true death.

You will be Geordie's servant, I told her. Instant disgust filled her and she went rigid. *Not that kind of servant,* I added hastily. *Geordie would never force you to do anything sexual. He's a good kid and I think he'd be a good master.* I never thought I'd ever think that about the adolescent, yet I found it was true. *You'd have to obey him, but I doubt he'd give you any orders that you would object to. While you'd have to drink blood to survive, you won't need to kill anyone.* The last point that I was about to add would be her greatest concern. *You'll also have the need for sex, but you can choose who you want to sleep with.*

As expected, she came close to vomiting at that last point. Mastering herself, she showed a maturity that I hadn't expected from a sixteen year old. *So, my choice is to either die, or live as a vampire forever?*

Pretty much, I agreed, secretly glad that she understood her choices completely. Her humanity was gone forever no matter which choice she made. It was up to her whether she would live or die.

Taking another brief look at Geordie, she met my eyes again. *You promise to erase my memories of being held captive by those men?*

I promise. I'll wipe any memory of you being hurt at all. You'll think you were hit by Geordie's car by accident and that he saved you because he couldn't stand the thought of you dying.

Is that true? She sent me a look of heartrending vulnerability.

It is.

She gave me a tiny nod. *I want to live, even if it means I will no longer be human.* I sensed her sorrow and loss at no longer being human and her determination to survive at all costs. She might be small, but she was a fighter and I admired her courage.

Concentrating hard, I sorted her memories into different sections. It became easier when I thought of her brain as a computer and her memories as files. I found every file that related to her capture and subsequent torture and erased them completely. I also wiped out the murders of the three small children and replaced those memories with her being hit by Geordie's car. As far as she'd know, she'd been pushed in front of his vehicle and he'd turned her to save her life.

While I was there, I stripped away her need to kill and eat humans and toned down her blood hunger to a manageable level. In the space of a few moments, I changed her from being an uncontrollable fledgling into a vampire that might have been several months old, one that was still young yet was old enough to control herself.

Stepping back, I released her mind. Her eyes remained cloudy for a moment before clearing. "Hi, Gabrielle, I'm Natalie." I held out my hand to her as if this was our first meeting. "It's nice to meet you."

Shaking my hand, she gave me a timid smile. "It is nice to meet you, too. Geordie hasn't told me much about his friends." She gave the teen an affectionate smile that left him slightly dazed. I almost felt his tentative love for her reach out and slap him up the back of the head. It was instantly obvious that he was going to fall head over heels for her.

Everyone was staring at us with varying degrees of astonishment. What I'd just done had gone far beyond mere hypnotism and had vaulted directly to mind control. I sent them a warning glance and they schooled their expressions to a pleasant welcome.

"Come, Gabrielle," Geordie said to his servant, "I will show you to the bathroom."

Glancing down at her bloodstained hands, she nodded. "I would like to wash my blood off." It wasn't her blood, of course, but she didn't know that. I couldn't undo what she'd done to the three poor kids, but she at least wouldn't remember the deed.

The pair disappeared upstairs to the second floor and into the bathroom that I had yet to see. Once the hot water was running, Geordie sprinted back down to us and we moved into a huddle.

"How is it possible that Gabrielle is so rational so soon after being turned?" Igor asked.

I gave them a quick rundown of the steps that I'd taken to repair her mind. I spoke at barely above a whisper so she wouldn't overhear me.

"She was raped and tortured for several months by five different men?" Geordie asked. He felt sickened by the news and his feelings were shared by everyone in the group.

"Yeah, but she doesn't remember any of that," I said bleakly. "She thinks she was pushed in front of your car. I wiped her memory of killing the kids, too, so we'll have to be careful not to bring that up around her."

"Did you also blunt her blood hunger?" Gregor asked. He was trying to be blasé, but I sensed his disquiet that I had the power to alter someone's behaviour so drastically.

"I thought it would be better than leaving her a starving, mindless eating machine," I said almost acerbically. "Don't worry, Gregor, I don't intend to mess with anyone else's mind. Not unless I'm forced to," I added softly.

"This new ability of yours is disconcerting," he said. "If anyone else were to have this level of hypnotism, I would be very concerned." He already was and he was trying very hard to hide it from me.

"I'm Mortis," I reminded him. "Fate has given me the powers she thinks I need to keep the humans safe. If she thought I'd use them in a bad way or for my own gain, she wouldn't have given them to me in the first place." If I went rogue, Fate would find a way to destroy me somehow and I wasn't about to risk that.

Cocking his head to the side, Gregor thought through the logic of my statement and came to the same conclusion. His smile was relieved and he offered me a bow of apology. "I am sorry I doubted you, Natalie. You are correct, of course. You just did what you thought was necessary."

I waved his apology away. "I'd be just as concerned if someone had the ability to control me like that," I admitted.

"We know you would never harm us, Nat," Geordie said and shot a glower at Gregor. "You have my undying thanks for saving Gabrielle's sanity." He hugged me and I felt a tremor run through his body. His relief at not having to kill his servant almost overwhelmed us both.

The shower shut off and we returned to our seats, pretending we hadn't just had a secret meeting. We were all smiles when Gabrielle shyly stepped into the room. Now that she wasn't covered in blood, I saw how pretty she was. Taking a seat on a dining chair next to Geordie, they made a cute couple. Gabrielle leaned against the teen and her expression was very close to adoring. While she was shorter than me, we were roughly the same size. Even our hair was similar, long, brown and slightly curly. Geordie stared at her as though she was the most beautiful girl he'd ever seen and a sob threatened to choke me. He'd loved me almost from the first moment that we'd met, but now his affection was directed at someone else.

Get a hold of yourself, my inner voice said in exasperation. *The kid was pining for someone of his own to love and now he's found her. You should be happy for him!* As always, my alter ego was right. Gabrielle might take my place in Geordie's heart, but I knew he'd always love me, just as I would

always love him. We were family now and no one could
take that away from us.

Chapter Seven

After we'd all introduced ourselves, we chatted briefly, then I gave Igor a subtle signal. He nodded imperceptibly in response. We had work to do and I didn't want Gabrielle to hear our plans. She could know nothing of what we were about to do. I'd wiped the memories of her capture away and I didn't want her to know about the task that we were about to undertake.

Igor motioned to the two teens. "Come on you two, let's get you settled into your new home." He stood and the young couple followed him to the door. Geordie sent me a look of profound gratitude and blew me a kiss on his way out. I kept my smile in place until the trio disappeared. Igor had handed Geordie the key to his house before leaving. He was sacrificing his need for privacy to his apprentice. He'd most likely bunk down with some of the other soldiers until they reshuffled into another house. The

Russian had earned his right to live alone, if he so chose. He'd been willing to share a dwelling with Geordie, but he wasn't going to cramp the teens' style.

"I sincerely hope that we're going hunting for the animals that held Gabrielle captive," Ishida said with quiet distaste.

"You betcha," I replied with grim promise. "She wasn't alone in the dungeon where she was kept. Other girls are being held there, too." Now that I knew there was more than one victim, I couldn't leave the girls to their fate. It might have been my job to save them, but I was far from alone in my need to free the captives.

"Do you think you'll be able to locate the cells?" Gregor asked. Kokoro's expression had turned fierce and I sensed her loathing at the thought of any person being tortured and held against their will.

"It shouldn't be a problem," I replied. I had Gabrielle's memories to guide me. "Who wants to come with me?"

Luc was the first to step forward and everyone else joined him. No one wanted to miss out on the retribution that was about to rain down on the perverted humans. Keeping the picture of Gabrielle's cell in my mind, I willed us to appear inside the dank confines of a dungeon back in France.

The cell door was still locked and it appeared that the torturers weren't yet aware that their prisoner had escaped. The remains of a piece of bread sat on a rusty tin plate. It had been eaten by either rats or mice. Only a small slice of crust was left. The captives had a bucket to use for their waste and nothing else. They didn't even have a pallet to lie on.

Ishida hunkered down beside the shallow ditch that Gabrielle had first deepened, then wormed her way out of. "I can barely believe she managed to claw her way out through that." He shook his head in disbelief. She'd left skin and blood behind and her escape hadn't been easy.

A scream rent the air, bringing us all to high alert. "No. Don't. Please!" a young girl moaned. Her pleas cut off as someone slapped her.

Red light from my eyes bathed the walls as my rage flared. Far more controlled than me, only a faint hint of red stained Luc's eyes as he kicked the door open. The lock snapped and the heavy wooden door splintered down the middle. It banged open and hit the wall almost hard enough to leave an imprint in the aged bricks.

"What was that?" a startled male voice asked from the far end of what sounded like a long hallway. "Jean-Claude, go and see what made that noise. We wouldn't want any of our girls to escape." He gave a low laugh that made my flesh crawl. The girls in the nearby cells whimpered in fright.

"But, it's my turn with her next," Jean-Claude whined. He grunted when one of the others punched him none too gently. "Fine! I'll go! Just don't use her up completely before I get back."

Leaning through the doorway, I peeked up and down the long, wide hallway. The walls, floor and ceiling were made of bricks that were so old they were beginning to crumble. Twenty cells lined the underground dungeon and almost all of them were occupied. Judging by the smell of fresh death, two of the cells held corpses. Those two were now beyond our help and my fists clenched in anger as I stepped out of the cell. Gabrielle's prison was towards the end of the hallway. The single bulb was far enough away that I was shrouded in shadow.

Jean-Claude emerged from a cell at the opposite end of the hallway. Casting a regretful glance through the doorway, he shut the door, then hurried towards me. Short, chubby and not particularly handsome, his light brown hair was thinning and a scruffy beard did little to hide his weak chin.

No girl in their right mind would want to date this loser, I thought as I caught a whiff of his unwashed flesh and filthy t-shirt and pants. *No wonder he has to resort to taking them by force.*

Standing in near darkness, my black clothes helped me to blend in with the shadows. I kept my eyes shut so the red glare didn't give me away. I opened my eyes when Jean-Claude was only two steps away. Blinking at the twin red orbs that suddenly appeared in front of him, the rapist gave a gasp of alarm and tried to run. Moving almost too fast for even me to follow, Luc popped up right behind him. The human bounced off him and fell to the floor.

Higgins darted forward then went down to one knee and clapped his hand over Jean-Claude's mouth to muffle his screams. "Do you want me to kill him?" he asked me quietly as he hauled the human to his feet.

A quick and painless death would be far too merciful for these animals and I shook my head. "No. Keep him alive, for now." I had another plan in mind, one that I thought my friends might approve of once they heard it.

Jean-Claude sagged in relief to hear that he wasn't going to die. He started babbling madly, pleading to be released and promising us riches if we let him go. I couldn't understand his muffled speech, but I read the promises in his mind. They were lies, of course. He had no job, no savings and zero prospects. The instant that he thought he had the upper hand, he'd try to kill us.

He succumbed to my evil allure without protest and went still when I mentally ordered him to be quiet. Seeing the will drain out of the torturer, Higgins let him go and unconsciously wiped his hands on his cargo pants. Jean-Claude stared ahead with glazed eyes, bereft of the ability to think for himself. I wasn't going to give him the chance to flee and had laid a thick layer of hypnotism over him.

Four more fiends were in the cell where their latest acquisition was being held. I'd gleaned from Jean-Claude that the men were brothers and that they'd captured the poor girl only hours ago. Her young life had already been ruined beyond repair. I saw through one of his brother's eyes as she was brutalized for what would be a final time.

Motioning the others to follow me, I left my lackey where he was. He wouldn't move unless I commanded him to. He belonged to me now, far more so than any of these girls had ever belonged to him and far more permanently if I willed it.

Once again, Luc did the honours and kicked the heavy wooden door open. It had been made to open outwards, not inwards and it didn't react well to the treatment. The wood splintered and fell to the floor in pieces. Three men made startled noises and turned to fight for their lives. They were armed with knives. They were the very weapons that they'd used to disfigure their latest prisoner. The fourth man buckled his pants then backhanded the naked, sobbing girl into unconsciousness before climbing to his feet.

Standing side by side, Luc and I apparently didn't appear to be very frightening. The humans' eyes crawled over me and they exchanged glances. I was wearing my usual jeans, t-shirt and black leather jacket, all of which highlighted my curves. Silently, they agreed to kill Luc and then to make me their latest toy. While hand to hand combat would have been satisfying, I wasn't going to risk accidentally killing them. That wasn't part of my plan at all. I captured them all without bothering to make eye contact. That was no longer necessary anymore. I could now bamboozle any human, or vampire, with a mere thought.

"Go and stand in the hallway," I ordered them. Like robots, they obeyed.

Voices began to call out from the other cells when the girls realized that strangers had arrived. Some spoke English, but most were French.

"Please, help us."

"Save us!"

"Get us out of here!"

I counted sixteen different females in the other cells. Including Gabrielle, the unconscious girl and the two dead girls, all twenty of the cells had contained captives. *How could these men have gotten away with this for so long?* Delving into the mind of the oldest brother, I discovered that they'd been capturing, torturing and killing girls for over a decade. None had ever been questioned about the girls' disappearances. If Gabrielle hadn't thrown herself in front of Geordie's car, God only knew how long they'd have continued their sick hobby.

Luc took me in his arms when I shuddered. My need to rend these men to pieces brought my battle lust to the surface and my eyes blazed an even brighter scarlet.

"Can the girls be saved?" Luc asked me quietly.

Venturing into their tortured minds, I knew none of these girls and young women would ever be able to live normal lives again after the pain and degradation that they'd suffered through. Even if I managed to repair their minds and wipe away what had been done to them, their bodies would still be irreparably scarred. While none of their limbs were missing, they'd never be able to look at themselves in the mirror without wondering what had happened to them.

"They can be saved, but I'm not sure they'll want to go on living looking like that." I pointed at the disfiguring wounds on the latest victim. Blood sluggishly oozed through the makeshift bandages that had been administered to her recently. Her torturers wanted to keep her alive for a long time, hence the attempt at first aid. A knot had risen on her jaw where she'd been backhanded. Her head had hit the ground pretty hard when she'd landed and she'd be out for a while. Scanning her mind, I made sure she wasn't suffering from a brain injury. She would wake up with a headache, but her skull didn't seem to be fractured.

Gregor entered the room and stared down at the girl in pity. "At first, I couldn't help but think that tinkering with a person's mind was wrong," he said in a low voice. "Now that I have seen the atrocities that have been inflicted on these girls, I understand your decision to alter Gabrielle's memories." He met my eyes and his also glowed red. It was rare to see him lose control even slightly. I knew even without reading his mind how deeply affected he was by the sights that we'd all just witnessed. "Will you give each of these girls a choice to join us?"

While I hated the idea of creating more vampires, I couldn't deny them this choice. Fate had led us here, so it obviously wanted me to be in this quandary. "Does everyone agree that this is the right thing to do?"

My friends crowded into the doorway and Ishida was the first to respond. "It is what I would do."

Danton seconded his statement. "This has the feel of destiny and it seems right to me."

Kokoro looked at the unconscious girl with pity and understanding. "We should take them out of here as quickly as possible."

Higgins and Wesley just nodded grimly. They'd brought their guns along, but the weapons hadn't been needed.

Kokoro was right, we had to get the girls out of these cells. Men would be the last beings they'd want to see, so it took some intricate concentration to position everyone where I wanted them. Moments later, the surviving girls were in the main bedroom of my new home. Startled shrieks rang out when they realized they were suddenly no longer in the cells. I put a calming blanket of hypnotism over them, cutting off the screams as quickly as they'd begun.

I'd shifted my friends into the living room downstairs so that the captives wouldn't have to be confronted with any other males just yet. I'd also brought along the monsters that had become our prisoners. They waited downstairs, hypnotized so heavily that they were unaware of their surroundings.

I'd shifted Kokoro into the room with me. Laying a hand on my arm, she spoke quietly. "I will find something for the girls to wear." She wasn't gone long and came back with an armful of linen. She handed out towels and sheets to all but the girl who was still unconscious. That one she gently covered with a towel.

Filthy, battered, scarred, half-starved and traumatized, the victims stared at me through wounded eyes. They varied in looks, but were all either in their teens or their early-twenties. They were all pretty, or had been before they'd been disfigured.

Hatred for the men that had reduced them to shattered wrecks welled within me and Kokoro placed a calming hand on my shoulder. "Make them your offer, Mortis."

Chapter Eight

Reminded of my duty, I reached into the mind of the unconscious girl and brought her awake. Already beneath my spell, she sat up, tucked the towel around her body and watched me without speaking. If I hadn't already calmed her mind, her frantic screams would have pealed out, drawing my soldiers from the village to investigate. Her screams were locked within her mind along with the horror at what she'd just endured. Her emotions were battering to free themselves. The sooner I erased the memory of her torture, the better off she'd be.

"My name is Natalie and I'm a vampire," I said in French, since most of the girls were natives of the country where they'd been snatched. I saw recognition on most of their faces. I was well known pretty much all around the world, but it was from infamy rather than fame. I might have saved the humans several times over, but I hadn't exactly been portrayed as a saint by the media. Especially after turning the US president into tiny chunks of meat. That was going to be hard to live down, even if it had been justified.

"I'm going to give you a choice. I can wipe the memory of your abuse away forever and return you to your normal lives, or you can choose to become one of us."

One of the women looked down at her scarred arms bitterly. "You might be able to take our memories away, but what man will ever want us now?" She spoke in French, but she was Scottish, going by her accent. She was the oldest of the group at twenty-three.

"Your scars will fade if you become the undead," Kokoro said. Her expression told us that she knew this from personal experience.

"What will become of us if we choose to let you turn us?" the Scottish woman asked. Her French was pretty good, but her accent made it hard to understand her.

"You will become soldiers in my army."

"I'm not a soldier," the recently awoken girl said. "I'm just a normal girl."

"So was I, once," I told her dryly. "Now I'm Queen of the Vampires, or something a lot like it." The prophet had foretold that I would rule our kind, so I wasn't being purposefully pretentious.

"Do you promise that we will be pretty again?" another girl asked. A jagged red scar ran from the corner of one eye down to her jaw. The muscles had been severed and her face sagged on one side. She was younger than the others at barely thirteen.

My dead heart went out to her and I stepped forward to hug her. "I promise that you will be far more beautiful than you'd ever be as a human. I also promise that I will protect you from harm."

She let out a sob and nodded her assent as a tear rolled down the furrow of her scar. "Make me forget and make me pretty again, Natalie. Please." Her request was echoed by all of them. Like Gabrielle, they all wanted to live, even if they technically wouldn't really be alive at all.

"I'll have to do this one at a time," I said. "But I'll work as quickly as I can. What is your name?" I asked the girl who was still wrapped around me.

"Renee," she replied shyly.

"You'll be the first, Renee." She looked up at me gratefully, but only the right side of her mouth moved in a smile. "You'll have to feed when I turn you and I brought five snacks along."

She might be young, but she was far from stupid. "Is it the pigs that raped us?" Her tone was hard with hatred.

"Yes." Fright warred with the idea of retribution on their faces. "You won't remember them by the time you turn and they'll just be walking blood bags to you."

"I like that idea," the Scottish woman said. Her hair was flame red and her skin milky pale. At the moment, her eyes were pure green and were decidedly lovely. Their beauty was marred only by her fury and shame. "My name is Simone and I put my hand up to be second."

"I'll be right back," I told her and escorted Renee into the room next door.

"I'll ready one of the men," Kokoro said and headed for the stairs.

Sitting Renee on the bed, I stared into her eyes and deepened my hypnotism. It took only a few minutes to wipe away her memories of being snatched on her way home from school and carried to the torture chamber. In short order, her mind was clean of horror. I planted a false memory of her being sick and near death as I bit into my wrist and offered her my blood.

Renee drank, then her body convulsed as she was invaded by the substance that powered me. My blood had turned yellow, but it wasn't pure Viltaran and only a few nanobots were transferred to her. They would multiply and permeate her veins, but she wouldn't turn into a grey skinned clone. She would become a lesser version of me, just like my male soldiers had.

By the time her blazing red eyes snapped open, Jean-Claude was kneeling before her. I lifted his hypnotism just as her scarlet gaze fastened on him. He began to scream as her delicate, yet now far stronger hands reached out and pulled him in close. His shrieks became piercing as her fangs tore into his flesh.

Ishida held the man firmly, watching with approval as my latest minion became one of us. Ishida would be an excellent mentor for the younger girls. I just hoped he didn't persuade all of them to join him in bed once their flesh hungers rose. Then again, some of the teens were too young for most of the soldiers, so maybe it was better this way. I mentally shook my head that I'd inadvertently just created a harem for the former emperor.

"I know what you are thinking, Nat," Ishida said with a small smile. "You know that I will treat them like princesses."

"I know," I admitted grudgingly. I'd witnessed how well he treated his human harem. "If they're willing, I'm not going to stand in your way." It would be up to the girls who they wished to share their flesh hungers with. Maybe they'd take a shine to some of the other men. It was hard to predict who would appeal to them. Frankly, I felt uncomfortable thinking about it at all.

"My bedroom will require some remodelling," the adolescent teased. "I'll need a far bigger bed."

"I'll see if I can arrange it," Luc said dryly from the doorway. "But first, we should see just how many of these ladies will wish to live with you."

Nodding his agreement, Ishida led Renee away. A dreamy smile of contentment hovered over her now perfect mouth. Just as I'd promised, her mind was free from terror and horror and she was already far more beautiful than she had been as a mortal. She was barely into her adolescence, but she was old enough to be able to cope with her flesh hunger when it eventually rose.

In a production line that reminded me of when I'd first turned my soldiers, I transformed the minds and bodies of all seventeen girls. As promised, Simone was next. Escorting the next man to become food for my newest fledglings into the room, Igor arrived just after I'd fed her my blood. The Russian started when he saw Simone's face and an image rose in his mind. Apart from her hair, Simone looked a lot like his long dead wife. Not that cavemen and women had marriage ceremonies.

Turning to me, Igor saw my surprise. "Did you see my memory?" he asked me, shaken.

"She looks just like your wife," I agreed.

Eyes opening, Simone sat up and her red gaze fastened on the man that had repeatedly brutalized her. That memory was gone, but her hunger was fresh and new. Igor forced the man to his knees and held him while I lifted his hypnotism. Igor had been advised of who the men were and why they, and the girls, were here. Satisfaction emanated from him as the torturer struggled in his grip. My minions weren't gentle when they fed for the first time and a jagged wound marred his neck when Simone was done. Each of the men would take their turn over and over to feed my fledglings. It would take a lot of blood to satisfy them and I couldn't think of anyone who deserved to be drained to death more than these scumbags.

Igor offered the freshly made vampire his hand and she took it and rose gracefully. "I am Simone," she said in English. "Who are you?"

"I am Igor," he said with a stiff bow. It was a toss-up which accent was harder to understand.

Simone's flesh hunger wasn't ready to rise yet, but she smiled in appreciation. As unhandsome as Igor was, he appealed to her on some level. She linked her arm through his and he sent me a panicked look before leaving the room. He dragged the prisoner behind him like a recalcitrant puppy.

I gave Igor a fake commiserative smile, secretly glad that his abstinence of the past fifteen thousand years might not hold up for much longer. *Did you have something to do with this?* I sent the thought out and received a sly chuckle deep in the recesses of my mind in response. Apparently, Fate had decided that Igor had punished himself for the deaths of his family members for long enough.

"Why are you smiling?" Luc asked me as he led in the next girl to be converted.

"You probably won't believe me, but Igor just met a doppelganger of the love of his life."

He looked momentarily shocked, then gave a quiet laugh. "My old friend has been alone for a very long time.

I wonder how he will adapt to being one half of a couple once more?"

He'd probably fight it, but Fate had made her decision and Igor would just have to live with it. Privately, I thought this was a good sign that we might actually prevail against the still largely unknown threat. Three of my previously single closest friends suddenly had a female, or more than one in Ishida's case, to call their own. All I had to do was make the right decisions and hopefully the inhabitants of Earth would remain safe.

Fate was dangling a carrot in front of me in the shape of happiness for my small family. If I screwed up, there was a good chance that our happiness would disappear right along with the entire human race.

Chapter Nine

There was still an hour or so left before dawn by the time I finished transforming the girls into my fledglings. Some reshuffling would have to be done to ensure that they all had a place to stay. My men had all taken turns driving into the city to feed. We only had nine cars, so they'd set up a roster.

None of the soldiers had any idea of what had transpired this night. Higgins and Wesley headed down to the village to fill their comrades in. It would be strange for them to have women in their ranks once more, but the girls would hopefully fit in. Maybe they could even become warriors in time and with extensive training.

"I must admit," Gregor said as he dumped the fifth lifeless body on the living room floor, "I did not foresee anything like this happening. I thought our numbers were being strictly controlled."

"It does seem rather strange that eighteen females have joined our team in the space of one night," Kokoro agreed.

"I'm pretty sure Fate planned this," I said. No one seemed surprised by that revelation.

"Does Simone truly resemble Igor's deceased wife?" Kokoro asked. Danton's ears practically pricked up at that, but I trusted his discretion. He was good at keeping secrets after a lifetime spent taking care of a prophet that had foreseen some pretty horrible things in store for our species. The prophet had known far more about our destiny than he'd written down in his journal. Maybe he'd been instructed to keep most of the information to himself. If I'd known of the awful tasks that I'd be forced to do, I'd have lost my will to continue a long time ago.

"I saw a picture of her in Igor's mind and Simone looks just like her," I confirmed. "His wife had brown hair rather than red, though."

"Is Fate orchestrating mates for us all?" Gregor asked with a hint of suspicion. I caught a fleeting glimpse of doubt that his love for Kokoro had been his choice.

I shrugged then nodded. "It sure looks like it. Now maybe you can understand the dilemma I had on Viltar." Back then, Fate had been more subtle about pairing us up. She now appeared to be throwing caution aside. "Geordie ran over the type of girl he seems to prefer, Ishida might very well have just gained another harem of girls that are around his age and Igor has just met possibly the one woman he'll be able to allow himself to love."

"I do now see why you doubted whether your feelings for me were real," Luc admitted. "Does this mean that you were right all along?"

Gregor pondered the question and I was relieved by his response. "I do not think so. I believe we are merely being given the opportunity to meet the person, or people," he said with a tiny smile, remembering the bevy of young girls around Ishida's age, "who would suit us best."

Kokoro showed how perceptive she could be with her next statement. "This is incentive for us to do our utmost to protect the humans, isn't it?"

Again, I nodded. "It sure seems like it. If we do everything we can to keep the flesh bags safe, then maybe we can be happy. If not, then…you get the drift."

"Before Kokoro and I bid you good night, there is something I think you should see," Gregor said and crooked his finger at me. He'd taken a few moments to explore and had found something of interest. Kokoro accompanied him from the living room into the hallway, wearing a look that I couldn't decipher. Both hid their thoughts from me and I didn't try to pry them free. For one, it would be rude, for another, I didn't want to be caught deliberately snooping in their minds.

Luc slanted me an inscrutable look and nudged me after the pair. The house was larger than it had seemed from the front. Reaching a door at the end of the hall, I realized another room had been added on to the dwelling. It stretched the entire width of the house and was large enough to host a sizable party if we'd been the sociable kind. A door over to the right led outside.

Coming to a stop just inside the room, I was riveted by the sight of a large sheet of canvas hanging on the back wall. A library scene had been skilfully painted on it. A chair sat on a small stage in front of the canvas. All that was missing was a round table bearing watermarks where some kind of liquid had sloshed over the edges and the scene would have matched my dream exactly.

"Does this look familiar?" Kokoro asked me, knowing full well that it was.

"Very." I stared at the backdrop for a few moments, then mounted the stage. "I'd bet my life that this chair is maroon and is made of some kind of dark wood with gold paint inlaid in it." Whisking the sheet off, I waved away the dust particles that were unleashed and beheld the chair from my dreams.

"I'd bet there were once several cameras trained on this stage," Gregor stated. "This room has the appearance of a television studio."

"I wonder what was filmed here?" Kokoro mused.

Recognition flared in Luc's eyes. "Two decades ago, the manager of the property requested permission to film a weekly segment on the production of wine in the nearby vineyards." He shook his head in bafflement. "I'd forgotten all about that and had never seen the show for myself. It only ran for a few weeks before the segment was cancelled."

"Why would I dream about this place?" I wondered out loud. Luc wasn't the only one who was baffled. What could an old studio possibly have to do with the future of the planet?

Examining the stage, Gregor was as blank as I was feeling. "I will think on this, but for now we must retire to our new home." He offered Kokoro his arm and she took it with a shy smile.

"We will see you in the evening," Kokoro said and they took their leave.

Danton took the opportunity to leave as well and then there was just Luc and me left. All thoughts of nooky abandoned me when I remembered the five bloodless corpses that were stacked in the living room. Their deaths had been prolonged and painful and it still hadn't been justice enough for the hell that they'd put their victims through.

Reading the anger on my face, Luc correctly surmised what I was thinking about. "What are you going to do with the bodies?"

"I'd like to leave them in a garbage dump, but I don't want to risk their discovery." There was really only one place that I could think of where they'd never have a chance of being discovered.

We left the studio and walked back down the hall to the living room. I concentrated and all five bodies disappeared. I didn't go with them to see them off. The destination that I had in mind was a random spot of nothingness in deep space. Now that they were dead, I couldn't sense them anymore, so I had to trust that they'd gone where I'd willed them to go.

"Where did you send them?" Luc asked.

"They're space junk now," I said with a smirk.

"What a fitting place for them to spend eternity," he replied. "I only hope their souls are being tortured in hell."

I agreed with his sentiment and slid an arm around his waist. "How about we take a shower together and have loud, satisfying sex?"

Scooping me into his arms, he took the stairs three at a time. "I like the way you think."

Steam quickly filled the small bathroom when I turned on the hot water. I didn't bother with the cold water. My leather jacket would be ruined if I left it in the bathroom, so I ducked into the main bedroom just down the hall and stripped down to my skin.

Luc was waiting for me in the shower when I returned to the bathroom. He sent me a smouldering look that made me heat up deep inside my core. He beckoned me to join him and I stepped inside the small enclosure. Turning me around, he dug his fingers into the knots in my shoulders and leaned down to kiss my neck. There was barely enough room for both of us, but we'd make do.

It never seemed to take much to get me into the mood. Luc's hands and mouth were the only aphrodisiac that I needed. When his hands moved down my torso then slid around to cup my breasts, I moaned my need. Soapy and slippery, his fingers tortured me, then one hand slid down lower.

A master of the art of pleasing women, Luc sensed it when I was about to lose my last thread of control and turned me around. Dazed and on the edge, I barely had time to brace myself before he lifted me, pressed my back against the wall and drove himself into me. I wrapped my legs around him and held on tightly.

Our faces were a mere breath apart as he pounded a rhythm that was hard and fast, just the way I liked it. My head went back to rest against the wall and my hands gripped his shoulders when I reached my peak. I barely managed not to scream and let out a strangled moan instead. While our house was set apart from the others, everyone would be able to hear my screams. I didn't want to suffer the embarrassment of the entire team knowing what we were up to.

Shuddering against me, Luc rested his forehead against mine. "It seems I will have to construct a house further away from the village," he said. We both remembered his promise to one day take me somewhere where no one would be able to hear me scream out my pleasure.

"I'm going to take you up on that when this is all over," I told him, hoping that there would eventually be an end to our constant struggle against the forces of evil.

Chapter Ten

While Luc had to dry himself off the conventional way, I reduced myself down to particles and was nice and dry when I re-formed my body. I changed into clean undies and a t-shirt, wishing I'd been able to bring more clothes along on our sudden and unexpected trip to Italy. None of our new recruits had any clothing at all, apart from Geordie's servant. If Gabrielle was up to it, maybe she could join Kokoro and me on a shopping trip. A girly night out wasn't something I'd ever been a part of before, but there was a first time for everything.

I wasn't particularly tired, but most of our band would fall asleep once the sun came up and there was very little we could do until the mysterious threat appeared. Lying down and trying to sleep would be better than sitting around worrying.

The village had been constructed for humans rather than our kind and the curtains were far too flimsy to suit our needs. Luc picked up the wardrobe and carried it over to the window. It did an effective job of blocking the light that would shortly enter the room and attempt to fry us.

Wearing only black boxer shorts, he climbed into bed and patted the mattress in invitation. "A penny for your thoughts? You seem to be a world away."

I realized I'd been staring at him without really seeing him and smiled. "Sorry. I was just thinking that Kokoro and I will need to go on a shopping spree tomorrow. The girls will need clothes."

"Then it is a good thing that I have amassed a small fortune," he said as I climbed into bed beside him.

"How small is your fortune?"

"I am worth just over one hundred million dollars," he said carelessly.

I stared at him to see if he was joking, but he was serious. "Trust me to have to die to meet a multi-millionaire," I said almost beneath my breath.

It took several hours before I finally fell asleep. When I did, it was deep and dreamless. I received no hints of what was to come and I was starting to worry. Usually, my time was spent facing one disaster after another. I wasn't used to the inactivity and it was making me nervous.

I was up long before the sun went down for the day. Luc also woke early and joined me in the living room. Drawn to the window, he shaded his eyes with his hand and squinted through the glass at the sunset. He was riveted by the beauty of the valley that he'd never expected to see with his own eyes again. While the last rays of the dying sun were painful for him to behold, at least he didn't burst into flames, or start giving off steam.

I left the couch to stand beside him. "I can see why you wanted to come back here," I said and put my arm around his waist.

Hugging me to his side, he gave a silent wistful sigh. "I have travelled all over the world and this is still the most beautiful place that I have ever seen."

"It beats the heck out of Viltar," I replied and he slanted an amused smile at me. Even our planet's driest, most lifeless deserts would seem like a paradise compared to the planet that our alien ancestors had turned into a ruined husk.

"I would like to accompany you ladies into the city," he said. "It has been some time since I last fed."

I couldn't help but tense up at the thought of him putting his lips on another woman. Unfortunately, feeding from humans was a necessity for both of us. Vampire blood couldn't give us the sustenance that we needed. "Maybe we should all go. The guys will need more clothes as well."

Appreciating that I hadn't made a fuss about his need to feed, he nodded. "I will make sure to bring my credit cards along."

"If I'm the Vampire Queen, then I guess you must be the treasurer," I joked.

Pulling me in close, he leaned down and gave me a thorough kiss that made me see stars. "I would hope that you think of me as your King, my wife."

Geordie burst through the door with Gabrielle right behind him. "When did you two get married?" he demanded.

Normally, his question would have come out sounding jealous, but instead he was just hurt that he hadn't been invited to our phantom wedding. Gabrielle's hand was held firmly in his and she stood close at his side. The sun had only gone down a couple of minutes ago, yet all of my fledglings were already awake. Geordie's infusion of Viltaran blood must be to blame for his servant also being awake already. As far as I knew, I hadn't altered anything other than her memories and her uncontrollable craving for blood.

"It's just a joke," I explained as the rest of our friends began straggling up the hill.

Igor stalked through the door and he wasn't alone. Simone came right behind him, almost close enough to be the Russian's shadow. He murmured something to her, then headed straight for me. I hid my smile as he took me by the arm and marched me towards the studio. Luc wasn't about to be left behind and followed us. He closed the door to give us a semblance of privacy from the others.

"I want you to order your servant to leave me alone," Igor said with quiet desperation. He made sure to keep his voice down so that he'd remain unheard by the others.

"Why?" I asked him bluntly and just as quietly.

"I am already responsible for Geordie, I do not need someone else following me around. One apprentice is more than enough."

His excuse was pathetic and I very nearly rolled my eyes. "I don't think Simone wants to be your apprentice, Igor," I said dryly.

"I don't care what she wants," he said in a harsh whisper. "This is about what I want and I want to be left alone."

Luc placed a calming hand on his friend's shoulder. "I have known you for seven centuries and I do not believe that you are a selfish man, Igor. This young woman needs someone to guide her through her new life and she has chosen you for the task."

"She is not my responsibility." Igor's black eyes darted between us, searching for help.

"I beg to differ," I said. "I might have sired her, but I'm not going to control her thoughts and actions. She chose you and you're going to have to suck it up and do the right thing."

As close to being stricken as I'd ever seen him, his shoulders slumped. He didn't hear Geordie slip into the room. "I do not want or need a woman in my life," Igor said in a tone that came very close to sounding self-pitying.

Frowning, Geordie stepped up and slapped Igor up the back of the head. Eyes almost bugging out of his head in outrage, Igor slowly turned around and loomed over his apprentice. "Did you just strike me?" he asked in an ominous tone.

"Yes," the teen said, standing his ground, but quailing visibly. "You were acting like a child, so I treated you like one. I have nothing but respect for you, Igor, but you are disappointing everyone with your selfish desire to remain alone."

Despair threatened to overwhelm the Russian again. "Do you not see? I do not deserve to have someone care for me!"

"It's a bit late for that," I said. "We all care about you."

His glare was almost scornful. "You know what I mean."

Crossing his thin arms, Geordie did his best to look down at his mentor despite being several inches shorter. "Your master made you kill your wife and children and you're afraid to love anyone again in case they're taken away from you," he said bluntly. "It's been fifteen thousand years, Igor. You have to let your family go and allow yourself to move on."

"What if I don't want to move on?" Igor seemed almost terrified of the idea. I'd never seen this side of him before and I found his distress to be strangely endearing. He'd always been so strong and dependable. It was weird to see him unnerved by one young woman.

"Fate has given you this opportunity, old friend," Luc said gently. "It is up to you whether you will accept the offer, or if you will reject it and continue to spend your life alone."

As if summoned, Simone opened the door. The look she sent Igor spoke of her vulnerability. She'd borrowed some of his clothing, but her feet were bare, giving her a waifish air. "I just wanted to say that I know I pushed myself on you and that you don't really want me around. I'll back off and leave you alone from now on."

Frozen in indecision, Igor said nothing as his potential mate turned to walk away. Geordie lifted his hand threateningly and sent his mentor a glower.

Surrendering to destiny, Igor darted forward. Simone started when his hand closed around hers and she turned to him uncertainly. "I do not want to be alone any longer," he whispered.

Simone smiled tremulously. "Neither do I."

Too self-conscious to kiss Simone on the lips while we were all watching, Igor contented himself with a peck on her cheek instead.

Geordie waited until his mentor and Simone had left the studio before succumbing to soundless dry sobs. He turned and stumbled into my arms and did his best to muffle his weeping. He was feeling a mixture of joy and sadness that the man who'd been a father to him for his entire undead existence now had someone more important in his life.

"Now you know how I feel," I said when his sobs petered out.

Looking around, he realized it was just the two of us in the room. Luc had left to give us some privacy. "You are truly sad that I have made a servant?"

"Of course. I was the person you loved the most and now you have someone else to care about."

His lips trembled, but he managed to control himself. "I did not even think how turning Gabrielle would affect you," he whispered.

"I'll get over it," I said ruefully. "I'm just glad that you're happy now and that you've found someone to love."

Nodding thoughtfully, he took my hint. "Then I shall be happy for Igor as well. He deserves my support after caring for me for so long."

"How are things going with Gabrielle?" I asked.

He turned coy and smiled shyly. "It is going well, *chérie*. We are very compatible." They should be, since they were roughly the same mortal age. "Her flesh hunger has not risen yet and I am not going to pressure her into sex when it does rise. I hope that she will choose me to satisfy her hunger. If she doesn't, then I will help her find someone who appeals to her."

I controlled the urge to screw up my nose at the thought of the teens having sex and gave him a supportive nod. "Good idea. You might be her master, but she'd end up hating you if you forced her to do anything she didn't want to do."

Wise beyond his years at times, he nodded his agreement. "I want Gabrielle to love me for me, not because I forced her to care for me."

"She will, Geordie. I'm pretty sure she already does."

He beamed at that and we linked arms as we left the studio. The object of our conversation narrowed her eyes when she saw us enter the living room together. Her suspicion disappeared when her master hurried over and planted a kiss on her temple.

"They make an adorable couple," Luc said from right behind me.

The pair could almost have passed for any normal love-struck teens. Only their pallor and Geordie's unnaturally dark eyes gave them away.

Ishida entered the living room with Renee at his side. Like Igor, he'd given her some of his clothing. He hadn't sired the girl, yet he'd stepped up to take responsibility for her. As the youngest of our newest members, she'd need the most guidance. At that thought, several more of the younger girls entered the room and moved to surround the former emperor. He sent me a glance and shrugged. *It appears that these ladies feel comfortable around me,* he thought at me. *I do not mind taking them under my wing.* All six of his soon-to-be harem members were young, slender and beautiful, just his preferred type. I had to give him credit, he didn't openly smirk at his good fortune. I nodded imperceptibly to let him know that I'd received his message.

One by one, the rest of the new additions to our family made their way up to the house on the hill. Higgins and Wesley escorted the stragglers, while the bulk of my men remained in the village. They knew that they'd be informed of any developments if and when they arose.

Most of the girls were still wearing sheets or towels. I'd wiped their memories of how they'd come to be naked and I'd also erased their curiosity on the topic. I was about to rectify their lack of clothing and asked the question that most females liked to hear. "Who wants to go shopping?"

Chapter Eleven

Corporal Higgins stepped forward after the eager replies from the girls died down. "I saw a department store in the city that should meet our needs."

I nodded my thanks to my right hand man. "Let's gather the others and I'll teleport us all there."

It would have been faster just to zap us all straight to the village, but I wasn't quite that lazy. Luc didn't bother to lock the door as we filed outside. He'd instructed Maria to keep the human staff away. Besides, there wasn't really anything worth stealing inside even if someone did come to investigate.

My men gathered on the lane at Higgins' shout, but jogged back to their homes to leave their weapons behind at his order. We'd be able to hypnotize any humans we encountered into forgetting they'd seen us. Guns wouldn't be necessary. Far less trusting than Luc, they all locked their doors securely.

"Are we all ready?" I asked and received nods from most and curious expressions from the new girls. They'd been out of their minds with terror and pain when I'd whisked them away from captivity. To them, this would be their first trip via teleportation.

Using the image from Higgins' mind, I relocated our group to the department store in the nearby city. Shouts of alarm from shoppers and staff members rang out. They were quickly quelled as I sent out a blanket of hypnotism over the entire building. Sounds of surprise came from my newest fledglings when they saw that they were in a new location.

"What just happened?" Simone asked Igor, holding onto his arm tightly as if she was suffering from vertigo.

"Natalie can shift both people and objects using her mind," he explained.

"What *are* you?" the Scottish woman asked me rhetorically. I hoped it was rhetorical because I didn't have a simple answer for her. I didn't really want to have a philosophical discussion about the pros and cons of being Mortis right now.

The shopping centre had four levels and it was far grander than I'd expected. The floors were faux marble in shades of black and white. Ornate columns supported the ceiling and massive chandeliers hung in the centre of the complex. Tiny tables with two chairs each sat in the food court on the bottom level. I didn't recognize many of the fast food restaurants. Human food was the last thing we needed, so we headed for the escalators.

I mentally instructed the shoppers and staff to ignore us as we split into two groups and separated. Luc herded the men in one direction and we females went in the other. I'd donned jeans and a t-shirt for this trip. My distinctive red leather suit hung neatly in the wardrobe of our new home. While I loved the suit, it tended to stand out a bit too much.

Kokoro led the way into a store that caught her eye. The clothes on display in the windows were elegant, expensive, feminine and beautiful. She chose a few outfits and I handed over one of Luc's credit cards so she could purchase them. Kokoro wore a contented smile as we headed for a store that better suited the young women in our midst. Being far less mature than I should have been, I also chose my outfits from that store. I was twenty-eight in mortal years, but looked several years younger and could get away with wearing the trendy clothing.

There were far fewer girls than guys, yet we still took far longer to choose our new wardrobes. I sensed the men gathering outside and glanced out through a window to see them waiting patiently for us in a quaint little courtyard. The department store was about to close for the night by the time we were finally done. Now wearing clothing instead of linen, the girls were far happier. Shopping was usually an excellent way to put females in a good mood.

Everyone was hungry, including me, so we paired up and spread out in search of food. My men knew well enough to bamboozle their meals into forgetting that they'd been snacked on. Ishida couldn't handle all six of his girls at once, so five of them reluctantly paired up with my soldiers, while Renee stayed with the former emperor.

I trusted my men to take good care of the girls. They were all trained to be protective of anyone they saw as being weaker than themselves. I was the only female vamp that was stronger than even the biggest and toughest male undead. Kokoro was less powerful than me, but the added vitality of the Viltaran blood in her system made her stronger than the average male of our species.

As agreed, everyone would meet back in the courtyard of the department store when they were done feeding. Luc and I remained behind to watch over the bags and other assorted equipment that had been purchased. I was highly unsurprised to see a television for every home, as well as other electronic devices they felt they couldn't do without. Several people had opted to buy computer consoles and games. No doubt, one of the bags full of goodies would belong to Ishida. He had to assuage the boredom of waiting for action somehow.

"That one is yours," Luc said and pointed at one of the bags sitting beside a large, brand new TV. Taking a peek inside, I saw the latest gaming console and a bunch of games. The top one was a zombie game, which made me smile. "Consider them to be a wedding gift," he said with a wink.

"Aw, and I didn't get you anything."

"You are the only gift I need," he replied and pulled me in for a deep kiss that made my toes curl.

"Get a room, you two," Charlie called, instantly shattering our mood as he loped into sight. He and his partner were the first to return. Geordie's shrill giggle meant that he wasn't far behind and that he'd overheard Charlie.

"Friggin' vampire hearing," I muttered. There was rarely any privacy when our kind was near.

"Let's find a meal," Luc said and lifted my hand to kiss my knuckles.

Now that someone else could guard our treasures, it was our turn to feed. We walked arm in arm down the street, waving greetings to our kin as they returned.

Reaching an apartment building, Luc raised his eyebrow in query and I sent out my senses. Delving the structure, I located a young couple that were slumbering peacefully. Taking Luc by the hand, I willed us up to the fourth floor and into the couple's bedroom.

Our prey didn't even wake as we knelt on either side of the bed and sank our fangs into their necks. The female moaned and arched back against Luc as he fed from her from behind. The image conjured up pictures of what I wanted him to do to me. My emotion flowed through to the human that I was drinking from and a boner rose beneath the sheet. Luc's eyes crinkled at the corners at the sight as he laughed silently.

Finished with my snack, I stood and Luc broke his contact with the woman. As the couple came awake and rolled towards each other in a frenzy of sexual need, I teleported us back to the courtyard. Feeling full of need myself, I checked to make sure everyone had returned, then whisked us all, plus our packages, back home.

I zapped Luc and me directly into our living room, leaving everyone else on the laneway outside of their homes. Luc barely had time to set the TV and his bags down before I was on him. I broke my body down momentarily and left my clothes in a heap on the floor. Luc didn't have the same ability and I was in too much of a rush to wait, so I tore his pants off. Eyes dark with desire and hunger, he didn't protest when I tackled him to the carpet. His head went back, exposing his neck as I settled on top of him and began to move. The pace that I set had us both catapulting towards orgasm even faster than usual. He made an exclamation of intense pleasure when I bit him. Knowing how horrible his blood tasted, I didn't actually drink. The sensation of my fangs in his flesh was enough to send him over the edge. Then it was my turn to be on the bottom and his teeth were slicing into my vein. He sucked hard and I spun into ecstasy in a dizzying rush.

"That just never gets old," I said when I was capable of speech again.

"I pity vampires who can't bite their mates," Luc agreed.

That was the vast majority of our species. I wasn't sure if our five closest friends had tried to ingest the blood of our own kind yet. I doubted they'd try, due to the fact that it was strongly ingrained into them not to bite another vampire for fear of a horrible and painful death. Luc's blood tasted like arse, but it was hard to resist biting him now that I knew how good it felt for both of us.

Ruefully picking up his tattered pants, my one true love shook his head. "This is the price I have to pay for falling in love with Mortis."

"Would you rather I was all gentle and demure?" I asked curiously.

"No," he replied immediately, which eased my sudden worry about my utter lack of finesse. "I love your eagerness and lack of pretention."

He'd lived amongst the haughty courtiers for centuries and they'd perfected the art of being pretentious. In comparison to them, I guessed I was a breath of fresh air.

Donning new clothing, Luc went about the task of setting up the TV and other electrical devices that he'd bought. Not only had he invited us into his home, he'd also spent tens of thousands of dollars on us all. I felt a wave of love sweep over me at his kindness and generosity. Coupled with his intelligence and looks, he really was the perfect man for me. I still wasn't sure how he could love someone as strange as I was, but I wasn't going to argue the point. We were a matched pair and nothing was ever going to tear us apart. Not if Fate wanted us to save the precious human race yet again.

Chapter Twelve

We spent the next few evenings watching movies. Cuddled against Luc's side on the couch, I could easily see us spending the rest of our undead lives together.

"Will you teach me how to kill zombies?" Luc asked.

Thrown for a second, I realized he was talking about electronic zombies. "I'll try, but Ishida is the true master of computer games. He taught me everything I know." I'd spent four months on his island learning how to use my samurai swords and hanging out with the ruler of their nation. Ishida had been a lot stiffer and more formal back then, but he'd still been a kid at heart and had wanted someone to play with. The fact that he'd chosen me to be his playmate didn't say much for my level of maturity.

Moving away from the topic of computer games, Luc brought up a good point. "Perhaps Ishida and Kokoro would be willing to teach your soldiers how to use swords."

It was an excellent idea. My soldiers were all proficient at using guns, but it couldn't hurt to train them to use swords as well. Their nation might have been destroyed, but Ishida and Kokoro could pass on their knowledge to the foreigners that they'd once hated. Most of my men were American rather than European, but they'd have no doubt been enemies to the Japanese vampires.

"I'll ask them if they're interested," I said and kissed his jaw to show my thanks for thinking of our whole team. "Where are we going to find enough swords for everyone?"

"The internet would be our best bet. I will begin to search for weapons when we rise tomorrow night and you can speak to Ishida and Kokoro."

We needed something to do to keep us busy while we waited for disaster to strike and weapons training was an excellent idea. While I was happy that we had a chance to rest after our ordeal with the octosquids, I couldn't relax. Something was coming that would turn the Earth upside down. I wished I had a hint of when and where it would happen.

We settled down to sleep just as the sun was about to rise, but it took a long time before my eyes closed and I finally drifted off.

Waking, I shivered at an intense cold that burrowed its way inside my very bones. I had to force my eyes open and ice crackled when they finally did. After drinking deeply of the blood of our ancestors, the cold no longer had the power to bother me. I was puzzled how it could be affecting me so strongly now.

Staring up at the white tiled ceiling, something was very wrong, but I hadn't figured out what it was yet. Lifting my head, my hair was stuck to whatever I was lying on and came free with a brittle snapping sound. Glancing down my body, the first thing I noticed was that I was naked. The second thing I noticed was that my breasts were gone and that I'd grown male genitalia. Before I could descend into a panic, I realized I'd dreamed myself into the body of a male vampire.

Letting out a relieved sound, I lifted my head higher and examined the object that I was lying on. My borrowed body was strapped down to a hospital bed by thick metal bands across the chest, abdomen and legs. Strong leather straps also held my arms down and a cannula was taped to the right one. An IV stand lurked at the foot of the bed. An empty blood bag hung from one side of it.

Curious rather than alarmed, I looked beyond the bed and IV stand. A wide window at my feet immediately caught my eye. I peered through the thin veneer of frost that had formed due to the intense cold. Scientists in white coats bustled around the room on the other side of the glass. One stood in front of a machine that spun rapidly in dizzying circles. It slowed and stopped and several small test tubes were removed. A thick black substance was inside each tube. It was a substance that I instantly recognized.

Large refrigerators with glass doors lined the back wall. Inside were dozens of test tubes and all were filled with vampire blood. It was too much liquid to have come from one lone vampire. Turning my head to the left, I saw that I wasn't alone in the room. Twelve metal containers stood side by side. Hoses sprouted from the tops and they were welded securely to the floor. The containers were made of thick glass that had been filled with ice. Murky, hard to make out forms were trapped inside the cylinders. Squinting at the closest container, I made out a face beneath inches of ice. Red hair had frozen around the familiar milky white face. Even as a vampsicle, Millicent still managed to look arrogant.

Eleven of the containers were occupied. One lone vessel stood empty, ready to encase the final member of the group of courtiers that I'd dropped off in China at their request. Obviously, their choice of location had been a bad one. I had serious doubts that any of the courtiers had willingly allowed themselves to be imprisoned in ice. I also suspected their blood wasn't being drained from their veins by their choice.

I tried to read Millicent's mind, but couldn't. All of the vampsicles were impervious to my mental probe. I figured being frozen had something to do with it. Delving into the sluggish mind of the body that I was currently occupying, I identified it as belonging to Thaddeus. He'd retreated into a near coma from the enforced cold. Normal vampires couldn't function when they were frozen. The scientists had used that weakness against them.

Thaddeus didn't budge when I tried to will him to safety. I wasn't really surprised by my failure to rescue him. This was just a dream after all and my dark mojo only worked when I was awake. I really wanted to know what trouble these idiots had gotten themselves into, but couldn't do so while I was asleep.

With that thought, I woke from my slumber. It was now nearing nightfall and it would be dark in another couple of hours. Luc was still asleep and I didn't want to wake him. I sent out a cautious thought to Gregor and found him also dead to the world, so to speak. It seemed that I was on my own this time. I'd have to decide what to do about the twelve imprisoned courtiers without assistance from the others.

Dressing as quietly as possible, I zapped myself into the living room. *Remember what usually happens when you go out on solo missions,* my inner voice warned me, as if I needed it. In most instances when I went on adventures by myself, I ended up neck deep in trouble. I had no reason to believe that this time would be any different.

Undecided as to what I should do, I sent out my senses in search of Thaddeus. I found him in the same state that I'd dreamed him in. His mind was closed to me from being half frozen and I needed to know how they'd managed to get themselves into their bind.

I could have teleported him straight to me, but I opted to go to him instead. An instant later, I stood beside his hospital bed. It was easy enough to snap the metal bands around his legs, abdomen and chest. I freed his right arm from its restraint and was working at freeing the left one when a scientist spotted me.

"One of the creatures is loose!" she screamed in Chinese.

Darting over to the wall, she slammed her hand down on a bright red button. With a hiss, a freezing cold substance jetted down from sprinklers that popped out of concealment in the ceiling. The substance coated everything in the room, including me. Instantly immobilized, I couldn't even twitch a finger.

What the hell is this? My inner voice had an answer for me. *I think its liquid nitrogen. You know, the stuff that freezes things solid.* I'd seen more than one movie where a container of the stuff was broken open and froze hapless people or evil monsters. I also remembered what happened if they received a trauma such as being shot. They tended to shatter into a million pieces.

While I was used to my body breaking down into small chunks, Thaddeus wouldn't survive the process. I had to be very careful if I wanted to keep him whole. Already frozen inside their containers, Millicent and her crew would probably be safer where they were, for now. I'd concentrate on freeing Teddy and myself and would come back for them later. While my body was unable to move, my mind was still free. Before the scientists could enter the room and figure out who I was, I shifted myself, Thaddeus and his hospital bed back to Italy.

Inordinately glad that no one was awake to witness my latest calamity, we appeared in the living room of my new house. I tried to break my body down into tiny molecules and it stubbornly resisted my mental command. There was only one way to free myself quickly from my frozen state.

Choosing an abandoned field several miles away, I teleported high into the air then let myself drop. A small crater formed when I landed. Just like in the movies, I shattered into tiny shards and chunks of frozen flesh. The sun would shortly fall, but enough light remained to thaw me out quickly.

An instant before I could burst into flames, I reduced myself down into particles and returned to the house. I re-formed my body in the living room and found that Luc had already risen. He no longer had to wait for nightfall to awaken from the unnatural slumber that felled all but my close friends and me each day. His eyebrows rose when I appeared beside him. My clothes hadn't survived the fall and I was buck naked.

"Do I even want to know what happened while I was sleeping?" he asked.

"No, but I'll tell you anyway." First, I needed to dress before our friends showed up, which would be any moment now since the sun had dipped down below the horizon. I teleported into our room and quickly chose a new pair of jeans, t-shirt and brand new black leather jacket before returning to Luc's side.

Drawn by some strange instinct that they were needed, Gregor and Kokoro were the first to arrive. They paused in the doorway and examined the half frozen lump on the equally frozen bed. "Is that Thaddeus?" Gregor asked. He could usually puzzle out any problem that he encountered fairly quickly, but this one was beyond even him.

"Yep," I replied. "You should see the condition Millie and the others are in," I added. "Does anyone have any idea how we can safely thaw him out?" Sunlight had worked for me, but it would kill Teddy. That option was no longer available anyway now that night had fallen.

"I doubt a hairdryer will do the trick," Kokoro said. That struck me as funny and I sniggered.

"What is so amusing?" Geordie asked as he barged inside. Ishida came next, followed by Igor, Danton, Higgins and Wesley.

"Where are the girls?" Kokoro asked.

"They're having a 'female only party'," Ishida said, making the required quotation marks with his fingers and rolling his eyes.

Geordie glanced at the now closed door with an indulgent smile. "They feel the need to bond." Now that they'd mentioned the party, I heard rock music coming from the village and the high pitched sound of excited female voices.

I'd been left on my own after I'd been turned. It had been an unsettling experience to suddenly find myself a creature of myth and legend. Granted, I'd only been alone because I'd killed my master. It would have been nice to have had someone to share my experience with. I'd been lucky enough for Luc to stumble across the mausoleum on his quest to hunt down Silvius. Of course, that had all been part of Fate's plan, but I hadn't known that at the time.

"It's just as well they are otherwise occupied," Gregor said. "I doubt they'd wish to see this." He gestured at the grotesque sight of the slowly thawing vampsicle. Teddy's still sluggish thoughts were beginning to quicken. He'd soon become aware of us.

Ever practical, Igor had a solution. "We need to immerse him in water." He gave the courtier's arm an experimental tug. Stuck solidly to the hospital bed, Teddy wasn't coming loose anytime soon.

"There is a small lake nearby," Luc suggested. "It should be large enough for us to be able to submerge the entire bed." He hadn't seen the lake in a very long time and I picked up on his thought that he hoped it would still be there. For all he knew, the owner of the property might have had it filled in.

Kokoro had put aside her black leather and had donned a tightly fitting white dress. It wasn't one of the kimonos she was used to wearing, but it suited her. She wasn't perturbed by the idea of traipsing around in her new dainty shoes. The rest of us were dressed casually, except for Gregor, who was once more wearing a brown tweed suit. He and his love were well matched when it came to style.

"We will need rope," Igor said and turned to me. "I left some in the garage on Gregor's estate. Could you retrieve it?"

Reaching out with my thoughts, I pictured the rope and it landed on the carpet with a thump. Igor picked it up and hefted it over his shoulder. "Let's go," he instructed me and I transported us to the lake that was prominent in Luc's thoughts.

The lake was on private land and had escaped being turned into a tourist attraction. It was small, as he'd described, but the water was clean and tranquil. I didn't recognize many of the trees and shrubs that surrounded it. That came as no surprise, since I barely recognized the plant life of my own country.

A small space at the edge of the water had been cleared and a dock led out onto the surface. An old, weathered rowboat bobbed at the end of the dock. It was a peaceful, picturesque scene that was ruined only by us monsters. Now that we were here, the scene had turned sinister. Instead of a romance movie, the lake would now have been more suitable for a horror flick.

Igor tied one end of the rope to the hospital bed then carefully looped the other end around Thaddeus' left foot. He had to be careful not to break anything off. Unlike us, Teddy wouldn't be able to reattach his limbs.

The rope was long enough for Igor to be able to stand on the shore while the bed and its occupant went under. Luc helped Igor carry the bed to the edge of the water. It crackled and popped as it became submerged. We left both the bed and Teddy under the water until the rope finally moved in Igor's hand.

Proving just how resilient our kind could be, Thaddeus quickly thawed out and emerged from his hibernation. His head broke the surface and he thrashed around in a circle. Coming to a stop, he realized that he wasn't alone and turned to us. He momentarily froze when he recognized us.

I couldn't help but be suspicious when he immediately attempted to swim to safety. It was useless since I could teleport after him far more quickly than he could run. Gregor and Luc exchanged cynical glances. Teddy had just indicated that he thought of us as unfriendly. We hadn't done anything to incur this kind of reaction, so that meant he and his crew had most likely done something wrong.

Igor wasn't about to let Teddy escape. He yanked hard on the rope and the naked vampire flew through the air and flopped onto the shore before us. Naked and extremely pale, he looked like a beached fish. Cowering on his side, Teddy drew his legs up and covered his face with his hands. He made small keening noises as he waited for his torture to begin. I knew most vampires were afraid of me, but I'd never had this kind of reaction before.

Luc knelt beside the ex-courtier and put his hand on the man's shoulder. He flinched then stilled when Luc spoke. "Calm yourself, Thaddeus, we do not intend to do you any harm."

I had the distinct feeling that we would be far from friends with the courtiers when we learned exactly why they were being held in that lab. I couldn't discount the possibility that torture might very well come into play at some stage.

Slowly moving his hands away from his face, Teddy cautiously studied Luc's expression then swept his gaze across the rest of us. He dropped his eyes guiltily when he saw me. "I believe that that will shortly change once you learn what we have done," he said softly. "Millicent made a grave mistake. She trusted the wrong human and I am very much afraid that the entire world will now pay the price for our actions."

Chapter Thirteen

Gregor spoke to me before Thaddeus could tell us his story. "Can you retrieve Millicent and the rest of her people?" he asked.

I could, but I wasn't sure that I wanted to. Gut instinct had already warned me that they'd betrayed us somehow. Teddy's confession had boosted the feeling. I wasn't a big fan of saving my enemies if I'd only have to destroy them later.

"I will accompany you," Luc said, clearly expecting me to do the right thing.

Heaving a mental sigh of capitulation, I teleported us both back to the Chinese laboratory. This time, I aimed for the room on the other side of the frosty window. I'd expected to face chaos and panicked humans upon our arrival. Instead, the lab was deserted. In the few hours that I'd been gone, they'd evacuated the staff and had removed some of the equipment from the lab. I was glad to see the eleven specimens still remained. If I didn't get them out of there, the scientists would probably return and they would no doubt recommence extracting their blood.

Luc examined the now empty fridges that had been left behind. They were too large to be easily shifted. Finding little of interest, he crossed to the icicle covered window. He peered through the glass at the ice and vampire filled capsules then glanced at me. "Will you be able to free them?"

Since it should now be safe to enter the other room, I shifted us both to the other side of the glass. Millicent's eyes were open and seemed to glare right at me. I knew she wasn't aware of me, yet my dislike for her intensified. She had been behind whatever scheme had landed them in this predicament.

I didn't need to read her mind to know that her hatred and jealousy of me were to blame for her actions. Some of the ancient vampires had megalomaniacal tendencies and she seemed to be one of them. I'd sensed that she was a sneaky cow. If I'd bothered to delve into her thoughts deeply, I could have prevented whatever disaster was about to befall us. I'd been warned by both the prophet and my dreams that something bad was coming. Now it was probably too late to stop it.

Considering my options, I decided it would be far easier to try to teleport just Millicent and the ice that encased her and to leave the capsule itself behind. Aiming for the centre of the lake in Italy, I concentrated and she disappeared. One by one, I broke all eleven courtiers free, then willed us back to our friends.

Igor had retrieved the hospital bed from the lake and I sent it back to the lab. I also sent his rope to the trunk of his car. He gave me a nod of thanks when I advised him of that fact.

Thaddeus was still dripping wet and he was shivering from being frozen for God knew how long. I took pity on him and sent my mental probe back to the department store in the city. Twelve towels would be found missing from a store. Luc had already spent a lot of cash in the establishment, so I didn't feel particularly guilty about the theft.

Eyes wide with fright, Teddy took the towel and wrapped it around his torso like a sarong. I deliberately didn't probe his mind to find the answers that we were all seeking. I wanted to hear the information directly from Millicent, since she was the ringmaster in this particular farcical circus.

"How did you do that?" Thaddeus asked, teeth chattering slightly.

"Do what?"

"Appear and disappear and conjure things out of thin air. Are you some kind of witch?"

He smiled cheekily, attempting to lighten the mood and failing miserably. I wasn't anywhere near in the right frame of mind to be entertained, but that didn't mean I had to be rude. I'd almost forgotten that not everyone knew of my new talents and answered his query. "I can teleport people and objects now."

"How?"

I understood his utter bewilderment, since I was still occasionally surprised by the things that I could do from time to time. "I learned how to teleport on Viltar."

"Did the aliens give you this ability?" His natural mischievousness was more muted than usual, but his curiosity couldn't be as easily tamed.

"Not directly. They just made it possible for me to learn how to do it." It had taken the beheading of Geordie for me to unlock the skill of teleportation. That had been the second worst thing that had happened to one of the people I loved. The worst had been seeing Luc blown into small pieces. I sincerely hoped I didn't have any more skills to learn, because I never wanted to witness anything that horrible ever again. I also didn't want to go through the anguish that seemed to be required to learn how to use my hidden talents.

It only took half an hour for Millicent and her clique to thaw out. They surfaced at roughly the same time and were bewildered to find themselves no longer imprisoned in the lab. Millicent's eyes tightened when they passed over me. Her gaze went straight to Luc and stayed there. She swam to the shore and emerged from the water, revealing her magnificent nakedness. Ignoring me completely, she oozed sexual invitation as she sashayed towards my beloved.

A beautiful woman who was used to bending men to her will, she couldn't even comprehend the idea that Luc wouldn't fall for her charms. Especially now that they were on display right in front of him. She considered me to be too skinny and far too flat in the chest area to really be able to entice a man.

A memory of her and Luc in bed together surfaced and her lips curled upwards. "Lord Lucentio," she purred, "I do not know how you managed to free us, or where we are now, but I wish to thank you from the bottom of my heart." She took his hand and held it to her considerable bosom.

Igor's hand clamped down on my elbow before I could take a step forward and press my palms against her face. The need to use my holy marks to pop her head like a boil was hard to resist. I forced the mental picture of her twined in Luc's arms from my mind. That had happened centuries ago and Luc had only slept with her because his master had ordered him to. If he'd had a choice, he'd have fled from the mansion entirely rather than force himself to bed the Court harpies.

"I was not the one who saved you," my one true love said coldly and extricated his hand from her clasp. "You have Natalie to thank for that."

Bracing herself, Millicent's expression changed from flirtatious back to condescending. "I see." She turned her icy gaze on me. "Then I suppose I should offer you my thanks."

Thaddeus ambled over and handed her one of the fluffy white towels. She took it and might as well have been holding the skin of a rat for all the enthusiasm she showed. Realizing he'd been rescued sometime before the rest of them, her gaze sharpened. "What have you told our esteemed rescuers, Teddy?" she asked in a sickly sweet tone as she deigned to don the towel.

"I haven't told them anything," he said irritably. "They haven't asked me any questions yet."

"We were waiting for you to thaw out, *Millie*," I said, emphasizing her hated nickname. I stifled a snigger at her instant rage at my mocking tone.

"Perhaps, when we have bathed and have donned suitable clothing, we might be able to discuss whatever is on your mind," she said and sniffed in displeasure. It was completely unnecessary, since we couldn't produce mucus anymore. It was just one more way for her to show her perceived superiority over me.

"How about we discuss it now?" I contradicted her. "Thaddeus said that you'd trusted the wrong human and that we're all going to pay. What did he mean by that?"

Sending a sharp glare at the man she thought of as her lackey, she drew herself up to her full height. "I thought you didn't tell them anything," she hissed accusingly. He ignored her ire and she reluctantly turned back to me. "I mistakenly believed that a Chinese scientist might offer us shelter if we reached an accommodation with him."

"Yeah, that worked out really well for you," I said sarcastically. "They turned eleven of you into ice blocks and kept one of you in a near frozen state so they could drain your blood."

Fear momentarily flickered over her features, but was quickly replaced by bluster. "It was *our* blood being taken. What concern is that of yours?"

"You didn't just give them your blood, did you?" I'd skimmed her mind and had seen something hidden deep beneath the surface. I probed it loose and her secret bubbled up for me to read. I saw an image of a plastic cup full of bright yellow blood that contained the alien nanobots. "You gave them my blood as well," I said and it was my turn to use an accusing tone.

Guilt appeared on Thaddeus' face and he hunched his shoulders. "We thought we could trade a sample of your blood and ours for our safety. We didn't expect them to turn us into lab rats."

J.C. DIEM

Dread stiffened Gregor's spine. "They performed experiments on you?" Everyone who'd suffered at the hands of American scientists tensed up at that question. These courtiers had made themselves our enemies by making the wrong choice, but none of my friends would wish painful and degrading experimentation on anybody.

Teddy shook his head while Millicent grimly wrapped the towel around herself. "No. We were asleep or frozen most of the time, but I think they just took our blood."

"There were dozens of test tubes in the lab," I advised them. "Why would they need that much of your blood? Why would they need *my* blood at all?"

"If they siphoned so much of your blood out of your veins, why do you appear to be healthy?" Ishida asked. The American scientists had drained half of the teen's blood and had attempted to replace it with human blood. The experiment had been a failure, but they hadn't let that stop them. His body had been a withered husk and he'd aged horribly during the process. Viltaran blood had restored him to his youth as well as giving him the few extra perks that we seven shared.

"They fed us regularly," Teddy explained. "It must have replenished our blood quickly enough for them to continue extracting it." None actually remembered having their blood stolen. Their brains went into stasis as soon as their body temperatures had been lowered to just above freezing.

Gregor's dread increased and Geordie shivered in reaction. The teen drew closer to my side and slipped his hand into mine. "What are you thinking, Gregor?" he asked in a small voice.

"I have a very bad feeling," the sophisticated one said. "The Chinese scientist had access to normal vampire blood and to Natalie's blood. I would be willing to bet they also have some of the nanobots that were left over from the Viltaran invasion."

His dread spread to me and a memory of a brief encounter that I'd had in Las Vegas surfaced. "The creatures in my dream were like the doberclone," I realized out loud. I knew they'd been familiar, but I'd almost forgotten about the dog. It had been transformed into a creature that was a blend of a Viltaran clone and a vampire. It had become a hybrid monster that had never existed before and that I'd hoped would never be seen again. That hope had been in vain and I finally realized exactly what we would be facing.

Geordie was both puzzled and curious. "What is a doberclone, *chérie*?"

"It was a normal Doberman before it attacked me. It bit me and was also shot by a nanobot dart at almost the same time." My blood had already been changed from being extremely deadly into something else by then, so that explained why the dog hadn't expired. "Instead of dying, it became a cross between a vampire and a clone."

My friends were horrified by the idea and Danton closed his eyes against the images that my tale had conjured. I had more bad news for them. "According to the Viltarans, non-intelligent life forms that are converted into clones are always automatically destroyed."

"Why?" Corporal Higgins asked.

"Because they turn into vicious, uncontrollable killing machines that can turn on their makers."

They'd die if they killed their makers, but they were too mindless to realize it. In this instance, they'd been manufactured rather than turned. In effect, they had no masters and no one to control them at all.

Geordie summed up our predicament. "We're screwed, aren't we?"

Chapter Fourteen

"Tell us everything," Gregor instructed Millicent in a tone that brooked no argument.

Ignoring him, she turned on me. "This is your fault, *Mortis*!" She hissed my title with all the venom that she could muster. If she'd still been able to produce saliva, she'd probably have spat at me.

"I can't wait to hear this," I muttered just low enough for only my confidants to hear me.

Geordie sniggered and Millie rounded on him. "You are also at fault, servant boy! If not for you, we wouldn't have been forced to seek asylum from the Chinese. We would have had our rightful place at Natalie's side!"

Staring at her wordlessly, I had to clamp down on my automatic fury at her deluded self-importance so I could conjure up a response. "That might have been possible if we were living in a parallel universe, but it was never going to happen in ours."

"We courtiers are far more suitable companions for you than these…dregs of society that you have gathered together!" She swept her hand across my motley crew, almost losing her towel in the process. She held it loosely and it hovered on the verge of exposing her breasts again.

"These dregs are my family, *Millie*." Her eyes narrowed at the jab. Now it was Thaddeus' turn to try to hide his amusement. He secretly hated Millicent and was tired of being beneath her overbearing control. "These people mean far more to me than you ever could," I continued. "I don't give a crap about anyone's pedigree, but we both know where you really came from anyway." I tipped her a slow wink and she grew very nervous.

"I don't know what you're implying."

I had to admit that she looked very regal even when she was just wearing a towel. "You and Geordie have a lot in common. You both grew up dirt poor on a farm. Yours just happened to be in Poland."

"Who told you that?" She'd pretended to be an aristocratic Englishwoman for so long that she almost believed the lie herself.

"You're *Polish*?" one of her minions asked incredulously, as if she'd just discovered that Millicent carried a rare and disfiguring disease.

Thaddeus barked a laugh and clapped Millie on the shoulder. "Don't worry, love, you're not the only one who's been lying for all these centuries." He grinned at her and the others. "My real name is Petrov and I'm from one of the Slavic countries whose name has changed multiple times over the past couple of centuries." He turned his grin on Gregor. "Ask your questions and I will do my best to answer them."

Millicent turned her back on all of us and stalked to the edge of the water. I wasn't worried that she would try to make a break for freedom. There was nowhere on this planet that she would be able to hide from me.

"Who was this Chinese scientist?" Gregor asked. "Was it someone in the military?"

Shivering when a breeze tried to flip his towel open, Teddy shook his head. "He was a civilian scientist by the name of Chan Wei Lee. He'd put out feelers asking for vampires to aid him in his research shortly after you lot were ousted from the planet. Naturally, his government were concerned about his research and immediately began hunting for him. He went into hiding and only re-emerged when the aliens invaded Manhattan and you returned from your decade of banishment."

His amusement disappeared and he turned more serious. "When it became obvious that we wouldn't fit into your little cadre of friends, Millicent concocted the idea of selling your blood to Dr Lee."

I remembered handing over a cup of my blood to her when I'd been creating my small army of fledglings and the icy look in her eyes when she'd taken it. I also remembered Thaddeus hunching over the bundle that he'd been carrying when I'd dropped them off in the underground parking lot in China. I might have handed her my blood, but he'd been the one to squirrel it away.

"Dr Lee had procured some of the yellow goo the robot army used to turn humans into those ugly grey monsters," Thaddeus explained. "He intended to use your blood, our blood and the yellow goo to experiment on animals."

"How could you possibly think that that would be a good idea?" I asked him.

"We only discovered the full extent of his plan after we'd been incarcerated," Thaddeus said in an effort to defend their actions. "They locked us in a room with twelve containers and lowered the temperature and began to freeze us. We overheard some of the lackeys talking about Dr Lee's intended experiments through the window."

"How long were you held captive?" Luc asked.

"Since the day that Natalie teleported us to China," Teddy confessed.

"That was only a few weeks ago," Igor said. "How many creatures could they possibly have created in that short space of time?"

My intuition took over. "I don't think they've created any, yet. I'm pretty sure the abandoned monastery in my dream is where the actual experiments will take place." That was where the new undead would be birthed and where our nightmare would begin.

"We need to find this monastery and stop the disaster before it happens," Ishida said.

I probed Thaddeus' mind for an image of the mad scientist, but came up blank. None of the twelve prisoners had actually met Dr Lee. They'd only had contact with his lower level lackeys. I had a feeling the mad scientist was in the wind and no one would be able to tell us where he'd gone into hiding.

"We can perform an internet query on both the monastery and Dr Lee and see if that will help us narrow our search down," Gregor suggested.

"What are we going to do about them?" Geordie asked and pointed at the bedraggled vampires.

I knew what had to be done, yet I turned to the others to seek their opinions. Their expressions said it all. These twelve ex-courtiers were the remnant of the old way of life. Their discontent had led us to the very threat that we would now have to locate and destroy. I read their doom in the eyes of my friends and allies. "What do you suggest we do, Geordie?" I asked.

Geordie's narrow shoulders bowed beneath the weight that I'd just placed on him.

Spinning around, Millie squawked in rage. "You dare to leave our fate in this lowly servant's hands?" She stalked forward, shoving her minions out of the way and leaned down so her face was a bare inch away from mine. "What right does he have to decide whether we are to live or die?"

"By the right of being my conscience," I replied. "Geordie?" I prompted, maintaining my eye contact with the courtier.

Despite his treatment at Millicent's hands, sorrow settled over him. "Kill them all," he said softly. Obeying his command, my hand shot out.

Millie's eyes widened and she looked down at her chest. I'd moved so fast that she didn't even feel it when my fist punched through her flesh just above her towel. Fishing around inside her chest, I wrapped my hand around her heart and yanked it out. Thick, black goo squirted between my fingers and oozed down my hand as I squeezed the muscle to a pulp. For two seconds, she stared uncomprehendingly into my eyes then her heart disintegrated and the rest of her followed.

Before the remaining eleven ex-courtiers could flee, Higgins and Wesley fired their weapons. I hadn't even realized that they were armed. Their weapons were a part of their uniform and I barely noticed them anymore. I felt a moment of regret when a bullet tore into Thaddeus' chest. Geordie had made the call and it had been the right one. I shifted my small group backwards a bare instant before the former courtiers exploded. I broke my hand down and re-formed it, ridding myself of Millie's remains.

I'd secretly known from the moment that we'd first met them that they'd end up this way, yet I'd hoped I would be wrong for once. My instincts had been true, which was proof that I needed to listen to them more often.

Igor put his hand on Geordie's shoulder when the teen bowed his head. Geordie had a servant of his own to take care of now. For the first time in his lengthy life, he knew the true weight of responsibility.

"Let's return to the village," Ishida suggested. "We have an internet search to run."

It was probably a good thing that the girls had chosen to have a bonding party tonight. They couldn't get into much mischief with dozens of protective soldiers in the houses around them. Ishida was philosophical that his home had been chosen to host the party. It made sense, since six of the girls lived with him. The event would keep them busy while we embarked on our hunt.

I returned us all to the house on the hill and Ishida switched on the laptop that Luc had bought for us both. We crowded around the couch to watch as he searched the internet for abandoned monasteries. He found plenty of ruins, but none had creepy stone statues holding sacrificial bowls.

China was a big place and I simply didn't have the capacity to search over a billion people's minds to see if they knew Chan Wei Lee. Ishida ran a quick search on the scientist, but no photos of him were available. I pictured the cells beneath the monastery and the laboratory all too well. I'd only caught a fleeting glimpse of the creatures that had probably already been created by now. I now knew what they were, or at least that they'd started out as some kind of animal before they'd become monsters.

"This is useless," Geordie complained when Ishida had located all of the monasteries on record. Throwing himself back in his seat, his bottom lip pooched out in a pout. He was adorable when he sulked, but he'd mope even more if I told him that. "Wherever it is, the monastery isn't on the net."

"You still can't sense any new undead creatures anywhere?" Kokoro asked me.

Indulging her unspoken request, I closed my eyes to better focus and sent my senses out across the globe. I counted nearly two hundred and thirty vampires. All but eight of them were right here in this village. The others were scattered throughout Europe and were lone souls who preferred to keep to themselves. I quickly scanned their minds and none were homicidal maniacs. They stayed beneath the radar and didn't leave corpses in their wake. That might change eventually, of course and they might one day become a problem.

Opening my eyes, I shook my head. "Nothing else is showing up on my radar." There was disappointment all around at my reply.

"I wonder why you can sense humans, aliens and even robots, but not these creatures?" Igor said.

Gregor looked thoughtful then came up with a theory that sounded plausible enough. "Perhaps Natalie can only sense creatures that possess a human level of intelligence."

"Are you saying that if these things are animals, then Nat won't be able to sense them at all?" Geordie asked.

"So it would appear," Luc responded.

"If that is the case, then we are in serious trouble," Higgins said. "How are we going to find these creatures if Natalie can't sense them?"

"We will discover them the old fashioned way," Ishida said. "We'll have to wait for them to start eating people."

"Just like the good old days," Geordie said. His mouth smiled at his lame joke, but his eyes reflected the dread that we all felt. We'd become so reliant on my strange and wonderful powers that we were lost without them. We'd be practically blind and crippled when hunting down our new adversaries. Any advantage that I had as Mortis wouldn't be of much help to us now.

Chapter Fifteen

We watched the news diligently as several more nights passed. No news was reported anywhere in the world that even hinted that our enemy had risen.

I wasn't the only one who was growing antsy from the inactivity. My men were showing signs of boredom and unrest. Ishida and Kokoro agreed to teach the art of sword fighting to anyone who was interested in learning it. Luc hunted down dozens of samurai swords on the net and I teleported him to wherever they were in the world so he could buy them. This meant we needed cash, so we took a trip to a private vault in a bank where he had a few million dollars stashed.

Retrieving the money was easy enough. I simply zapped us inside the vault, then waited for Luc to stuff a bag full of dough. I then shifted us to Tokyo where the first swords were waiting to be purchased. Tokyo had been spared by the octosquid attack, but other parts of Japan hadn't fared so well. It would take a long time to rebuild the cities and the population that had been destroyed or eaten.

Igor took on the job of weapons maintenance. He procured the necessary tools, then made sure each sword was sharp and in its best possible condition. Kokoro and Ishida held classes nightly in a field behind the village.

I taught Luc how to kill zombies and he quickly outstripped me in skill. Life was idyllic, but I knew the peace and tranquillity wouldn't last. Each time I lay down to sleep, I expected to dream about the coming disaster. The dreams I had were normal rather than prophetic. Most centred on a nuclear war or some other disaster that was about to happen because I was sitting around playing computer games instead of doing the job that I'd been created for.

My female fledglings, and Gabrielle, all succumbed to their flesh hungers on the same night. I sat on the couch beside Luc and tried not to cringe each time a cry of pleasure rang out from the village. Renee was only thirteen years old, yet she'd already experienced hell at several men's hands, not that she remembered the abuse. I trusted Ishida to initiate her into the pleasures of the flesh. With six girls to satisfy, he had an extremely busy night. Maybe it was a good thing that he was used to bedding several girls at a time.

Igor was the most deeply affected by the change in my servants. He'd fended off Simone's advances so far, but he couldn't fight her off any longer when her hunger rose and awakened his own. Luc sent me sympathetic glances each time I winced as the Russian sent out an image of what

Simone was doing to him. I saw many images that night and all had been inadvertently beamed to me by far too many people. I could barely look anyone in the eye the next night, especially Igor. It had been far too long for him and he couldn't keep his grin from rising when he came to visit us.

Fortunately, most of my soldiers had missed out on the display. They'd asked me to transport them into the city as the first lusty moan had pierced the night. I wished that I'd been able to join them. A few had stayed behind, sacrificing themselves to the young women. They'd been chosen by my newest servants and all had been happy to help out. Charlie had been one of the chosen and he'd worn a constant smug smile for hours. His smile withered a bit when the girl chose someone else the next night. Not all vamps were monogamous. Just like humans, some liked variety.

One of us was hard at work while the rest of us played computer games, or learned how to use the swords. Danton was determined to chronicle my story, but he had limited knowledge on how to use computers. Writing my memoirs was going to take time and typing it out seemed like a good idea, but he had to peck and hunt for the correct keys. With his highly attuned memory, he learned how to touch type after only one lesson from me.

I also taught Danton how to surf the net so he could take his turn searching for news. He was surfing through the headlines as Luc and I were playing a computer game in our living room. Gregor and Kokoro were snuggling on the other couch, having a rare night off from training the troops when Danton spoke. "This is curious." He was sitting on one of the armchairs with his computer in his lap. His brow was furrowed and I sensed his concern.

Luc paused the game and I was glad to have a reprieve from constantly losing against him. Put a sword in my hands and I was a genius. Put a game controller in my hands and I became a bumbling klutz. "What have you found?" Luc asked.

Danton stood and moved to the end of the couch. Taking a seat, he placed his laptop on the coffee table. Gregor and Kokoro left the second couch that we'd added to the living room and stood behind us. We read the news headline and Luc and I shared a worried glance.

"I believe this might be the sign that we've been waiting for," Danton said quietly.

I read the headline again, silently agreeing that he might be correct; Entire Town in India Missing. Evidence of Foul Play Detected.

A small town to the north of India had been abandoned several nights ago, according to the article. When no one had been heard from after a couple of days, the police were sent in to check on them. The remote mountain village had only contained three hundred people, but every single one of them was gone. While blood had been found in most of the homes, no body parts had been left behind.

It was a disturbing story, yet I was almost glad that we had our first inkling that the specimens had broken free from their cages. "This sounds like the disaster we've been waiting for," I said.

Fate wasn't going to be happy that three hundred of the souls that I was supposed to be keeping safe were already dead. I held no hopes whatsoever that any of them were still alive. While humans, vampires, aliens and even robots had the capacity to reason, animals acted on instinct. They'd slaughtered the inhabitants of the village and had then hidden the bodies somewhere. They were smart enough to cover their tracks, which meant they were craftier than I'd expected.

"Why would they remove the bodies?" Kokoro asked.

Gregor had already thought of an answer and he seemed disturbed by it. "Whatever animals they'd once been, perhaps killing humans is considered to be taboo for them. They are most likely acting on instinct." He echoed my thought almost too well.

"Should we investigate the town?" Luc asked.

Gregor nodded. "We five can take a quick look to see if we can find any clues."

From the cries and moans coming from the village, the rest of our friends were busy and wouldn't appreciate being interrupted, unless the matter was urgent. With the villagers already dead, there was no need to drag everyone along with us. Higgins, Wesley and some of the other men had driven into the city and wouldn't be back for at least another hour. We five were on our own.

I wasn't about to leave the house without my weapons and called my swords from the bedroom to me. Danton gave me an admiring grin when they appeared in my hands. "I do not suppose you could call my weapon to me?" he asked me hopefully. Gregor lifted his brow in enquiry as well.

It took only a few seconds of concentration then we were all armed with either swords, or with the guns that we'd stolen from the British soldiers. I donned the sheaths and my swords crisscrossed my back comfortably.

Danton hefted his gun, already comfortable with using the weapon after a short amount of practice. I'd shifted our entire team to a remote location several times so they could practice their skills. Even the newest arrivals had at least some proficiency with the guns and swords now. Luc had managed to procure one sword for everybody. I was the only one who tended to use two. My kin were as well armed as they could be and I still wasn't sure if it would be enough. I wished our troops still had their death rays, but they'd been confiscated when they'd been arrested. We had only seven of the Viltaran weapons left now.

With the image of the news clip fresh in my mind, we appeared a short distance away from the small rustic town in northern India. The houses were more like huts, but satellite dishes and electricity could still be found even in this remote location.

A single policeman remained behind to guard against looting or the merely curious. They needn't have bothered. No one had come to investigate the town, at least no humans had anyway. The policeman sat in his dilapidated, rusty car with the doors locked. He was afraid to move in case the things that had attacked the village returned. I sent him an order to fall asleep until morning and he gratefully complied. He slumped backwards and his head came to rest at an awkward angle. He'd have a stiff neck when he woke, but that was his problem, not mine.

"Do you sense anything?" Luc asked quietly.

Wary and ready for anything, I searched the town and surrounding area for signs of life or unlife. "I'm not picking up anything." Apart from us, I couldn't sense, see or hear anyone or anything in the immediate area.

"Let's take a look around," Gregor said and started towards the nearest hut.

Made of stone walls and thatch roofs, the dwellings weren't even close to being inviting. Inside, we found colour and warmth in the decorations and throw rugs. We were close to the border of Nepal and it was cold up in the mountains. The floors were covered in animal skins, possibly goats or deer.

The first hut told us little. Furniture had been knocked over and streaks of blood left a grisly pattern on the floor. A meal still sat on the table. I counted five plates, but saw no signs of the inhabitants.

We spread out and searched the small town, then met up in what was probably the village common. An ancient stone well with an aged bucket took pride of place. We stood near it in a small circle. "Did anyone find anything?" Gregor queried and received four negative replies.

"I did notice something," Luc said. "There are no animals anywhere. I saw signs of pig pens and other enclosures, yet not a single animal remains in the village."

Gregor nodded. "I noticed that, as well."

I hadn't, but I wasn't about to admit my woeful lack of attention. "Do you think they were killed and carried away as well?"

"I doubt it," Gregor replied. "It is more likely that they have been recruited."

Danton frowned at that possibility. "You believe that the specimens have turned all of the domesticated animals of this village into their servants?"

"It is a possibility," Gregor said. "The rat that bit Natalie turned its companion," he reminded us. It had been an accident, but if one animal had managed it, then others might be able to as well.

"Since this village was apparently the first one to be attacked, it makes sense that the monastery must be nearby," Luc suggested. "We should retrieve the others and search the area."

"Do you think that will be necessary?" Danton asked. "Would it not be best for us to hunt the creatures down and eradicate them rather than waste time inspecting where they originated from?" Staying true to his nature, he'd chosen more white shirts and plain brown trousers for his wardrobe. He shivered slightly as a breeze ruffled his fringe of white hair. The altitude of the town made it too cold for most of our kind.

It was my turn to answer him this time. "If I've learned anything about our destiny, it's that nothing is ever that easy. If we were meant to hunt these things down without jumping through a series of hoops first, they'd be standing in front of us right now."

Gregor backed up Luc's idea. "It could be useful to learn exactly what type of creatures we will be dealing with. If we're lucky, Dr Lee might have left some notes behind."

It was highly doubtful that the mad doctor had survived the breakout of his unholy creations. They wouldn't currently be running wild if he was still among the living.

Chapter Sixteen

I returned to Italy alone. The others opted to remain behind and begin the search for the monastery. While Gregor, Kokoro and Luc were immortal, Danton was as susceptible to death as any normal vampire. Luc didn't want to leave the monk wandering around the hills alone, so he paired up with him.

Corporal Higgins, Sergeant Wesley and the rest of my soldiers who had taken a trip into the city returned to the village shortly before I did. My sudden appearance was a warning that something had happened. Exiting from the cars, they jogged over to me.

"Have you located the threat, ma'am?" Higgins asked. He could tell by my expression that something serious had happened.

"Danton found a news report of a village near Nepal that has mysteriously been emptied of its inhabitants," I said grimly. "Gather everyone together and make sure they wear warm clothing. We're leaving in five minutes. See if you can find an extra jacket for Danton." He would begin to seize up from the cold before too long.

Snapping a salute, they split up and started banging on doors. I heard groans of disappointment from some of the ladies, and Geordie. Despite their protests, everyone was clothed and armed and had gathered on the laneway before their time was up. As ordered, they wore coats to ward off the cold that they would shortly be feeling.

Ishida's harem was clustered closely around him. Each girl carried a weapon that looked far too big in their tiny hands. More mature than the others, Simone held her gun confidently. She rarely left Igor's side and he'd spent a lot of time training her privately, not that he was a weapons master. He seemed content to have her near and even reached out to touch her cheek affectionately.

Geordie saw the gesture and turned away so his mentor couldn't see his bottom lip tremble. He was happy for Igor, yet he was still smarting that he was no longer the most important person in Igor's life.

"I take it we're going to Nepal?" Ishida asked. The soldiers had given them only a brief outline of our mission.

"Not quite. It's a village in northern India, near the border of Nepal," I replied. "I'm pretty sure the monastery is somewhere around there and we only have a couple of hours left to find it." India was a few hours ahead of us and time was running out. "My dream told me the ruins are near a cliff, so be careful not to step off the edge."

With that, I shifted the group to the empty streets of the village. My soldiers cast curious glances at the police officer who was slumbering in his car. His snores could be heard from several streets away. I nodded at Higgins and Wesley and they took charge of the search operation. Splitting our people up into small teams, they sent them out to look for the ruins. Higgins called for Danton, received an answering shout and hurried over to hand him the spare jacket.

I searched alone, walking through the tall grass and stepping over rocks and piles of dung made by unknown animals. They had most likely become hybrid clone-vampires. I wasn't particularly concerned when I found nothing of interest. My instincts told me that we were in the right place. Someone would eventually stumble across the scientist's lair.

A shrill whistle rang out after nearly an hour had passed, drawing everybody to the top of a distant hill. Charlie waved to me and I teleported over to him. "I think I found it," he said excitedly and pointed at a wall just ahead. Most of it had fallen long ago and only a small section still stood. A distant mountain range beyond the ruins looked familiar. It was another sign that we were in the right place.

Just like in my dream, the ruin was near the edge of a cliff. Reaching the crumbling structure, I made out the half-dead vines that covered the grey-brown stone. A robed figure stood in a cut-out section of the wall. It held a large, shallow bowl. The full moon shone through the gap behind it, throwing the statue's face into shadow. The hood of the robe covered the top half of its face. It hid all but its unsmiling mouth and square jaw.

"This is definitely the right place," I confirmed. One of the soldiers clapped Charlie on the back and the redhead smiled smugly at having been the one to locate our goal.

Luc threaded his way through the crowd with Danton on his heels. Together, we walked towards a rectangular opening in the ground. A set of stairs led down into a darkness that wasn't quite absolute. A faint light appeared at the bottom, beckoning us downward.

"What is that?" Renee asked and pointed at a large sheet of metal lying in the grass. Her eyes were sharp, I hadn't even seen it.

"I believe that is meant to cover the stairs," Gregor said.

That must have been what had trapped me inside the stairwell in my dream. Not that I'd tried to escape, since I'd known I was supposed to examine the underground lair. Now I was here in the flesh, but I wasn't alone this time.

It was highly doubtful that any of the specimens were still in residence. Still, I wasn't about to take any chances just in case they were lurking somewhere nearby. "I want most of you to stay up here and to keep watch," I instructed the group. "Whatever these things are, they don't show up on my radar, so I won't be able to warn you when they're about to attack."

"You're in charge, Charlie," Higgins said to his friend then he and Sergeant Wesley stepped forward. They were my right and left hand men and they'd earned the right to follow me into danger. Luc slanted me a sardonic look, but he didn't object to their overprotectiveness. They'd been trained for combat and backing up their leader had been their main purpose when they'd been alive. Just because they weren't human anymore didn't change that aspect of their personalities.

Danton wasn't about to be left behind and stepped forward as well. The rest of my close friends also joined us and we began the descent down four flights of rough stone stairs. Hand crafted and at least several hundred years old, they were uneven and varied slightly in height. Some of the stones had come loose, making our footing treacherous.

A long corridor stretched out ahead of us when we reached the bottom of the stairs. The smell of wild animals was strong and emanated from the cells on each side of the hallway. I glanced inside the barred window of the metal door to the left. Straw was piled in a corner. Excrement stained the walls in random patterns that looked like they'd been drawn by toddlers.

"You always take us to the nicest places, Nat," Geordie complained. Ishida did his best to muffle his snigger. The other teen's shrill giggle echoed around the hallway. Igor threatened them both with his open palm and they sobered. I understood their nervousness and their need to release their tension. Unfortunately, I was supposed to be an adult and didn't have the luxury of being childish, so I kept my amusement hidden for once. Luc slanted me a glance, knowing I was trying hard not to laugh. Sometimes he knew me too well.

At the far end of the corridor, a heavy metal door awaited. Just like in my second dream of this place, the door was slightly ajar. It swung open all the way when I pushed it and Luc levelled his weapon. The weak bulb in the hallway behind us didn't reach the lab and it was pitch black inside. My eyes adjusted quickly and I saw empty cages, oversized hospital beds and smashed lab equipment. We filed inside to inspect the room.

"Ten cages," Gregor mused. I did a quick count and came up with the same number.

"I'm really starting to dislike the number ten," Ishida said darkly. "There were ten banished disciples, ten octosquids and now we face ten escaped specimens."

The parallel hadn't even occurred to me and a superstitious shudder worked its way down my spine. I was glad to be distracted from my sudden and unwelcome thoughts of doom when Igor pointed at a splatter of blood on the floor. The drops had dried to a dark brown stain. "I see drag marks," the Russian said and followed them to another door.

A smaller corridor on the other side contained more cells. They were all empty, but showed recent signs of occupation. The wild animal smell disappeared and now I smelled something else coming from the cells. It was a strange blend of odours that I couldn't quite identify. Now that we had an inkling of what Dr Lee had been up to, I figured the smell was a combination of Viltaran clone and vampires, mixed with whatever animal had been experimented on.

The blood trail led us into a large room where over a dozen bodies were piled up inside. The deceased were Chinese and wore the typical white coats of scientists. The bodies were missing their heads, which had been discarded carelessly in a corner. From the stench and signs of decomposition, the corpses had probably been there for at least a couple of days. We were lucky the ruins were so cold, otherwise the smell would have been unbearable.

Igor and Gregor hunkered down beside the white coated man on the top of the pile. Twin holes had been torn in his chest and blood stained his coat. Igor's expression remained impassive as he searched the man's pockets and pulled out a wallet. Not much bothered him, not even patting down a slowly rotting cadaver.

Opening the wallet, he examined the driver's license then handed it to Gregor. After a few moments of scrutiny, they exchanged a look and stood. "We've found the elusive Dr Lee," Gregor said. "It appears that he was gored by something before having his head bitten off. The creature then fed from his neck, draining him dry." He mimed picking up an object and holding it above his head while he fed.

Geordie's weak stomach betrayed him and he made quiet gagging sounds. Ishida patted his friend on the back consolingly, but his face was pinched with worry. "Just how big are these escaped specimens?" he asked.

"They're huge," I replied bleakly. They'd been mostly hidden in shadows in my dream, but I'd had a pretty good impression of their size. I doubted they'd have any trouble at all at picking a human up like a bottle of water and drinking from the stump of their neck. I distinctly remembered how large the creature's mouth had been. My entire head could fit inside its gaping maw.

The bodies that lay piled together had all died the same way, being gored, then decapitated. The enormous lab rats had escaped and had turned on their captors. After killing the scientists, they'd escaped through the staircase and had attacked the town. Even ten voracious monsters couldn't have eaten three hundred humans without help. Gregor's hunch that they'd turned the domestic animals in the village was probably correct. If my blood had been mixed with theirs, then their minions would have turned almost instantaneously. The only question was whether they were mindless, ravenous eating machines, or if they'd managed to retain control of their blood hunger.

These creatures had a head start of several nights on us and we had no idea which direction they'd taken. While snow would seriously hamper a normal vampire's movements, I wasn't so sure that it would affect the specimens and their lackeys the same way. They could cross the range, passing through Nepal and straight into China, which was the most populated country in the entire planet. Or they could head south deeper into India, which was the second most populated country on Earth. They could also head east into Pakistan, or north into whatever other countries were close by. The choices were many and we had no clues to follow.

Remembering how quickly the rat that had bitten me had turned its companion, I shuddered at the thought of what might happen now that the threat had finally become known. Thousands, then millions and ultimately billions of animals could spread across the globe with the sole intention of feeding their hungers.

Whatever these experiments were, they didn't much resemble the Viltaran clones that made up at least part of their DNA. They hadn't eaten the humans' meat and had instead drained them of their blood. They were vampires, just like us. The only difference was that they lacked the intelligence to be reasoned with. There would be no peace between our species. We were in yet another kill-or-be-killed situation.

Most of the lab equipment had been destroyed in the initial feeding frenzy, but some of the larger pieces were still standing. Luc opened a door of one of several large refrigerators and pulled out a test tube. It was full of black vampire blood. Kokoro opened the doors of the other fridges and discovered the rest of the courtiers' blood that had been stolen from them while they'd been half frozen.

"We should destroy these samples so no other curious humans can perform experiments with them," Kokoro suggested.

"I'll take care of it," I replied and the test tube in Luc's hand disappeared. One by one, I cleared the fridges of their stolen contents and willed the courtiers' blood far away.

"Where did you send the test tubes?" Geordie asked.

"Space junk?" Luc said with an eyebrow raised.

"Space junk," I confirmed.

"That was a good idea," the teen said. "No one will find them floating around out there."

Ishida spotted a laptop bag lying beneath some junk and scooped it up. He took a peek inside and brightened. "This is labelled 'property of Dr Lee'. Let us hope that it will prove to be useful."

Dawn was nearing and it was time for us to go. I wasn't the only one who was happy to leave the spooky monastery behind. Geordie sent a glance back over his shoulder as we retraced our steps and let out a shiver. He gave me a sheepish smile and I briefly hugged him to my side. "I am glad to be leaving that place, *chérie*," he said.

"Me, too." He brightened at my confession that I'd also had the heebie-jeebies. The place had been even creepier in person than it had been in my dreams.

"Did you find anything?" Charlie asked when we appeared at the top of the stairs.

"Ishida found a laptop," I informed our team. "Hopefully, it'll tell us something that we can use."

Knowing our luck, it would be heavily encrypted and we wouldn't be able to understand a word of whatever was stored on the hard drive. *You managed to read the Prophet's journal,* my alter ego reminded me. Maybe I would be able to read even data that had been encrypted.

Once everyone was back on the surface, Higgins knelt and reached for the metal sheet. Igor touched the soldier on the shoulder and handed him several small devices that he'd pulled out of his pocket. Geordie craned his head over his mentor's shoulder to see what they were. His eyes went wide when he realized what Igor intended to do with them.

Higgins glanced up at me, raising an eyebrow in enquiry. "Do it," I confirmed then gestured for everyone to back away from the blast zone.

With a shrug, Higgins depressed the small red buttons on all six of the explosive devices then threw them down the stairs. He slid the heavy metal sheet over the opening and stood.

"You'd better move us further away," Igor said calmly.

Obeying his warning, I teleported my team to the bottom of the hill an instant before the explosions went off. Most of us covered our ears with our hands, grimacing in pain at the barrage of noise.

Bright orange flames roared up through the stairwell as the metal sheet was blasted into the air. The ground rumbled and the top of the hill became slightly smaller as the area above the secret lab caved in. The ancient monastery's walls buckled and fell, leaving no sign of the ruins behind. One of the girls squeaked in alarm when the metal sheet landed with a thump. It would take a far larger piece of metal to cover the hole that had been left behind after that explosion.

"Those explosives were more powerful than normal," Ishida said and turned a slightly accusing stare on Igor for not giving us a heads up.

"I may have modified them a little," the Russian admitted and held a thumb and finger a short distance apart. "They are now roughly four times stronger than they were."

"You could have warned us," Higgins muttered.

"Consider yourselves warned," Igor said and gave my soldier a rare grin.

Chapter Seventeen

Back in our village in Italy again, most of our team dispersed to their houses. The rest of us headed to the overseer's house. Ishida took a seat on our worn couch and fired up the laptop that he'd found amongst the ruins. For a scientist, Dr Lee was woefully lax with security. He hadn't set a password or any type of encryption on the computer. He must have believed that his lair was too well hidden to bother with the precautions.

Ishida opened up a list of files and searched through them until he found what we were looking for. Opening a lengthy document, he read through it, then recounted what he'd discovered. "The specimens started out as gorillas," he said. "Silverbacks, to be more precise."

He clicked on a folder and a series of pictures appeared. He enlarged one and a gorilla looked back at us. Its eyes were disturbingly human and contained a cunning intelligence. Ishida opened the other photos so we could examine them all. Going by the small notations beneath each picture, half of the specimens were male and the rest were female. They were far larger than a normal human in sheer muscle mass. Even when they were unconscious and had been stretched out on a table, they were taller than an average sized man.

Ishida read through some more information and was silent for a moment. "Dr Lee spent the past few weeks studying vampire blood and the Viltaran nanobots. He only began to experiment on animals a few days before his death. To begin with, he successfully changed some lab rats into a new species."

Pictures accompanied the reports. They showed the rapid transformation of a normal white lab rat into a nightmare combination of clone and vampire. Far larger than it had been, the rodent's teeth and claws had lengthened and its ears had become longer and curled at the ends. Its fur had disappeared and its skin had turned a dull grey colour. Its eyes were still black rather than red.

Ishida resumed reading from the report. "Dr Lee didn't stop there. He was curious about what would happen if he mixed Natalie's blood into the formula." The next series of photos depicted the disturbing changes. My blood had made the next few rats larger, uglier and stronger. Their eyes glowed red and stared directly into the camera with an evil malevolence. Their skin was greenish-brown rather than grey.

"Only three days ago, Dr Lee decided he'd perfected his formula and began to create a different type of specimen." He cast a look at me. "After destroying the lesser experiments with fire, he only had enough of your blood left to turn these ten gorillas into…whatever they've become now."

We saw what that was for ourselves in the next series of photos. Geordie made an exclamation of disgust as Ishida enlarged one of the pictures. Gone was a male silverback gorilla and in its place was a gigantic creature from my worst nightmares.

Completely hairless, it had the batlike nose of a Viltaran and the long, curled ears that we'd come to loathe. Its jaw had lengthened into something like a snout and its fangs were several inches long. Scarlet eyes glowered at the camera with hate and hunger. Its body was vaguely humanoid, but a spiny ridge ran along its back.

A close-up of the ridge revealed wickedly barbed spikes that would cut through flesh easily. Slabs of muscle on its chest and flanks had hardened into something close to armour. Its hands had turned into claws that were twice as long as its teeth. Instead of feet, it now had cloven hoofs. Somehow worst of all, long, slightly curving horns sprouted from its forehead. This creature was beyond a mere imp. It was far worse than that. *I think the word you're searching for is 'demon',* my alter ego said helpfully.

Wordlessly, Ishida opened the other nine photos. The gorillas had all been turned into Dr Lee's insane idea of the perfect specimen. They weren't quite identical in appearance, proving that they weren't clones and were an entirely different species altogether.

"Why do they have horns?" Geordie asked. Hunched forward on the edge of his seat, he was almost physically pained by the sight of our new adversaries.

"Good question," Ishida said and read the file on the demons in more detail. "It seems that Dr Lee wasn't content to just use vampire blood and the alien nanobots. He also mixed the DNA from several different animals into his cocktail. He used DNA from bears, goats, alligators and even himself."

"That would explain the claws, horns, cloven feet and scaly armour," Gregor mused.

"What was Dr Lee thinking?" Kokoro said in bewilderment. "Surely he knew how dangerous these creatures would be if they managed to break free." Which they most certainly had. Now we would have to hunt them and their minions down and eradicate them before they became a worldwide menace.

"He was a megalomaniacal fool," Ishida responded after rapidly reading through more of the files. They were written in Chinese rather than Japanese, but he obviously knew how to read them. "He was consumed with the idea of creating his own army of indestructible beasts. He believed that if he mixed his blood with the rest of the cocktail of ingredients, they would have to obey him."

"That is pretty crazy," Geordie agreed. "He was a human, not a vampire. Only a madman would have believed these creatures would be forced to follow his commands. How would they even be able to understand him?" He shook his head at the deluded rationale of the deceased scientist.

"Dr Lee performed many experiments on dozens of small animals," Ishida said as he continued to read. "He concluded that Natalie's blood is the key to rapidly turning his specimens into vampires. Anything that is fed the blood of one of the silverbacks turns into the undead instantly. So does anything else that is bitten by the second specimen, and so on and so forth."

Everyone glanced at me and I mentally slapped myself up the back of the head for being stupid enough to have given Millicent my blood. The scenario we were facing was exactly what the prophet had warned me about. This situation was the very one that I should have been trying to avoid. I'd idiotically handed over the means to destroy the entire human race to my enemies.

Ishida opened another file and we had a glimpse of what we could expect to battle ahead. Creatures in all sizes and shapes were recorded in the files. It was hard to tell what they'd been before their transformations. The mixture of my blood, nanobots and the blood of the mutated silverbacks had created servants that almost defied description. All were hairless, had red eyes, fangs, claws and greenish-brown skin. Only the gorillas had horns, so at least they'd be easily identifiable once we found them.

Gregor's fist rose to its usual position beneath his chin as he went deep into thought. I'd promised not to snoop into my friends' minds, but I was drawn into his thought process anyway. More rapidly than I'd have ever been able to, he sorted through the facts and drew conclusions that would never have occurred to me.

Seeing how his mind worked, I was awed by his instinctive ability to see the disaster from all angles. He foresaw a wave of undead animals sweeping across the globe and turning the planet into an empty wasteland. He also saw the humans retaliate with nuclear weapons, which had the same effect and the remnants of their species were forced to live beneath the ground. That was the exact scenario that I'd dreamed of. He didn't come up with the third alternative of the promised near utopia that Fate had dangled in front of me. Apparently, not even his imagination could stretch that far.

"Are things really that dire?" I asked him, revealing that I'd been snooping inside his head. "There has to be a third choice. There must be, because Fate told me we could somehow win."

"It may already be too late to stop this disaster," Gregor said gravely. "The Prophet warned you to be vigilant and to watch over your home. I now believe that he wasn't talking about anything as simple as a house, or even one country in particular. I think he was talking about the Earth as a whole. We were too late to stop the specimens from escaping and they have already commenced building an army of undead. Think of how many animals exist just in India alone and how many minions they can convert." Dead silence reigned as we contemplated the disaster that would shortly unfold. "If you cannot sense them, then we cannot anticipate where they will strike," he pointed out.

"Are you saying that there is no way for us to stop them?" Geordie demanded. "There has to be a way! Natalie will come up with something!" He turned pleading eyes on me and I'd have given anything to have been able to reassure him that we'd win this war. "You're Mortis," he reminded me. "It's your job to save the humans."

"I know," I said wearily. "I just don't know how I'm going to pull it off this time."

Igor's practicality came to the fore. "We have one tool at our disposal that should be of some assistance." He pointed at the laptop. "We might not be able to get ahead of the creatures, but we can at least narrow down the direction they're heading in. We will simply have to watch the global newscasts and be ready to act as soon as more disappearances are reported."

Gregor roused himself from the doom that was prominent in his thoughts. "As always, that is an excellent suggestion, Igor. In the meantime, our troops should continue to practice with their weapons and remain ready to leave at a moment's notice."

Geordie volunteered to take the first watch and returned to his home to monitor his laptop. Gabrielle would no doubt keep him company. I hoped the pair could keep their hands off each other long enough to check the news feeds every once in a while. As I'd expected, she'd chosen Geordie to be her bed partner. He was making up for his past two centuries of loneliness with frequent, and often loud, sex.

Accurately reading my doubt, Danton gave me a subtle nod before leaving. He'd also keep his eye on the news. I nodded my appreciation and saw everyone to the door.

Chapter Eighteen

Waking just before sundown the next night, Luc and I settled onto the couch to watch yet another old black and white movie. He preferred them to more modern movies with colour and actual speech, which proved that he was a dinosaur. He paused it after half an hour and cocked his head to the side. "We are about to have some company."

His hearing was sharper than mine, but I also heard voices approaching. We left the couch and opened the door to see my female minions heading up the path towards us. Even Ishida's harem was with them. It was rare to see his ladies away from his side.

Curious, I sent out my senses and found him sitting in his living room. A brief peek into his mind showed me he was happily playing a computer game. He was vaguely relieved to have some time to himself. Although he enjoyed being surrounded by his harem, he was beginning to feel a bit smothered by them. They lived in a small house and he had nowhere to retreat to when he wanted some time alone.

"We want to have a private training session with you," Simone told me when they reached the door. They all wore their swords in a sheath on their backs like I did. It was flattering to be emulated by my girls. They could use a gun if they had to, but they seemed to prefer using a sword. They all hero worshipped me, not just because I was their master, but because they thought of me as the ultimate female warrior. I might not have polished hand to hand skills, but I kicked arse with samurai swords. Plus, I was strong enough to rip just about any creature's heart right out of its chest.

Realizing that they wanted time to bond with me, I didn't turn the girls away. I didn't have any plans anyway, apart from getting Luc naked at some stage this night. "Ok," I agreed, much to their relief. I wanted them to know that they were important members of our team even if they were still fairly new. "Let's go to the studio at the back of the house." It should be large enough to accommodate all of us for a training session.

"I will see if Igor would like some company," Luc said and bent down to give me a thorough kiss before ambling towards the door.

We all turned to watch him walk away. One of the unattached girls made a sound of appreciation. "You're so lucky," she said enviously when the door closed behind my beloved.

"I know," I replied without a hint of smugness. I was well aware of how fortunate I was to have a man like Luc in love with me. I also knew what it felt like to be separated from him and I wasn't about to let that happen ever again. We were facing an unparalleled disaster, but I had to have faith that we would prevail. Otherwise, everything that we'd gained so far would be lost. This wasn't just about my happiness, it was about the welfare of our whole species. *No pressure,* I whined mentally as I led the way down the hall to the back of the house.

I'd never taught anyone how to use a sword before, so this was new to me. I lined the girls up and asked them to show me what they knew. They dutifully performed a series of blocks and slashes. I'd learned in one night what had taken them several weeks to grasp. Despite their lack of natural talent, I was still impressed with their progress. They were willing to learn and they were trying their hardest.

"We're sick of slashing at the air," Simone complained after I signalled them to stop. "We want to hack something to death." She laughed as she said it, yet I sensed her seriousness. "Igor won't let us chop up a real target because he doesn't want us to ruin our swords."

I knew of a real target that they could use, one that would repair itself whenever it lost a body part. "You can stab me," I offered.

Blinking at the suggestion, she shook her head as if she hadn't heard me correctly. "What?"

"I'll be your target," I told her. "I'm indestructible, so I'm your best sparring partner."

Knowing my reflexes sometimes reacted before I could stop myself, it would be too dangerous to use my real swords to spar with my students. I sent them to my bedroom then called a pair of Ishida's wooden practice swords to me from where he'd stashed them in his house.

Simone held out her hand for one, but I waved her back. "These are for me. You get to use your real sword." Her eyes lit up at the offer. Removing my jacket so it wouldn't be ruined, I readied myself. "Go for it," I ordered her and she attacked.

Sixteen young women formed a circle around us as Simone did her best to chop me to pieces. I deflected a lot of her wild swings and lunges, but allowed enough of them to get through for her to feel what contact with a real flesh and blood target was like. I also scored plenty of hits on her, reminding her that she could easily be hurt in return. The worst injury she suffered from my practice swords were splinters and a few bruises that faded almost instantly.

Stepping back at last, I bowed and Simone bowed in return. Her blade was coated in yellow goo. She cleaned it off with a soft cloth that she kept folded up in her pocket. Igor's influence was already starting to spread to her. She'd be as practical as he was soon.

My clothes were tattered in places and Renee stepped forward to finger a tear in my t-shirt. "Did it hurt when Simone stabbed you?"

"Not really," I replied honestly. "It takes a lot to hurt me nowadays."

"I've heard that you can reattach any body part that is chopped off," one of the other girls said in an awed tone. "Is that true?"

None of the girls had really seen what I could do yet and they'd only heard rumours. "How about I give you a demonstration of the kind of things that I'm capable of?" It was time for them to see just how strange I was.

They nodded eagerly, so I put the wooden swords down and obliged them. Holding onto my left hand with my right, I ordered Lefty to detach. My servants oohed and ahhed, then clapped when it waved at them before becoming reattached. They made noises of profound disgust when my clothes dropped to the floor and I became small chunks of meat. They were speechless when I broke myself down further. I became whirling particles that were almost too small to see even with our enhanced vision. Lastly, I formed a shadowy outline of my body, then poured myself back into my clothes and turned solid again.

"Are we ever going to be able to do any of that?" Renee asked and poked my arm to make sure that I really was whole again.

"Nope." They were disappointed with my answer, but I didn't want them to get their hopes up. Thinking that they might one day become invincible would be dangerous. It might lead them to take chances that they shouldn't.

"Luc, Igor, Geordie, Ishida, Gregor, Kokoro and I can heal any wound. The rest of you can heal most severe injuries, as long as nothing is hacked off, but we seven are the only ones who are truly immortal." Ishida's brood were happy to hear that he was indestructible, but none were happy with the news that they weren't.

"Why are you seven so different from us?" Simone asked me bluntly. I liked her forthright manner. She was only a few years younger than I'd been before I'd been turned.

"We, and a bunch of other vampires, were exiled ten years ago."

"I remember that," Simone said quietly. "You'd just finished saving Africa from a vampire invasion, then you suddenly turned rogue. We were told that you'd been sent to prison."

"We were," I said dryly. "We were imprisoned in a spaceship and were sent into deep space."

Renee's eyes widened as she put two and two together. "So, it's true that you're responsible for the aliens attacking Earth?"

I shook my head in denial. "Fate is ultimately responsible for everything that has happened, including our very existence."

They were understandably confused about that, so I gave them a quick rundown on how we'd come to be. I ended with our trip to Viltar and meeting the beings that turned out to be our ancient ancestors.

"Ok, I get why the seven of you are immortal now," Simone said. "But that doesn't explain why you are so different from the rest of us."

"I'm Mortis," I said with a shrug.

"What does that mean?"

"It's Latin for death," I replied. "A Romanian Prophet foresaw my coming a couple of thousand years ago and I guess he gave me that title. He said that I was destined to bring death to our kind, but that a remnant would remain."

"Are we that remnant?" Renee asked.

"Yes."

Most of them were flattered to be a part of a select group.

"Why do you have to go to the rescue of the humans all the time?" Simone queried.

"Because that's the real reason why I was created. I'm the guardian of the human race and it's my job to keep them safe."

"So, we have to find the monsters and stop them," one of the girls said. "We're your soldiers and your job is also our job. You have such awesome skills that we really can't lose with you in charge."

It was said so simply and with such belief that it almost brought a lump to my throat.

"Who wants to stab me next?" I asked, deflecting the group away from the fact that I might not be able to live up to their expectations. The last two groups of foes that we'd faced had killed millions of people worldwide. We were already several steps behind the silverback demons. They would quickly increase their numbers to plague proportions.

How many people are going to die this time? No one answered my desperate question. Even my subconscious remained conspicuously silent this time.

Chapter Nineteen

Igor's plan to monitor our laptops was a good one. We didn't have to wait long before we saw more news about the coming danger. Luc and I were teaching a class early the next night when Charlie sprinted over. "Higgins sent me to find you, ma'am." Our lesson was being held in a field a short distance from the village. Our students paused in their mock attacks, listening in as Charlie continued. "Gregor has found evidence of another attack."

I didn't waste time walking back to the village and zapped us all there instead. Luc and I barged into Gregor and Kokoro's home and found the rest of our friends already in attendance.

"What have you found, Gregor?" Luc asked.

"Unfortunately, it appears that the specimens have split up and have headed in several different directions," Gregor replied gravely. I caught another flicker from him of the doom that he felt coming. It was hard to remain positive when the smartest of us all thought we were screwed even before the threat had become widely known.

He's been wrong about our chances of success before, my alter ego said. *Let's hope he's wrong this time.*

I stood behind the couch with Luc at my side as Gregor brought up the first story on his laptop. I scanned the headlines over his shoulder. This story was eerily similar to the disappearances in northern India. The only difference was that this village was in Nepal. Once again, all of the humans and animals that had once inhabited a small town had mysteriously disappeared. Bloodstains and overturned furniture were the only signs of violence.

Three more stories in India told the same tale. One of the towns was to the south and the other two were to the east. God only knew where the other six demons were heading.

"Can you imagine the chaos that will ensue if these creatures attack a city the size of Delhi?" Kokoro said.

I didn't know how many people lived in the city, but it probably contained more souls than the entire population of Australia.

"What do you suggest we do?" Luc asked Gregor.

"We should teleport here," he leaned forward and pointed at a tiny dot on the screen. It was close to where the towns in eastern India had been attacked. "When we arrive, Natalie can send out her senses and see if she can pick up on a large number of lives being extinguished."

"Good plan," I said with genuine admiration. I'd never have thought of trying to sense the victims as they were perishing. Once again, he'd proven to be an invaluable asset.

"Your troops are armed and ready to go, ma'am," Higgins said. He came close to snapping me a salute. Igor shot a frown at Geordie before he could let out a nervous giggle. Chastened, the teen contented himself with a cheeky smirk instead. He liked the Americans, but found them to be highly amusing at times.

Stepping out onto the lane, I saw that my right hand man had been efficient at gathering our team. Everyone had assembled and they carried both swords and guns. I barely gave them the time to brace themselves before I carried us to the location that Gregor had in mind.

Being nearly five hours ahead of us, most people in the small town were asleep. Hearing the distant sounds of screams and guttural growls, their peaceful slumber wasn't going to last for much longer. Soon, the entire town would awaken and be reduced to a state of panic.

We ghosted into the shadows and I sent out my senses. I winced as I felt more human lives being snuffed out. Shifting us all further to the east, I landed our group into the middle of a feeding frenzy.

For a moment, we could only stare at the monstrosities that had once been ordinary animals. Their photos hadn't really done them justice. They were much uglier in real life. Moving with blinding speed, they brought fleeing humans to the ground and fed on them. They came in all different sizes and shapes. Some were almost recognizable, if now much larger than they had been.

I saw a pack of hybrids that had to have been dogs in their former lives. They were smaller than the doberclone that I'd inadvertently helped to create, but were no less vicious. One reared up, knocked an elderly man to the ground then sank its fangs into his throat. With a pained gargle, he died almost instantly. He was drained dry as two more dog imps joined in on the meal. I'd expected them to guard their meals viciously and was disturbed to see them sharing so easily. They must feel some kind of kinship then.

I already knew we were too late to save most of the population of the small town, but we could at least diminish the numbers of their attackers. I teleported the surviving civilians to a distant town where they would be safe before drawing my swords. "Open fire!" I yelled and my soldiers obeyed.

Bright orange light flared as explosive rounds hit their targets and reduced them to puddles of sludge. They had enough vampire blood in their systems to die like we did rather than leaving a messy corpse behind. The horde of misshapen abominations understood that they were under attack, but they didn't flee as I'd expected them to. Snarling their fury, they turned as one and ran straight towards us. Even my vampire soldiers with their uncanny strength and speed weren't a match for these monsters. They would be overwhelmed in seconds.

Making a split second decision, I whisked my friends and allies to the outer edge of the town. "Form a circle and work your way in," I instructed them.

My clothing would become a tattered ruin once I engaged the enemy up close and personal. They dropped to the ground when I reduced my body down to particle form and shifted into the centre of the town.

Whirling my swords in a vicious arc, only my eyes and hands remained solid as I waded into the crush of hybrids. Confused that their enemies and food had disappeared so suddenly, they milled around, vainly searching for a target.

I stabbed several to death before they became aware that they were under attack again.

Leaping, lunging and slashing with their claws, they tried to bite a substance that wasn't solid. They lacked the brains to realize that they couldn't kill me. My swords cut through their ranks with ease as shots continued to be fired by my soldiers. Scanning my small army for signs of panic, I made sure to shift them to safety whenever they were at the risk of becoming overwhelmed.

We'd destroyed roughly half of the horde before a roar raised the hairs on the back of my neck. Twin red orbs rose up above the fray as the demon in charge of this mob stood to its full height. It was hard to tell at this distance, but it appeared to be around fifteen feet tall. Even the outline of its body was enough to give me nightmares.

Its bellow seemed to be an order for its minions to fall back. I tried to read its mind, but all I could sense was rage and hunger. I was surprised when the undead critters turned tail and ran. They moved so quickly that our bullets had little chance of hitting their targets. Those of us who still carried death rays had more luck. Bright violet light flared and we zapped a few dozen of them before they moved out of our range.

The Viltarans' protocol to destroy all non-intelligent life forms that were exposed to their nanobots might not have applied to these creatures. These minions were definitely death machines, but it appeared that they could be controlled after all.

Intuition told me that my blood was to be thanked for this development. I'd had an epiphany at a casual remark that Kokoro had made during one of our battles with the octosquids. The blood bags that I'd used to top up my strength had spoiled, which had surprised Geordie. Kokoro said that anything could spoil if it wasn't stored correctly.

I now wondered if my blood had been altered during the hours that Millicent had held onto it. She'd had no way of keeping it cool after stealing it from me. Perhaps the nanobots had begun to malfunction slightly without a host body to inhabit. It was possible that my vampire blood had superseded the micro robots enough that the mutants were forced to obey their master. If so, then this was the only bright light in a sea of darkness. I'd half expected the hybrids to go their respective ways after being created and for complete chaos to reign. It seemed that we were dealing with controlled chaos instead.

Mutilated, mangled and sometimes headless, the drained corpses of over a thousand people lay strewn throughout the town. The gorilla didn't get the chance to hide the evidence of its attack this time. I wondered if their instinct to hide their deeds would eventually fade once they grew used to dining on human blood.

Surveying the carnage, Higgins made an observation as I called my discarded clothing to me and poured my particles inside them. "I don't think we have enough ammunition stockpiled to fight these things."

So far, we'd only encountered one of the packs that were roaming the country and we'd used up a lot of bullets and explosives in the process. There were nine more of these demons and their packs out there and we'd just failed miserably to stop this one. We couldn't be everywhere at once and I despaired that we were somehow supposed to end this disaster with a minimal loss of human lives.

I don't think it can be done, I admitted to myself. Now that this silverback knew how deadly we were, I doubted it would command its minions to attack us again. It would simply flee when we encountered it again and it would most likely choose another town to attack. Even we couldn't keep up with them once they ran. They didn't appear on my radar, so the only way we had of tracking them was the method Gregor had already suggested. I'd have to pick up on large numbers of people being slaughtered before we'd know where to strike next.

That plan sucks, my subconscious said in disgust.

Do you have a better idea? It remained silent at my question. *I didn't think so,* I thought sourly.

Chapter Twenty

We returned to our base to restock our ammo and took a few moments to procure more death rays. It was a strange quirk that I could will any item to me that I was familiar with. I didn't have to know exactly where they were, I just had to concentrate and draw them to me. I stole enough of the alien weapons to arm my male soldiers only. The girls would need to be trained how to use them before I'd bother to steal them one each. The death rays could destroy both metal and flesh, once they were turned to the correct setting.

My soldiers were pleased to have their hands on the advanced weapons again. They were far superior to anything the earthlings had created so far. Each man made sure the death rays were set to destroy flesh, then we waited for more mass deaths to appear on my radar. Several happened simultaneously, so it was back to India again. Choosing one of the towns under attack, we repeated our tactics of surrounding the enemy while I whisked any survivors away from harm.

The creatures didn't get a chance to attack us this time. Their master roared an order from the darkness and they fled before we could kill more than a couple of hundred of them. I caught a fleeting glimpse of the gorilla. It ran upright, towering several feet over most of its underlings.

I didn't get any sense that the silverbacks shared a telepathic link. This one just had fewer servants than the last science experiment and it was reluctant to allow them to be killed. It seemed that Gregor had been right when he'd assumed the silverbacks would recognize danger.

Before I could shift my army to the next location, I heard a strange fluttering noise. A second later, something slammed into my back. I was lifted into the air and the ground rapidly receded. Turning my head to see what had grabbed me, I realized I was caught in the talons of a gigantic prehistoric looking bird. Its feathers had been replaced by thin, leathery flaps of skin. It looked a lot like a pterodactyl, but I was pretty sure that it had once been a pelican. Now I knew what had swooped at me in my dream of the monastery before I'd been pushed down the stairs. *That's one mystery solved,* I thought in dazed amazement.

A red eye glared down at me and I sensed its intention to bite me in half. Drawing one of my swords, I shifted away a split second before its beak could slice me in two. Now crouched on the back of the bird, I held onto its clammy body with my knees as its beak clicked together and it gave a frustrated squawk. Then my sword sheared through its neck and it turned into a small waterfall of sludge. I teleported myself to safety before I could fall and splatter to the ground myself.

"What was that thing?" Geordie asked when I returned.

"A pelican, I think," I replied as I checked my clothes to make sure they were still intact. My jacket and t-shirt sported tears in the front and back, but they weren't in danger of falling apart.

"You should come and see this," one of my soldiers called out. He stood at the top of a nearby hill, looking down at something. Knowing that I wasn't going to like whatever was on the other side of the hill, I refrained from reading his mind.

Worry creased the soldier's brow and I understood his concern when we reached him. A large clearing was at the bottom of the hill and a huge circus tent predominated. The sides were shredded and were stained a dark reddish brown from a mass slaughter. Bodies lay everywhere and most were minus at least one limb. All sported claw or fang marks and had been drained of their blood.

My soldier gestured towards a dozen huge cages that were lined up to one side. Each one had been decorated with a painting of the type of animal that it had housed. None of the pictures were of anything as cute and harmless as a rabbit. "That could be a problem," he said and I had to agree.

Geordie pointed at one of the cages. "Lions."

Ishida nodded at another cage. "And tigers."

Igor indicated a third enclosure. "And bears."

Kokoro's hand rose to her mouth. "Oh, my!"

Most of my fledglings' heads swivelled incredulously towards the four, not quite believing what they'd just heard. I sniggered first, then everyone else started laughing.

Even Luc was smiling and Igor glowered at him. "What is so funny?"

Luc patted the Russian soothingly on the shoulder. "When this disaster is over, we'll have to introduce you four to the Wizard of Oz."

"There's no such thing as wizards," Geordie said sulkily. He hated being the brunt of a joke that he didn't understand. He'd brought this one on himself and had no one to blame this time.

Gabrielle hugged the teen and her adoration actually increased when he pouted. "They're talking about a pretty famous book and movie," she told her master. "You guys just accidentally quoted from it."

"Oh." Geordie grinned sheepishly then pointed at the largest cage. "Are elephants also in the story?"

My blood tried to run cold even as the shredded canvas walls of the tent parted to reveal the enraged former elephant. It was now almost the same size as the octosquid clones back on Viltar, minus the tentacles. Huge beyond belief, it lifted its misshapen head and trumpeted a challenge. Its tusks had multiplied from two to six and had grown to a full twenty feet long. Its trunk had shortened and had grown twelve inch long fangs on the end. Yard long claws dug into the ground, which shook as it stampeded towards us. Corpses were squished to a pulp beneath its feet, sending splatters of guts and gore in all directions. They looked like meaty pancakes and my stomach tried to revolt. Not for the first time, I was glad that I could no longer puke.

My soldiers opened fire and great gouges appeared in the mutant's thick hide. Its steps faltered slightly and my men kept up the barrage. If it could be hurt, then it could be killed. It just might take a few more bullets than usual to take it down.

Someone fired their death ray, but it only left a deep scorch mark in its side rather than disintegrating it. Its mass was too big for even the alien technology to kill it. Throwing an explosive would be too dangerous. It was moving too fast for us to lob the small grenades at it with any accuracy.

Firing with precision, six soldiers targeted the same spot and blasted a deep hole in the beast's chest. It finally went down to its knees and they closed in around it, staying a safe distance from its claws, tusks and fangs as they continued to fire. Rolling its scarlet eyes, the monster bellowed a final challenge, then flopped over onto its side.

Higgins and Wesley moved in. They used their death rays to zap their way deep inside its chest until they found its heart. Higgins fired violet blasts from his Viltaran weapon at the gigantic muscle, while Wesley fended off its trunk with his sword. When the heart became a small pile of ash, the vampiric elephant finally broke down into ooze, leaving my soldiers coated in noisome muck.

"Eww," Renee said and took a few steps away from the smell. "That's the most hideous thing I've ever smelled in my life."

Ishida's indulgent smile turned to horror when a dark shape came rushing towards her.

A second elephant had crept up behind us while we'd been busy killing its partner. With a squeal of triumph, it impaled my tiny servant on a tusk. The tip burst out of her chest, stained red with not just her blood, but the blood of the humans that it had gored before her.

I felt Renee's pain as if the injury had happened to me. The tusk had missed her heart by a fraction of an inch. She let out a shrill scream and held out a tiny hand towards Ishida. He leaped forward to save her, but I was faster. She disappeared from sight and so did Ishida. I teleported them both back to Italy where they would be out of harm's way. My servant's wounds would heal quickly enough and Ishida would keep her safe until she was well again.

Fixing its eyes on me, the gargantuan thundered a challenge and I accepted it. I moved my army backwards and stepped forward to battle the beast. I didn't reach for my swords, death ray or my gun his time. The weapon that I'd use for this battle was a part of me. It was one that no other vampire in creation possessed.

The ground shuddered when the hybrid broke into a run. Dirt flew as its clawed feet dug small trenches with each step. It opened its mouth wide and reached for me with its mutated trunk, eager to impale me and stuff me into its maw. I wasn't food, but it wouldn't let that small detail stop it from chewing me to pieces.

The dark power of the holy marks rose at my call. Filling me quickly, it almost ached for release. Lifting my right hand, I made the shape of a gun then pointed it at the monster and mimed shooting it. A spear of holy power shot towards the approaching creature in an invisible wave that stopped it dead in its tracks. Standing only a few yards away, it looked down at me in puzzlement. Then its body began to swell and it let out a buzzing bellow of agony. I shifted out of the blast zone just before it exploded. If I'd remained in place, I would have been coated in ooze and become even smellier than Higgins and Wesley.

Dazed and bewildered, my fledglings crowded around. "What just happened?" Higgins asked. Both he and Sergeant Wesley stood in a small space of aloneness due to their gore splattered states. My nose wrinkled when I caught a whiff of their stench. I had to agree with Renee, they did smell pretty hideous.

"Nat just killed it with her holy marks," Geordie explained and danced on the spot in excitement. "That was so cool! You shot it with a holy bullet!"

"It was pretty awesome," I said without a shred of modesty.

Before we could celebrate our victory, two more members of the menagerie came sprinting out from behind the tattered circus tent. Nowhere near as big as the hybrid elephants, the bears were still a frightening sight as they galloped on all fours. About the size of a van, their red eyes seemed almost too small for their massive heads as they simultaneously opened their fanged mouths and roared in rage.

"Zap them! Zap them!" Geordie screeched.

Using both hands this time, I called on my holy marks. I didn't have time to show off and simply lifted my hands and sent a blast of power at them through my palms. Both of the former animals stumbled, crashed into each other and went down. They shrieked in agony as their bodies swelled and I scrambled away moments before they burst.

My soldiers watched the trees, ready for the lions or tigers to show. A couple of minutes passed without incident and I turned to Gregor. "Do you think the gorilla left the elephants and bears behind as a trap?" I asked.

"Almost certainly." His reply didn't exactly come as a surprise, but I'd hoped my intuition had been wrong for once. "These creatures are proving to be far smarter than I'd anticipated." Instead of descending into gloom, his expression became crafty. His doubts about our chances of success hadn't faded, but now he was rising to the challenge that was before us. I read in his mind that he wasn't going to give up. After witnessing me ending the animals' lives without needing to put my hands on them, he had faith in my powers as Mortis. "It will be dawn soon," he said. "We should return to our village. I have the beginnings of a plan, but I need time to think it through."

Ishida's door burst open when he heard us return. Standing in the doorway, he glowered at me then crooked his finger imperiously. I wasn't about to trot meekly over to him so he could berate me in public, but I also wasn't going to humiliate him in front of the others.

Luc nodded his understanding at my need for privacy when I glanced up at him. "I'll wait for you in our house," he murmured.

I was still getting used to the idea that we had a house to call our own. "I'll be back soon," I said quietly.

Both the former emperor and I winked out of sight and reappeared on a hill that was far enough away for no one to be able to overhear us. Our conversation was going to be heated and I'd prefer not to have any witnesses.

"How dare you remove me from battle against my will!" Ishida said tightly. He was almost quivering with rage at being teleported away without his consent.

"I was under the impression that you care about Renee," I responded mildly.

"Of course I care about her!" Ishida threw his hands up then put them on his slim hips. "I care about all of my girls." Coming from any other male, that might have sounded possessive. Coming from Ishida, it was mere fact. He had room in his heart for many girlfriends, not just one.

"Then what would you have done in my place?" He was silent at that question. "Renee was badly wounded and I had to get her to safety. You seemed like the logical person to send with her, since you care about her more than anyone else does. Should I have sent her home alone? Should I have sent your other girls with her, when they were all equally petrified? I suppose I could have had one of my soldiers take care of her." His eyes flashed at that, but I didn't give him an opportunity to speak. "Like it or not, I am Mortis," I said coolly. "I have a duty, not just to the humans, but to my people as well. I simply acted in Renee's best interests, Emperor Ishida."

Ishida's shoulders slumped at being reminded of his former title and the responsibilities that had come with it. "I sometimes forget that I am no longer a ruler," he said ruefully. "I ruled for ten thousand years and it can sometimes be difficult not to have my every wish granted." Meeting my eyes, he offered me a deep bow. "Forgive me if I have offended you, Mortis. I promise that it won't happen again."

"Don't make promises you can't keep, Ishida," I said with a grin and he smiled in relief that I wasn't angry with him. "How is Renee?" I'd already scanned her mind and knew that she was fine. Her wound had healed and she was currently enjoying being fussed over by the other girls.

"She is very brave," he said with genuine affection. "At first, she thought she was going to die, but she began to heal quite quickly." Hesitating, he fought against ten millennia of protocol then stepped forward and hugged me. "Thank you for saving her, Nat."

"You're welcome, kiddo," the endearment slipped out before I could stop it, but he didn't take offense. I was careful not to treat Geordie and Ishida like children, most of the time. They might be young, but I considered them to be my equals as well as my friends. That might have been the most significant difference between me and most of our kind. I believed that a person's worth was based on their deeds, not on their status. Both teens meant more to me than I could ever express.

Geordie was anxiously pacing the lane outside Ishida's house when we returned. Everyone else had disappeared inside their homes. No one wanted to get caught up in any potential arguments.

Spotting us, he stalked over and checked that no one was around before speaking. "You two need to grow up and get a hold of your egos!" he hissed. "I don't care that you're both high and mighty rulers who are used to snapping your fingers and making people jump. You're more than that to each other now and you're supposed to be friends, so start acting like it!"

Ishida and I exchanged a glance then surprised Geordie by drawing him into a group hug. "We know," Ishida said. "But thank you for the reminder."

Geordie giggled in relief that we weren't at odds anymore. "I can't stand to see my two best friends fighting."

"We weren't fighting, we just had a difference of opinion," I told him. "I knew Ishida was pissed at me, so I shifted us away so we could yell at each other in private."

Ishida gave me another rueful look. "I am glad she did, because I made a total fool of myself."

"That's usually my job. I'm glad it happened to someone else for once," Geordie said and sniggered.

Ishida glanced at his house when the curtain was pulled aside. Several anxious young faces peered out at us. "I should check on the girls."

"Yeah, 'check on them'," Geordie mocked then gave his trademark giggle. I could practically feel the tension seep out of the village when they heard his laugh. If Geordie was in good spirits, then that meant I wasn't angry, or so they reasoned. Everyone was aware that the teen possessed a highly accurate mood radar. He was rarely wrong when it came to the possibility of conflict arising.

"We'll get together once Gregor has worked out his plan," I told the pair. With nods, they hurried to their houses. Unsurprisingly, they'd chosen houses next door to each other. Gabrielle opened the door clad only in her skin and smiled invitingly at Geordie. I wasn't sure that I was ever going to get used to the teen having a servant of his own. She meant far more to him than that, of course. She had become his other half and she was someone who he could cherish.

Clamping down hard on the urge to cry, I zapped myself into my bedroom to change out of my torn clothes. Geordie might never be an adult physically, but the teen was finally growing up and no longer needed me to look after him.

Chapter Twenty-One

Luc was waiting for me in the bedroom. As always, he was dressed all in black. He'd foregone his usual cashmere sweater in favour of jeans, a t-shirt and a leather jacket. The casual clothing suited him. More importantly, it didn't make me feel as if I was dressed far below his standards.

"Is everything all right?" he asked quietly.

Gregor, Kokoro, Igor, Simone and Danton were downstairs in the living room, so I lowered my voice as well. "Ishida threw a hissy fit about being removed from the battle, but he's ok now."

"Hissy fit?"

Luc's amusement made his lips curl up, which instantly captivated me. A dark eyebrow went up in invitation, but I shook my head. "While I'd love to rip your pants off and have my way with you, I have a feeling we're going to be too busy for that."

Right on the heels of that, Gregor spoke from below. "If you two lovebirds would care to join us, I'll outline my plan."

"See?" I said and Luc forced out a disappointed sigh.

"I'll see you downstairs." Lifting my hand, he kissed my knuckles, then ambled out the door.

I changed as quickly as I knew how, breaking down into minute molecules then pouring myself into a fresh t-shirt, jeans and my black leather jacket that was much like Luc's. It now sported a few extra rips and tears. I arrived seconds after my beloved and settled onto the couch beside him.

Nestled against Igor's side, Simone gave me a naughty wink. The Russian looked at me suspiciously when I smirked back at her. While it was handy having a couple of hundred male servants, friends and allies on hand, I was glad there were a few more girls around. I'd never really had female friends before and it would be nice to have some when this disaster was finally over. I just hoped Gregor's plan would work so there would be an 'after' to look forward to.

Gregor had found several articles of the attacks that had happened across India and Nepal. While we'd been busy battling the two groups of malformed animals, more towns and villages had been hit. We could see the general direction that the creatures were heading in. While I knew exactly how many humans had lost their lives, it was frustrating not knowing how many enemies had been created.

"By now," Gregor began, "we have to assume that at least several thousand animals have been converted into mutated vampires."

"Don't forget about the birds," I added dryly.

Gregor inclined his head in agreement. "The silverbacks have the capacity to create a vast army of undead underlings. Luckily for us, it appears that they are able to control their servants. They won't simply rise and immediately go in search of prey, but will have to attack wherever their masters direct them to."

Pondering the map, his eyes moved from one red mark where a town had been attacked to another, stopping in Nepal. "Unlike our previous battles with our various enemies, this time we have few advantages over them. We will have very little chance of getting ahead of them to halt their attacks before they can spread. We are simply too few in number to contain this threat. I am afraid that we require assistance from the humans once again."

My upper lip automatically lifted at the idea of being forced to rely on human support once more. We didn't exactly have a very good track record when dealing with the military. They'd turned on us every single time that we'd joined forces with them.

Gregor read my expression accurately. "I am not suggesting that we team up with them this time."

"What are you suggesting?" Luc queried.

"I propose that Natalie should take over a force of soldiers and shift them to the most likely place that the creatures will strike next." He pointed at a small town in Nepal that was closest to where the last attack had taken place.

Igor leaned forward to examine the map. "We will need at least a thousand soldiers to aid us. More would be even better."

"The Chinese have a large, well-armed army," Gregor said. He clicked on another icon and a new photo filled the screen. It was a map of China. He pointed at a tiny dot to the west that was closest to Nepal. "They have a garrison here that we can use as a practice run."

I realized it was necessary, but I didn't like the idea of using humans like puppets. I didn't kid myself that I'd be able to keep all of the soldiers safe. Many would die in the battles ahead, but many more civilians would perish if we didn't try to stop the hybrids. Frankly, we were desperate and I couldn't afford to turn down any kind of help.

While there was still plenty of night left where we were, dawn had already risen in India. The demons and their spawn would have gone into hiding by now. It was highly inconvenient being in a different time zone from where the attacks were being made.

Kokoro had the same idea and voiced hers first. "It would make sense for us to relocate to India. We need to be closer to the action, so that we don't waste any nightfall."

"I agree," Gregor responded and received supportive nods from Luc and Igor. "Can you find us somewhere safe to stay, possibly in central India?" he asked me.

"I'll try to find us something suitable," I replied.

Since it was daytime, I teleported to the centre of India alone. Choosing a large city, I could scarcely believe the sheer number of people that were crammed into the buildings around me. Most of the populace were just waking for the day and hadn't yet left for their prospective work places.

Finding the poorest part of town where I hoped I'd find a suitable hiding place for my troops, I remained hidden in the shadows as I searched. It didn't take me long to locate an abandoned building that had once been a hotel. I teleported to the top floor of the four-story building and sidestepped a ray of sunlight with a wince when it landed on my face. My flesh sizzled and burning pain tore through me as smoke rose. The putrid smell of burning flesh wafted from me. I turned my head into tiny motes and the injury was gone when I re-formed. *I wish I'd known how to do that the time I was half burned down to a skeleton by Ishida's people.* It had taken hours to heal that damage and I'd been in excruciating pain the entire time.

It wasn't just the ceiling that was in bad shape, the walls were, too. It wasn't the top four floors of the hotel that I was interested in. The basement beneath the building was my goal. I just wanted to make sure that the above floors weren't a popular place for the homeless to sleep in. I searched all of the rooms and found them to be dusty, but empty. The building should have been demolished years ago. We weren't in any danger of being discovered if we used this place as a hideout.

Coalescing inside the basement, I wrinkled my nose at the damp walls and dirt floor. It was far from a palace, but the two large rooms would serve our purposes well enough. Rats were the only inhabitants and they wouldn't bother us. I'd just have to make sure none of them bit me.

None of my friends or servants would ever let me forget it if I accidentally created my own army of vampire vermin. It was an almost tempting thought, but I couldn't speak rat, or any other animal language and I'd have zero ability to control them. *Scrap that idea then,* my inner voice muttered. It, too, had momentarily contemplated the possibility of a rival undead animal army.

"I found a place," I informed the others as soon as I reappeared on the couch beside Luc. "It isn't fancy," I warned them and described our new lair.

"We'll need a few basic supplies," Igor said. "We should take a quick trip to a camping store before heading to India."

It was well after business hours and the stores would be closed in Italy. That would actually help speed things up for us. We wouldn't be bothered by salespeople getting in our way. Luc had plenty of cash on hand that he could leave behind to pay for our theft.

We rallied the troops and I teleported us back to the ever popular mall. Only thirty of us could comfortably fit inside the camping store, so I left the bulk of our team in the courtyard outside. Igor organized the men into digging out every sleeping bag that they could find. I helpfully shifted the bags outside each time a new one was found. Igor kicked open a locked door at the back of the store and hit the jackpot with a large stock of sleeping bags inside. He lifted a brow at me and I did the honours. We cleaned the place out and Luc left enough cash on the counter to cover the cost of our illegal after-hours business.

"I'll shift everyone to India in stages," I said to my small army once we were all gathered in the courtyard.

"Why don't you just teleport us all there at the same time?" Charlie asked.

"Because it's daylight in India," Higgins replied for me. "We'll fall asleep as soon as we arrive and I don't particularly want to wake up with your face in my crotch."

Renee giggled first, then the rest of the teens joined her, including Ishida and Geordie. Luc elbowed me in the side and I choked off my own sniggers. "Like I said," I continued when I'd regained my poise, "I'll take you in batches." I turned to Higgins. "You're in charge of the soldiers while I'm gone." He gave me a brisk nod and a snappy salute.

My six close friends, Danton, his warriors and Gregor's guards were the only ones who were old enough not to be forced to succumb to slumber each time the sun rose. I carried us few to India first, bringing the female fledglings and the sleeping bags along as well. As expected, the girls collapsed the instant that we arrived. We spread the sleeping bags out in neat rows and shifted the girls onto them.

While the others continued to arrange the sleeping bags, I concentrated and brought another batch of soldiers to me. Soon, everyone had been retrieved and slept the deep sleep of the undead.

Danton and Gregor had brought their laptops along so we could keep up to date with the world news. Gregor had turned his off to conserve the battery, but Danton sat down cross legged on his sleeping bag and rapidly typed up the events that had just occurred.

He'd made a lot of progress at telling my tale and I was slightly disturbed about just how accurate it was. I'd informed him of the missing details of what had happened to me every time I'd become separated from my friends.

Everyone had chipped in with their version of what had happened so far and the chronicles were almost complete. All Danton had to do now was to stay close to me until the end. It was my profound hope that the story would have a happy conclusion and that it wouldn't end in utter disaster.

Chapter Twenty-Two

While word of the strange disappearances had begun to spread, no one, apart from us, had any idea of what was really going on. Worry only began to spread amongst the humans when several more decimated towns were found throughout the day. The ten demons had stopped hiding the bodies of their victims and their mutilated, drained corpses were simply left where they'd fallen.

I sensed the disturbance of the population of India when the tally of the mass deaths was broadcast on the news just before nightfall. Having whole towns emptied of their citizens had been bad enough, but any hope that they'd been kidnapped for some nefarious reason had just been dashed. Thousands of lives had already been lost and no one knew which town or city would be next.

A hush fell over the city that I'd chosen to be our base as the sun eventually faded from the sky. The authorities had seen enough evidence of the deaths to assume that vampires were behind the attacks. They had yet to learn that it was a different type of blood sucker than usual. I heard my name crop up more than a few times on the news as I was blamed for being behind the latest undead invasion. A bitter smile twisted my mouth as I accepted the responsibility. I was doing a lousy job of protecting my fragile human charges so far.

Luc correctly read my expression and folded his arms around me. "This isn't your fault, Natalie."

Resting my head against his chest, I shrugged guiltily. "It feels like my fault."

"Fate should have arranged for you to be able to sense these things if she wanted to prevent these casualties of war."

I held in a shudder at the torture that I'd have to go through to gain that ability. "I'll figure something out," I said, just in case Fate was listening. I already possessed enough talents and didn't want any more.

Higgins was the first of my minions to wake when the sun went down, but the others were close behind him. Simone's eyes settled on Igor and her flesh hunger rose. It triggered the rest of my female fledglings' hungers and quickly spread to my soldiers.

Acting instinctively, I sent out a calming thought, leeching the need from my fledglings in the process. "Sorry, kids," I said into the astonished silence, "but we don't have time for that right now."

Only Gabrielle wasn't affected by my mental order to put aside her flesh hunger. She was Geordie's servant, not mine and she was his to control. Unfortunately, he was new to being a master and had no control over his own emotions or lusts yet. Sending me a helpless glance, he didn't even try to stop the girl when she began to undress.

Gabrielle had no qualms about getting naked in front of the rest of us. Her flesh hunger overrode her need for privacy. It would have been easy enough for me to delve into her mind and quench her flesh hunger. The memory of how disturbed Gregor had been by my mind manipulation stopped me from doing so. I didn't have any qualms about switching off my own servants' hungers, but it would be rude to mess with someone else's servant.

While the others might be comfortable watching the pair get intimate, I wasn't. Transporting my army out onto the street next to the abandoned building, I tried to block out the sounds of their moans and the mental pictures that the teens were unknowingly sending to me. While we waited for the pair to gratify each other, I scanned the country for mass deaths. I found large numbers of people dying in nine different locations. The silverback in Nepal hadn't yet attacked. I was certain that it would target another town soon enough. I hoped to be there soon after it struck.

The instant that Geordie and Gabrielle had finished their sexual gymnastics and had clothed themselves, I shifted my army to a new location. We appeared in a garrison in western China. This was the place that Gregor had suggested we use as a practice run of kidnapping human soldiers and using them for our cause.

Spotlights came on and illuminated us standing in a grassy yard. I sent out a blanket of hypnotism before any shots could be fired by the panicked soldiers. Roughly five thousand men and women gathered outside at my mental command. They were all armed, but carried minimal ammunition. They'd need a lot more than one or two magazines each to take down the targets that I had in mind.

"Gather as much ammo as you can carry and return here in five minutes," I instructed them in their own language. I sent the command via my mind as well as with my voice. I'd have to shout for everyone to hear me and I wasn't in a shouting mood.

Five minutes later, they were lining up carrying backpacks that were heavy with bullets. The maximum number of humans that I'd ever tried to teleport at one time before had been a thousand. Sensing the first few distant deaths occurring in Nepal, I threw caution to the winds and zapped the entire mob straight into the death zone.

Staggering a step as dizziness swept over me, I pointed at the misshapen greenish-brown monstrosities that were swarming through the town. "Cut them down!" At my order, five thousand weapons were levelled and a barrage of bullets flew.

The gorilla had managed to create a gigantic horde of minions, which frankly didn't bode well for humanity. I cursed Dr Lee's arrogance for creating his experiments and endangering the world, yet I knew this couldn't have been avoided. The ten silverbacks had been fated to rise and to amass their armies and it was our destiny to destroy them.

I waited for the dizziness to pass before teleporting the surviving civilians to a distant city. Thankfully, there were only a few hundred people still left alive. I felt guilty about my relief that I'd only had a small number to shift this time. My energy levels had been depleted after transporting so many people at once. I wasn't up to shifting several thousand again just yet.

I'd arranged the soldiers in an arc at the south end of town and they moved in to enclose the beasts. Rearing up from the midst, their hideously transformed leader roared an order. Turning away from their meals, the minions attacked the soldiers while their master attempted to escape with a smaller group of followers.

I was waiting for the horned horror when it left the safety of the buildings and broke out into the open. Surprise flared in its scarlet eyes when it saw me, then narrowed in cunning as it weighed up its options.

With a gesture from one clawed hand, five of the demon's lackeys moved in to surround me. They moved with sinuous grace, padding silently on their taloned feet and twitching their long, snakelike tails. Wickedly barbed, their tails flicked towards me menacingly. Opening its mouth, one of the beasts hissed. Its head was several feet higher than mine and its teeth were as long as my forearm. I was pretty sure they'd once been lions and wondered if these had also been recruited from a circus.

With a grunt, the gorilla sent its troops in to tear me apart. Two of the five cats pounced and made startled sounds when they landed on empty ground. Teleporting right behind the demon, I had to leap upwards to stab my swords into its back. Reacting lightning fast, it whirled around before I could pierce its heart and the weapons were wrenched from my hands.

Lunging at me, its mouth swallowed my head whole and its teeth closed over my neck. I reacted quickly and my head disintegrated into a mass of whirling particles. Giving a growl of frustration when its fangs snapped together rather than ripping through my flesh, it shoved me backwards.

I re-formed my head in time to see the monster turning to flee. Again, I shifted myself to block its path. Bellowing in rage, it put its head down and charged me like a bull, aiming its horns at my chest. Calling my swords from its back to my hands, I threw them like spears. Piercing the creature's chest, they ripped through its heart. It stumbled and fell, but it wasn't dead yet.

Landing on its face, it skidded a few yards and came to a stop right in front of me. Rolling its eyes up to my face, it made a gargantuan effort to struggle to its knees. Even when it was kneeling, it was still taller than me. An all too human looking hand shot out, but grasped only my empty clothes as I broke down into molecule form. My particles entered the monster's mouth and zoomed down its throat and into its lungs. They bored through muscle, fat and flesh until they reached its wounded heart. Forming hands, I grasped the gigantic muscle and teleported myself free from its body.

Becoming whole and holding a heart that was larger than my head, I watched the silverback convulse. Its claws stretched out towards me. It refused to give up even as it let out a feeble gurgle then broke down into a puddle of ooze. Its heart disintegrated as well and splattered to the ground. I shifted my clothes away before they could become irreparably stained and re-formed myself inside them.

I'd almost forgotten about the five big cats and ducked when a claw swiped at my head. I called for my swords again and defended myself against their murderous revenge attack for killing their master. While the felines were quick, they weren't skilled at fighting as a team. They'd been locked up in captivity for too long and their hunting instincts weren't as honed as they would have been if they'd been raised in the wild. I didn't exactly fight fair, either. I teleported out of harm's way, then stabbed them from the side. A sword through an eye only angered these things. They were far tougher than a normal vampire or clone. Shooting them with my death ray did the trick and finally the five animals became puddles of slush.

I'd been keeping a distant eye on the main battle during my skirmish and we'd lost more troopers than I'd expected. Fully a fifth of the humans were dead, but they doggedly continued to fire at the biting, clawing monstrosities. I'd hoped the death of their leader would weaken their resolve to stay and fight. This wasn't the case and they gave no signs of relenting in their attacks. Now that they were no longer being controlled by the silverback, their need to feed became overwhelming and the soldiers were the only food around.

My much smaller vampire army was doing their best to help the humans. They'd formed ranks with the front row kneeling. The next row shot their death rays over their comrade's heads. Their method was proving to be very effective, so I shifted us all back a couple of hundred yards, then arranged the Chinese soldiers in the same way. They quickly cut down the remaining enemies until only sludge remained.

"Well," Gregor said as the gun smoke began to dissipate, "that went better than I'd expected." He turned to me. "Did you manage to kill the silverback?"

"Yep. He's deader than disco."

"You *do* know what disco is, don't you?" Simone said slyly to the oldest members of our team.

"It was some kind of strange human mating ritual, as far as I can determine," Danton said. His sly wink at Igor at the outbreak of giggles told me he knew exactly what disco was. He'd probably seen the Wizard of Oz as well.

"One down and nine to go," Geordie said. "Does anyone else suddenly have a sense of déjà vu?"

"I keep expecting Colonel Sanderson to turn up," Ishida agreed.

"You mean *General* Sanderson," I reminded him.

"That man did not deserve his promotion," Kokoro said darkly. "He deserved the fate that he suffered at your hands."

My female fledglings were instantly curious. Renee whispered a question to Ishida and he quietly told them what I'd done to Sanderson. A smile rose at the memory of my right hand crawling its way up his throat and dragging his intestines behind it. It was a moment that I'd treasure forever.

"I'm very glad you are on our side," Simone said and the rest of the girls nodded in agreement. I'd creeped most of them out with my bloodthirsty smile at recalling how much I'd enjoyed murdering Sanderson.

"The night will not last forever," Igor said and brought us back to the task at hand. "We should attempt to intercept another of these gorillas while we still have time."

Shifting so many soldiers at once had weakened me. I frankly wasn't up to moving the remaining four thousand troopers at the moment. "I'm going to need a snack first," I said and motioned to the closest human soldier.

Being beneath my spell, he stepped forward and eagerly offered me his neck. I drank enough of his blood to top up, then searched for a new target. I couldn't contain my wince as I sensed nine more towns being wiped out. I wasn't a miracle worker and it was impossible to save them all. Picking a town at random, I shifted my diminished army back to India and into another slaughter.

Chapter Twenty-Three

We weren't quite as successful during our second battle. My Chinese war puppets unleashed hell on the next batch of monsters and cut down their numbers drastically. Unfortunately, the demon in charge of this mob escaped before I could hunt it down. It was too clever to make its presence known and presumably slunk away to safety while we were fighting its lackeys.

Once the final abomination had been destroyed, I searched the empty town with mounting frustration. All I found was the drained corpses of the fallen civilians and puddles of goo. We'd lost fifteen hundred troopers this time and were now down to half of the original five thousand Chinese soldiers that we'd started out with.

"Did you kill the gorilla?" Geordie asked me when I returned from the search.

"Nope. It looks like it got away."

"At least it doesn't have any followers left," Sergeant Wesley observed. "It will have to make more minions before it can attack another large town."

"Unfortunately, there is no shortage of animals in this area," Gregor said.

"Did you see those things that looked like trucks with legs?" Geordie asked his mentor.

"I think they were cows," Igor said. It was hard to tell what some of these creatures had been before they'd become mutated. The cocktail of nanobots and vampire blood did wonders for transforming even cute and cuddly animals into repulsive monstrosities.

"What next?" I asked Gregor. "Do we try to save another town, or pick up some more soldiers first?"

Eyeing our diminished ranks, Gregor didn't waste much time debating about our choices. "We need to replenish our ranks and our ammunition. Can you find this garrison in China?" He pictured the place in his mind and it came to me clearly.

"It shouldn't be a problem. I'll leave you all here instead of taking you with me this time." It made sense not to cart them back to China with me. I could only transport so many people at a time, after all. I'd be able to bring more soldiers back with me if I went alone. "I'll be back shortly."

Zeroing in on the location that Gregor had shown me, I zapped myself into the compound and sent out a silent command. Soldiers ran to arm themselves and load up with ammunition before racing out to the yard where I waited. Lining up neatly, there were seven thousand men and women this time. Knowing my limits, I sent half of them ahead to India first, then returned with the second half.

Igor nodded his approval at our increased numbers. "How many soldiers do we have at our disposal now?"

"Nine and a half thousand," I replied. He and Gregor shared a look and I caught their mutual fleeting thoughts that we should split up. "We're not breaking into two teams," I told them flatly. "The gorillas are too smart and too dangerous to take on by yourselves."

"I would hope that we are far more intelligent than our quarry, Natalie," Gregor reminded me mildly. "I also think you are forgetting that we are immortal."

I hated the idea of being separated from anyone within my close circle, yet I grudgingly saw the sense of it. "Fine," I conceded. "I'll give you half of the Chinese soldiers."

Kokoro linked her arm with Gregor's. Her expression remained serene, but her eyes challenged me to try to argue with her decision to accompany him. Luc slid his hand into mine, silently reminding me that he hated to be parted from me. Gregor and Kokoro loved each other as much as Luc and I did. I gave in and sent her a reluctant nod of agreement.

Igor shook his head when Simone took an anxious step towards him. "It will be safer for you to remain with Natalie." He softened his rejection by leaning down and kissing her cheek, then gave me a direct stare. "She will make sure that you remain unharmed."

It was a subtle warning that he would never forgive me if I let anything happen to Simone. I nodded reassurance that I would take care of her. She might be his lover, but she was also my servant. I'd do everything in my power to keep her safe.

Geordie turned away and blinked eyes that would never be able to tear up. He was overcome with emotion at the sign of tenderness from his usually stern mentor. Igor had denied himself for far too long and he deserved to forgive himself for the deeds that he'd had no control over. His master had been to blame for the deaths of his family and Igor had gotten his revenge in the end. I suspected his satisfaction at murdering his master far outweighed my joy at ripping Sanderson's insides out.

The night was waning and we still had far too many enemies to defeat. Locating two towns that were being attacked, I instructed half of my human servants to obey any order that Gregor, Kokoro or Igor gave them, then sent them all away. I then whisked the rest of us to the second town.

It was far larger than the other settlements that had been attacked so far. Word of the attack hadn't spread to the entire small city yet. The hybrids had entered from the southeast and most of the citizens to the north and west were asleep. My troops surged through the streets, cutting off access to the rest of the town and trying to contain the threat.

Taking my army of vampires with me, I followed a hunch and transported us to the rear of the flood of misshapen monsters. As I'd hoped, I found our quarry directing the attack. Standing tall above most of the horde, the horned demon sensed us at its back and turned. I caught a flash of recognition from it. This was the first gorilla that we'd encountered. I was highly disturbed at how many animals it had recruited into its army considering we'd killed off its first batch of minions. Its lips wrinkled back from its fangs and its horns lowered threateningly. It wasn't going to run this time and intended to get revenge for its dead servants.

"That is one ugly mutant monkey," Ishida said and fired his gun. Even with its unnatural speed, the silverback still couldn't quite avoid the projectile as it galloped towards us. The round pierced the creature's shoulder and its arm was torn off when the round exploded three seconds later.

Losing the limb barely slowed it down. It took a further five explosives to send the beast crashing to the ground. Reminiscent of something from a horror movie, it dragged itself forward. Its scarlet gaze was locked on me, sensing that I was the greatest threat out of the pack of vampires that surrounded it. My swords stabbed through both of its eyes and it finally went still. I didn't relax completely until I pulled my swords free and it turned into a puddle of goo.

With the leader of the pack dead, we were now free to turn our attention to its minions. A flock of misshapen undead birds soared overhead. One went into a dive and disappeared from view. When it reappeared, it carried a struggling human in its beak. Landing on a nearby roof, it bit the civilian's head off and drank down the blood that gushed from his neck. Another bird soared over, intending to share the meal. It shied away when its rival snapped at it with its oversized beak. With a caw of anger, the second bird went in search of its own meal. Clearly, the hybrid birds were less amiable about sharing their food. Or maybe their ability to cooperate disappeared with the death of their master.

Leaving Luc in charge of the team, I teleported to the rooftop before the mutant could fly off. I wasn't sure what type of bird it had once been, but it was now the size of a large dog. It was trying to extricate the dead human from its talons and stood on one leg. Holding the other leg over the side of the roof, it shook its leg until the body came loose and fell to the ground below. Landing on a fence, the body was cut in half. Still attached by the ropy intestines, the two halves fell on opposite sides of the fence.

"Gross," I complained. My nose wrinkled in disgust and I wished that I could un-see that event.

The bird squawked in alarm when it realized it wasn't alone. Whirling around, its beak darted towards my face. Sidestepping slightly, my sword lopped its head off, ending its life instantly.

My holy marks were difficult to use when I couldn't lock onto a target with my senses, but the creatures were too far away to use the death rays on them. The bird's eye view at least gave me a chance to take pot shots at the deformed avian creatures that soared above the beleaguered town. I let the dark power build up, then shot a wide, but invisible stream towards the flock. Uttering panicked screeches when the power reached them, they flapped their featherless wings and tried to flee. Escape was impossible once they were caught within my death zone. Their bodies swelled like hideous balloons, then burst and a shower of sludge fell to the streets below.

Once again, my bamboozled Chinese soldiers were being slaughtered faster than they could cut down their enemies. I shifted them to a safe distance away where they could still shoot their targets. I ordered them to move backwards slowly and to keep up a steady stream of fire, then checked that my friends, allies and servants were safe. They were and they were also far enough away that they wouldn't get caught in the stream when I turned the holy marks on the monsters below.

A shudder went through any freakishly altered animal that was touched by my dark power. It was frustrating not being able to sense them and it was hard to tell whether I'd caught them in my snare or not. Screams, bellows and yelps of pain were accompanied by the wet popping sounds of their bodies being torn apart when I zapped them.

A piercing shriek from right behind me made me whirl around. Long, sharp talons punched through my chest and I was lifted off my feet by a mutant bird that had escaped my holy marks. My head automatically became ghostly when the kamikaze bird's beak darted towards my face. I pressed a hand against the cold, scaly skin of its unbeating chest and sent a pulse of power through it. It didn't even get a chance to swell before exploding, thanks to the direct contact with the cross that was embedded on my palm. My clothes were drenched in dead bird ooze before I could shift myself away.

Falling towards the ground in a dizzying rush, I stopped my descent by teleporting back to the rooftop. My human troops were at risk of being overwhelmed again. I shifted them backwards once more to give them room to shoot at the suicidally murderous creatures. The animal minions were far less intelligent than their masters. They didn't have the brains to realize that they should retreat. They were intent on feeding from the walking blood bags whether they were armed or not.

Finally, the last monster winked out of existence and we were free to join Gregor, Igor and Kokoro. We arrived just in time to help their soldiers cut down the remaining few dozen hybrids. Their troops had fared better than ours and they'd only lost a few hundred souls. I'd lost over a thousand soldiers, which made me think that I should just put Gregor and Igor in charge of each battle. I was supposed to be the leader, but there was no rule that said I couldn't delegate. *Come to think of it, I do my best work when I'm on my own and when I don't have to worry about everyone else.*

My inner voice had its opinion ready for me on the heels of that thought. *You also get into serious trouble when you're on your own and end up in horrible situations every time.* Sadly, my subconscious had a very valid point. Maybe it would be better to stay with my team after all.

Igor looked a little wild eyed when we gathered to compare notes. He, Gregor and Kokoro all sported tears in their clothes. Simone darted forward with a cry of alarm and hugged Igor. He patted her on the back, murmuring reassurances that he was unharmed. While their injuries had healed without a scar, the traces of black blood on their skin and clothing told us that they hadn't taken down the creatures without sustaining wounds of their own.

Gregor made a subtle gesture and Luc and I joined him and his ladylove. "It is a very good thing that we seven are immortal," he said in a low voice. Kokoro grimaced and put a hand to her neck. It was unmarked, but the dark stains on her shirt testified that she'd sustained a severe injury that would have killed a lesser vampire.

"Are you all right?" I asked. I could see for myself that she was fine physically, but I wasn't so sure about her mental state. While I was well used to being chopped up by now, my friends had far less experience in that area.

"I have shared an injury that both you and Geordie have suffered," she replied. "Being beheaded is a very unsettling experience." She flashed a series of images at me and I was treated to the sight of a silverback swiping at her with a clawed hand. She hadn't ducked fast enough and her head had been torn from her shoulders. It had been kicked, tromped on and chewed by another mutated beast before Gregor and Igor had finished off the ape and had reunited her parts.

Gregor drew her closer to his side. "It was quite a shock to see Kokoro in two pieces." She smiled up at him and put her hand to his cheek briefly. "You were right, Natalie," Gregor said with a hint of apology, "the silverbacks are too dangerous for any normal vampire to battle. Even we three were hard pressed to destroy it."

"We took it down in the end, but it wasn't easy," Igor said.

"At least you did a better job of keeping the humans alive than I did," I told him. "We've killed three of the gorillas now, but there are still seven of them left." Scanning the country, I winced at the numbers of people that had fallen. "Over three hundred thousand people are dead," I informed them. "With each night that passes, thousands more hybrid vamps will rise." That meant hundreds of thousands more people would die each night. The number would soon escalate into the millions.

"There isn't much more we can do tonight," Gregor said regretfully.

I could still feel humans expiring as their blood was drained from their bodies, but he was right. Dawn was on its way and I still had to return the soldiers to their garrisons. They would need rest, or they'd fall over in exhaustion and be eaten the next time they tried to battle the bloodthirsty hordes.

I scooped up my friends, allies and fledglings and deposited them in the basement of the abandoned hotel in central India. Next, I shifted the soldiers in two separate trips back to where I'd found them. I lifted my hypnotism so they could function without waiting for my orders. I didn't wipe their memories of the battles that they'd participated in. They at least would know that we weren't responsible for the deaths of the Indian and Nepalese people. I also returned the bodies of the fallen soldiers to their rightful country. It seemed like the right thing to do.

Returning to our base, I took a change of clothes out of my backpack. I phased into particle form to rid myself of the disgusting coating of bird goo. Luc frowned at the tears in my shredded jacket, but made no comment. He knew that nothing on Earth could kill me, yet he didn't like the thought of me suffering. I felt exactly the same way about him. Neither of us had much of a choice about any of this. We'd been made to endure this kind of pain so that the humans wouldn't have to.

Exhausted from expending so much energy shifting the humans backwards and forwards, I sank down onto the sleeping bag beside my one true love. Putting my head on his chest, I fell into a deep sleep. *Maybe I'll dream up a solution of how to stop this latest invasion,* I thought wistfully as I succumbed to darkness.

Chapter Twenty-Four

Standing in a grassy field, I turned in a slow circle and I wasn't alone when I came to a halt. A figure stood at the top of a familiar hill. It wasn't Luc this time, but was instead a female. She was just a shadowy figure, a dim silhouette that seemed as though she might blow away at any moment.

Long grass tickled my fingertips as I walked up the short hill towards her. I came to a stop a few yards away. She stood without moving, gazing out over the horizon, or so I assumed since I couldn't see her face. She wore a black hooded cloak that almost seemed to be made of darkness itself. Several strands of long ebony hair had escaped from her hood and were being teased by the soft breeze. There was really only one entity that she could possibly be.

"You have some difficult decisions to make soon, Mortis," Fate said in a hollow voice that sounded like it was coming from the far end of a long tunnel. "Your choices will affect the destiny of the entire human race."

"I know," I said unhappily. "It would be nice if someone would tell me what choices I should make," I hinted.

Turning, her face was deeply shadowed by her cowl. I caught a glimpse of depthless black eyes that would draw me in and hold me captive forever if I stared into them for too long. I averted my gaze before I could become ensnared like a hapless mortal.

"I have led you this far and I have made certain that you possess the knowledge and skills that you will need to prevail," she told me. "You have the power to succeed within you."

"Why are you telling me this?" I was already well aware that the fate of the world rested on my narrow shoulders. It seemed redundant for the mistress of destiny herself to show up and tell me this directly.

"This is the last time that we will have any contact. From now on, you are on your own and I can no longer guide you."

"What if I make the wrong choices?" I whispered. "What if I fail?"

"If you fail, then all will be lost." Her hollow voice spoke of despair, not just for the humans, but for every life on the planet, including my kin.

With that unsettling piece of wisdom, she faded to mist, then disappeared, leaving me a dubious gift. Three doors hung in mid-air over the precipice. They were a reminder of the results that I could expect from the choices that I would shortly make.

All three doors stood open and depicted scenes from my earlier dreams. The door on the left showed a town that was empty of life. Beyond it was another empty town and another and another. The villages, towns and cities all over the planet were overlapping each other and all told the same story. The humans were gone and the only creatures that still existed were the undead. The entire world had become a ghost town. Even the undead would eventually perish from starvation. The world would one day be devoid of animal and bird life. Nature would win and the plants and insects would be all that remained.

Behind the second door was the aftermath of nuclear war. Some humans still lived in caves deep beneath the ground, but the surface had become an uninhabitable ruin. It was a replica of Viltar, without the stinky yellow dust storms and evil alien overlords. The human race would slowly die out from lack of food and sunlight. They'd turned on each other and had doomed their entire species to death. Trees and insects hadn't fared so well in this scenario and the world was essentially doomed.

Door number three was the opposite of the first two. I saw towns and cities from all over the world just like the first door. This time, life seemed to be normal and the humans were relatively happy. There didn't seem to be any wars or global conflicts, which didn't seem possible considering how contentious humans were.

A new image in the third door caught my eye and I moved closer until I was teetering on the edge of the cliff. A tiny village had been added to the scene. It was our vampire haven in Italy. Its appearance told me that if I made the right choices and saved the humans, I'd also save my people. If not, then we would also cease to exist, or most of us would anyway. We needed blood to survive and we couldn't drink the blood of the undead.

The three doors turned misty then faded, leaving me with a weight on my shoulders and the destiny of billions of lives in my hands.

Waking, I felt the sun still high in the sky and knew I wouldn't be able to fall asleep again after that disturbing dream. Surrounded by the corpselike bodies of my fledglings, I opted to teleport into the next room rather than attempt to pick a path through them. Besides, I didn't want to wake Luc up. His face was serene and model perfect, as always. If he was dreaming, I hoped it was more pleasant than mine had been.

Gregor was the only other person still awake. He sat on a spare sleeping bag with his computer on his lap. He was hunched over a map of India, monitoring the attacks via the news feeds that were continually being updated. He glanced up when I appeared in front of him and patted the sleeping bag beside him in invitation. "Did you sleep well?" he asked.

"I did right up until Fate paid me a visit," I replied grumpily, but made sure to keep my voice down so I didn't wake our close friends. They all now slept like humans and could wake at will. That was just one of the perks that we'd gained from our time spent on Viltar.

"What did Fate tell you?"

"That I was on my own from now on and that I had to make the right choices or we're all doomed." It came out sounding gloomier than I'd intended, but how was I supposed to sugar-coat the possible end of the world?

"Perhaps we'd better keep that between us two," he said gravely. "Were you shown the same three possibilities?"

I nodded. "She added a picture of our village to the third door. The one that shows the Earth as a near utopia."

"So," he mused, "Fate is telling us that we should not give up hope. It is still possible that we can prevail."

He was trying to sound positive, yet he sounded pretty hopeless to me. Looking at the number of red dots on the map that indicated towns that had already been wiped out, it was difficult not to fall into despair. "How many people have died now?" I knew the number, but I needed to hear it from him.

"They've estimated that somewhere between three and four hundred thousand souls are either missing, or dead."

Anyone who had gone missing had simply been hidden by the mutated animals and could also be counted as dead. Those deaths were on my hands. I couldn't undo them and all I could do was try to prevent more people from dying. It was a given that I'd fail, of course. Once night fell, the undead would rise and they'd begin feasting again. It would take a miracle to halt this invasion and I didn't think God would hand over a miracle to us. We might be on his side, but we were still unholy monsters.

Seeing the red dots spread throughout India in random, unpredictable patterns, I came to a reluctant conclusion. "We need more human soldiers."

"That would be my recommendation." Switching to another picture, this time a map of the world, Gregor pointed out blue dots that he'd marked in most countries. "These are all of the military bases that contain at least a few thousand soldiers each."

I stored the knowledge away, knowing that it would come in handy. Several of the dots were in India. Since it was their country that was under attack, it made sense to use their soldiers to fight the invasion. "I was thinking I might start moving more soldiers into the worst affected areas." I was probably condemning the troops to death, but I didn't know what else to do.

"I agree. Try to shift as many soldiers as you can to these areas to attempt to pin the creatures in." He made a circular motion near the disaster zones. "I'd put more soldiers here." He pointed to a spot south of Delhi, since the hordes seemed to be heading towards it. "There are a great many animals in the larger cities. I shudder to think of just how large this undead plague of beasts and birds could become once they target somewhere like Delhi."

"Some of those mutants are gigantic." The former elephants and cows came to mind. "Where do they hide during the day?"

"I assume they retreat to the forests, or hide inside buildings."

I didn't know a great deal about India and had no idea what the countryside was like. I'd mainly seen small towns during our travels. The only large city I'd seen so far was the one we were currently using for our base. "I'll order the soldiers to keep their eyes out for daytime lairs and to burn any mutants that they find." Fire had always proven to be an effective weapon against our kind. We knew from reading Dr Lee's files that he'd used fire to destroy the specimens that he'd created. "I'm going to start kidnapping soldiers and move them into position. Wish me luck." Moving the soldiers into position before the sun went down might give us the advantage we needed. It beat sitting around twiddling my thumbs.

"Good luck," Gregor murmured, then I was gone.

I made a short jump to one of the military bases in India first. Standing deep in the shadows, I sent out a mental order to the twenty-thousand soldiers residing inside. Minutes later, they were armed and had formed into five orderly groups. Keeping Gregor's map in mind, I started zapping them to the towns to the south of Delhi that had been attacked.

I gave them the command to search for possible lairs and to burn anything that looked like a mutated animal. I also ordered them to use the same tactics that we'd used before. Forming ranks and shooting over each other's shoulders had worked well so far. This time, I told them to fall back regularly if they were in danger of being overwhelmed. My small army of vampires couldn't be everywhere to oversee the battles. This was the best that I could do to keep the casualties to a minimum.

Cleaning out all of the army bases in India, I then shifted to China and kidnapped some more troops. By nightfall, I had two hundred thousand soldiers from several different countries arrayed around India. A full hundred thousand were stationed near Delhi just in case any of the hybrids made it past the other soldiers to the south.

Teleporting four thousand soldiers at a time sapped my energy and I had to feed several times throughout the long afternoon. I fed for a final time to replenish my strength before heading back to the basement. My fledglings would awaken soon, but my friends were already up and were clustered together.

"How did you fare?" Luc asked, searching my face for clues on how well my mission had gone.

"I bamboozled a couple of hundred thousand soldiers and placed them where Gregor suggested. I guess we just have to wait for the enemy to strike now. When they do, I think we should try to hunt down the apes in charge and let the soldiers deal with the minions."

"That is a valid suggestion," Gregor said to back up my plan. "The gorillas are intelligent enough to realize they need large numbers to subdue the human population. From what Fate has shown Natalie, it appears they do not realize that creating so many minions will eventually result in the extermination of their food source. It is crucial that we cut the leaders down, or all will be lost." He'd just repeated the same sentiment that Fate had told me in my dream. A superstitious shudder worked its way down my spine.

Expecting to sense mass deaths popping up on my internal radar at any moment, I waited tensely. My small army was ready to be whisked into battle. Some of my soldiers were looking forward to the carnage that they were about to dole out. Feet shuffled impatiently when the minutes stretched out and nothing happened.

"Why aren't we moving, *chérie*?" Geordie asked.

"Because no one is dying yet." I felt dozens of lives being snuffed out around the country, but they were random murders or natural deaths rather than the result of animal attacks. It was disturbing to realize just how many murders were carried out in India.

There's something really wrong with humanity, I thought to myself. Their need to dominate, control and conquer was far too reminiscent of the bloodthirsty Viltarans. I'd made the comparison before, but that was before I'd rescued seventeen girls from the captivity of five depraved men.

Even if you do stop the gorillas, the humans are destined for annihilation anyway, my inner voice said morosely. *They'll end up destroying the planet one way or another.*

I didn't want to agree with my subconscious, but I couldn't help but do so. I'd been human myself once and I knew just how flawed they could be.

Chapter Twenty-Five

Minutes stretched into hours and there were still no attacks. Geordie's eyes glazed over from sheer boredom and I sympathized with him completely.

"Do you have any theories about why they haven't attacked anyone yet?" I asked Gregor.

Tilting his head to the side thoughtfully, he ran through the possibilities. "Worst case scenario, they might be clever enough to recognize the soldiers as a threat by now. Ordinary gorillas are able to understand and use sign language. These hybrids would easily be able to recognize an armed human on sight."

Geordie struggled out of his lethargy to query him. "So, they see the soldiers and then what? Just hide and wait for them to go away?"

"I imagine they will flee and choose somewhere else to feed and to build their armies."

"Please don't tell me I've made a huge mistake by shifting the soldiers into one general area," I said with a groan. Every choice I made would be crucial from now on and it seemed that I'd already screwed up.

"We need to be prepared for just such an occurrence," Gregor said and gave me a sympathetic look. He felt equally responsible, since I'd placed the men at the locations that he'd suggested. "While I can usually predict how humans, vampires and even aliens might react, I am afraid I cannot foresee where the gorillas will strike." His sense of guilt came through despite his even tone.

"This isn't your fault," I told him softly. "The fate of the world is in my hands and I'm not sure I'm up to the task."

Igor's hand connected with the back of my head in a resounding slap that staggered me forward a couple of steps. "You are Mortis," he said when I turned to face him. "You have the tools to destroy these things. Now stop doubting yourself and do your job."

"Thanks, Igor," I said dryly and resisted the urge to rub my scalp. The slight pain had already faded, but the sting of his scorn would linger for far longer. "You always know how to get me back on track."

"It's a gift," the Russian said stoically.

Geordie sniggered, then squawked in outrage when Ishida dealt him a slap. "What was that for?" he demanded.

Ishida shrugged. "I thought it would be fun and I was right," he said with a grin. His harem moved in protectively to surround him when Geordie took a belligerent step forward. "Careful," Ishida warned him, "they can be feisty."

"I know," the teen replied dourly. "Your house is right next to mine and I hear how 'feisty' they are every night."

"Don't worry, we *all* hear them," Higgins said and Renee let out a shrill giggle that sounded almost exactly like Geordie's. One of the other girls smacked her, then they became a giggling bunch of slap happy, shrieking harpies.

"Are you going to get them under control?" Luc asked me with a raised eyebrow.

First, I had to get myself under control. If I'd been human, tears would have been streaming down my face from my gales of laughter.

"Are you sure she's really Mortis?" one of Danton's warriors asked doubtfully, which made me laugh even harder. Danton was smiling, amused by my amusement. *I hope he doesn't put this in the chronicles.* He would, of course. Every embarrassing detail of my undead life would be noted down right up until the world came to an end. Unfortunately, that might happen all too soon.

The thought sobered me and my giggles trailed off. Sensing the mood change, my female fledglings ceased squabbling and watched me anxiously.

A feeling of doom swelled moments before I was staggered by the sudden sense of tens of thousands of people dying. Luc put a hand on my shoulder to steady me. "I take it the silverbacks have finally struck?"

"Yeah. It feels like a few of them have banded together and have attacked the same city." With the number of deaths that I'd just felt, it had to be more than just one demon and its lackeys at fault.

"Which city did they target?" Gregor asked, feeling the same dread that I did. He had strong intuition of his own and he already knew the answer.

I didn't want to reply, because it would seem more real if I did. "They've attacked Delhi," I forced out and he blanched. This was our worst fear. It wasn't just the number of civilians that would be killed that we were afraid of. It was the sheer number of domestic animals that would be transformed into the undead that was the real problem.

Taking a few moments to assimilate this information, Gregor shook his head dejectedly. "I had hoped to avoid this level of catastrophe, but now…"

It scared me when he trailed off into silence. I'd deployed the soldiers too far to the south and I wouldn't have time to move them all directly into Delhi now. Millions of people would lose their lives this night and countless others would die in the nights to come.

"We might not be able to stop the mutant minions, but we can at least try to hunt down the apes," I said. Gregor nodded, but he didn't meet my eyes. His hope that we might prevail against the hordes withered. He was back to believing that we would fail. I didn't blame him for his lack of belief in me, since I felt the same way. But I couldn't just throw in the towel and sit back and watch the populace being eaten. I had to act and act fast.

Teleporting my small private army to Delhi, I split us up and deposited my team on several rooftops near where the bulk of the deaths had occurred. The undead mob was moving northward, leaving a wake of drained and sometimes headless corpses behind them. Prehistoric looking birds soared overhead, diving for victims. Biting their heads off and drinking their blood in mid-flight, they dropped the drained bodies. Men, women and children rained from the sky, landing with jarring thuds and breaking apart upon impact.

There were far too many people in Delhi for me to be able to evacuate them all to safety. Screams of terror assailed us and my youngest servants let out sobs of pity for the victims. Sending out a mental command to the soldiers who were to the south, I knew they'd never arrive in time to stop the carnage. They could at least hunt for the mutants once the sun came up and they went into hiding.

"I think I just spotted one of the silverbacks," Charlie shouted from a nearby rooftop. Following his pointing finger, I saw a dark, malformed shape on the street below. It entered a shabby apartment building and I saw a hint of twin horns before it ducked inside.

"Keep watch for more of them while we seven take care of that one," I shouted. My soldiers nodded and spread out to watch from all four sides of their buildings.

"We should use our swords or death rays rather than our guns," Igor suggested. "We do not want to frighten the other silverbacks away if they are within hearing distance."

"Good point," I replied and reached for my swords. The guns would make far too much noise and would alert the other leaders and their minions that they were under attack.

Luc touched my arm and pointed at the front door to the apartment building. A long, low misshapen shadow slunk out into the open. Peering around with eyes that glowed red, it sprinted towards the slaughter to the north.

One of the gorillas was definitely inside and it was converting more animals to join its cause.

"Let's go kill it," Geordie said. He was far more proficient with weapons after the intensive training sessions that Ishida, Kokoro, Luc and I had given everybody. Danton and his warriors had also pitched in to help with the training. They weren't quite as elegant as us, but they were brutally efficient.

I transported us soundlessly into the lobby and directly into the path of three more freshly made minions. Snarling, the closest beast swiped at me with claws that would have taken my head off if I'd been any slower with my weapons. The snarl turned into a screech of pain when its paw flopped to the ground.

Roughly the size of hippos, all three hybrids had one goal in mind; to feed. They sensed that we weren't edible and were therefore a threat and must be eliminated. They sprang at me and two of them crashed into each other when I shifted to the side. I stabbed the third one through the chest. It let out a snarl, but it didn't go down. Luc's sword flashed into view and sliced into the beast's throat. Blood spurted, momentarily blinding my beloved. My sword intercepted the claw that slashed at his face and the creature flinched back.

Wiping blood out of his eyes with his sleeve, Luc shook his head as the three legged mutant limped in for another attack. Its head was still attached by a thread and had flopped backwards. It stared at us upside down through slitted red eyes, trying to maintain its balance on three legs. One of its back legs lashed out, missing us by inches. "They do not die easily," my beloved observed.

"They're too stupid to know when they're beaten," Ishida said as he ducked beneath a claw and lunged in with his sword. The beast yowled and tried to backpedal. The teen moved fluidly, drawing his weapon back then lunging forward to stab his adversary in the eye as Geordie stepped in to hack at its neck.

Luc and I separated, which momentarily confused our quarry. Undecided on which of us it should try to keep in sight, it chose me and did a clumsy backwards jump. I sliced both of its back legs off and it fell to its stomach, mewling horribly as its head flopped forward. Luc's sword flashed again and its head rolled across the floor.

Igor, Kokoro and Gregor engaged the third hybrid, working together to corner and kill it. The beasts broke down into slush as they were separated from their heads. We didn't have time to rest before another one appeared on the stairs.

"What were they before they were turned?" Ishida asked. He was calm on the surface, but he was shaken on the inside. Ten millennia of strictly controlling his emotions had given him the ability to mask his loathing.

"I believe they were cats," Igor replied.

"Bad kitty," Geordie muttered, then stared at me wide eyed when I sniggered. He was too frightened to find any amusement in our situation. I couldn't blame being turned into Mortis for my weird sense of humour. I'd always had the tendency to laugh at inappropriate moments.

Upstairs, the silverback became aware of us as it felt its lackeys die. A fresh wave of newly made monsters came for us as it fled. Crashing its way through a window, I heard the thud of its feet and shards of glass hitting the street. The rapid clip of cloven hooves resounded from an alley as it trotted away.

We didn't waste time battling the newly risen undead animals up close and instead used our death rays. The combined brilliance of our violet beams was almost too painful to bear. I had to blink spots away from my eyes when I teleported my small band of hunters into the path of the fleeing ape. It skidded to a stop when it found its escape route suddenly blocked. Scarlet eyes flicked from side to side as it assessed its chances of survival if it engaged us directly. Pausing, it glanced upwards, then almost seemed to grin evilly.

"Look out!" Simone screamed from the rooftop above us. I tilted my head back just as a flock of birds descended. Talons plunged into the bodies of everyone but me. I turned into dust motes and only my clothes were whisked up into the air this time.

Igor hacked the feet off the bird that had snared him and plummeted towards the ground. Simone screamed again, in terror for her beloved this time. I teleported Igor safely to the ground seconds before he'd have crash landed. He calmly tore the feet out of his chest then turned and engaged the horned beast. I rescued the rest of my friends from being carried off by the birds and they moved in to surround the now frenzied ape.

I was ready for the birds when they returned. Remaining as whirling molecules, I gathered the power of my holy marks and zapped the creatures from the sky when they dive bombed us again. Their bodies burst and turned to ooze, coating the buildings and street with noisome sludge.

Roaring for its newly made minions to assist it, the silverback darted forward and drove its claws into

Gregor's chest. He in turn used both hands to spear his sword through the tough armour on its chest and into the beast's heart. Luc ducked a swipe from the gorilla's other hand and stabbed his sword in beside Gregor's. It took two more stabs from Ishida and Kokoro before it finally went down. In true vampire style, its body only disintegrated once the weapons were removed.

I shifted myself so that I stood between my friends and the malformed hybrids that were sprinting down the narrow street towards us. Holding my hands up palm outwards, I unleashed my holy marks. With screeches and yowls of pain, they swelled, burst and left more smears of ooze on the buildings, street and parked cars. *I'd hate to be on the clean-up duty for this part of the city.* It was looking less and less likely that anyone would be left to clean up once this was all over.

My hands dropped when the wave of enemies disappeared. While we'd been deep in battle with a single ape, hundreds of thousands of humans had died. The undead hybrids had reached epidemic numbers and I feared that they now couldn't be contained. India was just the start of the invasion. Once they crossed the borders and began to spread out, no land would be safe from their all-consuming hunger.

Chapter Twenty-Six

Retrieving my goo-splattered, shredded clothing, I donned them with distaste. They were disgusting, but I didn't have time to shop for replacements right now. Shifting from rooftop to rooftop, we searched for more demons to eradicate and had no luck spotting them. It was a huge city and we couldn't search every inch of it.

"What do you suggest we do next?" I asked Gregor.

Brooding for a moment, he met my eyes and I read a distinct lack of hope within his. "You could shift the bulk of the soldiers here and find more help to try to contain the creatures."

"But you don't think that will help," Ishida said flatly. He'd learned to read Gregor and I sensed his disappointment that the most sophisticated of us appeared to have given up.

Gregor hesitated before speaking. "I fear the repercussions once word spreads of just how many lives have been lost this night."

"What repercussions?" Geordie asked suspiciously. Gabrielle clung to his side and his arm went around her shoulders protectively.

An image of a toxic and highly deadly mushroom cloud rose in Gregor's mind. "They wouldn't, would they?" I asked in a horrified whisper. *Of course they would,* my subconscious said. *This has been the real danger all along. It's only a matter of time before someone gets an itchy trigger finger and nuclear war breaks out.*

"Who wouldn't do what?" one of my soldiers asked.

"They are talking about the humans employing a nuclear solution," Igor said. His stark response stunned us all into silence.

"Isn't that a bit drastic?" Simone asked. She wasn't exactly clinging to Igor, but she stood very closely beside him.

"Not to the world leaders," Gregor replied. "Self-preservation is paramount. They will do whatever they think is necessary to save their people, even if it means destroying India entirely."

Kokoro's delicately beautiful face was drawn. "Once the first missile is launched, where will it end?"

"In complete annihilation," I replied. "The few humans who manage to survive will be forced to live beneath the ground."

"For how long?" Renee asked.

"It would take thousands, or maybe tens of thousands of years for the planet to recover," I said with a shrug. "People might never be able to live on the surface again. I had the sense that they'll eventually die out from lack of food and sunlight living in the caves."

"What happens if they don't send in their missiles?" Ishida queried.

"The mutants will kill everyone on the planet." It went without saying that this choice also sucked.

"How are we going to stop both of those scenarios from happening?" Higgins demanded. "Surely we can do something?"

My mind frantically searched for a solution, but I came up blank. There was only one plan that I could think of and ferrying in the extra soldiers had already failed. *Then increase the numbers of soldiers and spread them out more,* my inner voice ordered. I was glad someone had an idea, even if it was my alter ego instead of Gregor for once.

"The mutants will have to go into hiding soon," I reminded everyone. Dawn was nearing and it would bring a welcome, if temporary, reprieve. "I'm going to gather all the soldiers that I can find and bring them here. I'll give them instructions to hunt for the silverbacks and to cut down as many mutants as they can. During the day, they can root the undead out of their hiding places."

No one argued with my plan, but Geordie raised a good point. "What will we do?"

"We'll help out as best we can." It was a lame answer and uncertain glances were exchanged at my solution. I was supposed to be Mortis the Great and Terrible and I was leaving it up to the very creatures that we were tasked with saving to save themselves.

Dropping my private army back at our base, I was almost relieved to be alone as I arduously shifted the soldiers into Delhi. The slaughter petered out just before the sun rose, so I shifted the bulk of the armed forces to the epicentre of the kill zone and instructed them to search for the undead. The hybrids couldn't have gotten very far before they'd have been forced to go into hiding from the sun. With their freakishly large sizes, they should be easy enough to find. Our main problem was that they had millions of houses and buildings to hide in.

Grateful that Gregor had mapped out the military bases for me, I diligently went about shifting troops in bunches of four thousand at a time. When that became easier, I upped the number to five thousand. By the end of the day, I was able to teleport eight thousand humans at a time.

When daylight finally began to wane, I was reeling with dizziness. I lurched towards the closest soldier, in desperate need of food. Sensing my need, he offered me his neck. My fangs descended, I gulped down his warm blood and my strength increased with each mouthful that I swallowed. I fed from four different men before I'd replenished my lost energy. Darkness was about to descend, so I gave them their orders and sent them on their way.

I'd kept tabs on the troopers' progress. They'd located thousands of mutants hiding in buildings, basements and in burrows that they'd dug out. It was only a small fraction of the hordes that had to be hidden within the city. This war had become an international affair with soldiers from nearly every country assisting us with our battles. I didn't concern myself with the diplomatic faux pas that I'd committed by kidnapping foreigners and recruiting them to our cause. There was a good chance that no one would survive to be furious about having their men and women taken against their will anyway.

On a rooftop in the centre of Delhi, I hid from the setting sun in the shadow of a gigantic satellite dish. I waited for the undead to rise and for the slaughter to recommence. My bird's eye view gave me a disturbingly clear picture of the vast number of creatures that rose and took to the streets in search of food. Most of the surviving civilians had fled to the north, leaving behind only the soldiers to eat. I saw no sign of the gorillas as their minions flocked towards the north.

Proving that at least one of the apes had to be present, the mutated animals formed into six different groups. Each targeted a wall of soldiers. Following my orders, the troopers had formed into ranks. Beneath my spell, they couldn't give in to panic and flee. Instead, they held their ground and fired with precision. I mentally ordered the men that were to the south to converge on the mass of monsters. It was a waste of time, since it was obvious that they wouldn't arrive in time to be of any help.

My human henchmen made a valiant effort to stop their adversaries from escaping their trap, but they were overwhelmed by the flood of monsters. Thousands died while hundreds of thousands of mutants fled. I caught a brief glimpse of the demon in charge before it was lost from sight amongst the throng. It would be pointless to attempt to pursue it when I couldn't even pick it out of the crowd.

Dully watching the tail end of the six separate hordes as they disappeared into the darkness, I clenched my fists in fury. *I was just beaten by a monkey.* The realization stung more than I cared to admit. I'd faced a number of crafty vampires, Viltarans and octosquids before, yet none of them had ever managed to defeat me. I was glad I hadn't brought my small army along to witness my humiliation. It was bad enough that I knew how badly my butt had just been kicked.

Speaking of my kin, they'd probably be wondering where I was. I knew I had to return, yet my feet weren't moving. A nagging sensation in the back of my mind told me that someone was trying to contact me. I was too busy wallowing in misery to respond to their call.

The nagging became a buzzing then rapidly shifted from alarmed to terrified. Geordie's mind touched mine briefly as I allowed his message to filter through. *A nuclear missile is about to hit Delhi!*

His terror-stricken mental shriek snapped me out of my self-pitying doldrums. The rapid approach of a missile caught my eye as it streaked towards the city. My insides went cold when I realized that I had less than three seconds to act. With one bomb, millions of people who hadn't yet moved out of range of the blast zone would be killed. So would the soldiers that I'd moved in to combat the mutants.

Mentally locking onto the missile, I could think of only one way to stop it. Teleporting myself directly into the path of the bomb, I screamed in agony when it tore through my stomach and the tip exited from my back. Shifting away, I carried the nuclear device into outer space. I dissolved into miniscule particles and the missile came free. I left it to drift in space harmlessly.

While the pain had been excruciating, there was no sign of injuries or missing pieces when I became whole again. My body had the capacity to heal any wound, no matter how great or small. If the bomb had detonated, only myself and cockroaches, would have survived the blast.

Returning to Delhi, I was relieved to see it was still intact. More missiles could be on their way, so I gathered my courage and teleported back to my friends. They weren't in the basement as I'd expected and I found myself in the back of a moving truck instead.

Geordie let out a cry of relief when I appeared and instantly berated me. "Where were you? We called and called and you didn't come!" Taking in my shredded shirt, his anger turned to concern. "What happened to you?"

"I heard your message in time to catch the missile," I explained.

Igor looked at me in astonishment. "You literally caught the bomb with your body?"

"It seemed like the safest way to stop it," I said with a shrug.

Luc dropped his eyes to my bare stomach, but thoughts of sex were far from his mind. Reading his unspoken concern, I sat down beside him and leaned against his side. His arm came around my shoulders and held me tightly.

"Where is the missile now?" Gregor asked. He was slightly annoyed that I hadn't come when they'd tried to alert me to the danger. He was the brains behind most of our battles and I was just the weapon. I wouldn't be much use if I wasn't there when he needed to deploy me.

"It's space junk, just like the…" Realizing my female fledglings were present, I changed what I'd been about to say. "Like the other five sacks of garbage and test tubes full of vampire blood that I dumped in space," I said instead.

Nodding his understanding, Gregor returned to his laptop. "So far, only one missile has been launched, but we can expect more to follow."

"Who sent it?"

"The Chinese," Ishida replied. "One of the gorillas has recently invaded their country and has already destroyed two small towns." It must have moved at its top speed to make it all the way to China so quickly. I felt slightly ill at the possibility of just how far the undead could spread if the rest of the silverbacks decided to flee from India.

"The Chinese blame India for the attack, since the trouble originated with them," Gregor said. "I fear the Indian government might soon retaliate. Things changed after the First attempted to take over the world. They worsened when the Second and his fellow disciples created their armies of fledglings. The humans lifted their restrictions on creating nuclear weapons and now, nearly every country has at least a few bombs at their disposal. We are lucky that none were launched when the Viltarans invaded Manhattan and Las Vegas."

My worst nightmare was coming true. I put my hands over my face in a useless attempt to block out the disaster. The holy marks on my palms pressed against my cheeks, reminding me of what I was supposed to be. *What use are they? They aren't any help at all!* I kept the despairing thought to myself. Morale was already low and it would disappear entirely if I revealed just how close I was to giving up.

"Where are we heading?" I dropped my hands to ask when I'd mastered my emotions.

"Delhi," Igor replied. "We were on our way there to find you."

"Delhi is lost," I told them with brutal honesty. "The hybrids broke free and are heading in multiple directions."

"Did you encounter any of the silverbacks?" Kokoro queried.

"I spotted one briefly, but it got away." Admitting my failure was hard and no one had anything to say that could possibly make me feel better.

Gregor searched for solutions, but came up as empty as I had. I'd deployed and redeployed the troops and had chosen wrongly each time. I'd managed to get thousands of my war puppets killed for nothing and we were out of options. The truth that I'd already accepted suddenly became apparent to everyone. We were going to lose.

Chapter Twenty-Seven

Luc didn't allow me to descend into another bout of self-pity and attempted to rally us. "Our new priority should be to stop more missiles from being launched."

Gregor nodded. "Agreed. We need to convince the world leaders that nuclear war is not the answer."

By 'convince', he meant using hypnosis and that was where I would come in. *At least that's something I can do,* I thought bitterly. "How many people will I have to speak to?" I wasn't exactly an expert on which countries would pose the greatest threat.

"I suspect a full dozen or more countries will have their fingers hovering over the launch button right now," Gregor replied. "There are too many for one person to visit alone if we wish to avoid total disaster."

"What do you suggest we do?" Igor asked.

Gregor might be convinced that we were doomed, but he wasn't going to throw in the towel just yet. "I will give you each the names of two world leaders to speak to. Natalie can teleport us all to our first targets. Five minutes should be long enough for us to hypnotize the humans into keeping the peace. Then Natalie can transport us all to our second targets."

"Sounds good to me," I said, grateful that he'd concocted a plan to stop nuclear war. Out of the two threats to the planet that we were currently facing, worldwide holocaust was the greater danger. If Gregor's plan worked, we'd be able to stop that possibility from occurring. Then we'd just have the onerous task of halting the mutant undead.

"What about us?" Higgins asked. "What do you want us to do?"

I wanted to keep them safe, but his thoughts told me he wouldn't be happy if they were relegated to watching the battle from the sidelines. "Join up with the soldiers in Delhi and take down as many of the hybrids as you can," I instructed.

Relieved that they'd still be able to help, my soldiers and female fledglings nodded. The rest of my people in the trucks behind us would follow Higgins' orders. I just hoped he would be able to keep them safe while I was gone. Young in both mortal and vampire years, he was level headed and would keep his cool. He'd proven himself many times and I trusted his abilities. Sergeant Wesley was slightly older and he'd back up the corporal. Those two could handle things during our absence.

Gregor rattled off some names, most of which I'd never heard of before. We firmly memorized their faces when he showed us photos of our targets on his laptop. Unsurprisingly, he'd given me the current president of the United States to bamboozle. Since I was in the vicinity, he'd also given me the Prime Minister of Canada. My friends would be spread all throughout the world while they hypnotized their respective targets.

It took me several minutes to hone in on the leaders and to drop my close friends off one by one. I didn't have a watch and I'd have to guess when five minutes were up. Ishida was the last person I dropped off before I whisked myself over to the White House.

The new president was holding a meeting in a large conference room. Uniformed soldiers sat around a large, oval table. Men wearing dark suits and nearly invisible ear pieces stood in strategic places around the perimeter of the room. A large white screen had been mounted on the wall. A map of India was on display, showing the areas that had been decimated by the demons and their spawn.

"As you can see, we have little choice but to fire our…" The president froze when he turned and saw me. Shouts of alarm came from his bodyguards. One tackled the president to the ground and covered him with his body in a futile attempt to keep him safe. I didn't waste time trying to talk them into holding their fire and dropped a layer of hypnotism over the entire room. Hands that were reaching for weapons stilled, then fell limply to their sides.

"You will not send any nuclear missiles, or any other bombs, towards anyone unless I give you permission," I said to the group of Americans bluntly. Since I was never going to give them permission, no bombs would be sent.

"Yes, ma'am," my temporary human minions said as one.

Skimming the thoughts of the president, I shuddered at just how close they'd been to bombing not just India, but several of their rivals. They'd been absolutely certain that once India was hit, the US would become the next target. They'd been determined to destroy their potential enemies before any of them could take steps to eliminate them first. Kokoro's fears had been correct. Now that one missile had been sent, others would surely follow. I only hoped my friends would be able to stop utter disaster from occurring.

Too impatient to wait for the full five minutes, I left the dazed Americans and headed to Igor. He was waiting for me in Russia where I'd left him. He nodded to signify that he'd been successful then I zapped him to his next location. I'd already forgotten the faces and names of all but my targets. I had to skim the information from Igor's mind.

One by one, I shifted my friends to confront their second targets. Ishida had been given Japan and North Korea. He'd been in time to stop his fellow Japanese people from launching the few missiles that they'd reluctantly been allowed to stockpile by the rest of the world leaders. Unfortunately, as we appeared in the North Korean command centre, we saw that we were too late to stop them from firing their weapons. A gigantic screen was tracking the path of five missiles that had already been launched.

"Change of plan," I told Ishida and sent him to my target in Canada with a thought. "Hey, you!" I said to the North Korean leader and heads swivelled to me in surprise. Before anyone could shoot at me, I bamboozled everyone in the room. "Make the missiles self-destruct," I ordered the technicians that were standing at a console.

"We can't," one replied with deep regret and embarrassment that he couldn't meet my wishes. "They do not have that capacity."

"Then change their destination to somewhere in the middle of an ocean or into outer space."

"It is too late," the same technician replied and pointed at the screen. "Impact is in five seconds."

Turning to the screen, I realized the target wasn't India, which would have been bad enough. They'd aimed for five of the largest cities in the US, which was even worse. The North Koreans hadn't opted to attack the country where the undead threat had risen. They'd targeted the country that they thought of as their greatest threat.

I only had a split second to decide what to do, but I didn't descend into panic this time. I didn't have enough time to teleport myself to each missile. Instead, I reached out with my mind and willed them all into outer space. It was a much quicker and far less painful way of eliminating the weapons than catching them with my body.

My dreams had warned me not to allow any nuclear bombs to detonate on Earth. If I did, my mission to save the humans would fail. I knew I couldn't save all of them, but I could at least try not to let the planet itself be damaged.

Sounds of consternation were made when the bombs disappeared from the radar screen. "Do not fire any more missiles," I instructed the North Koreans. "Do not attack any other country." I was certain the South Koreans would appreciate that order. I wasn't exactly an expert on which countries hated each other, but even I knew that North and South Korea weren't on the friendliest of terms.

Sending out my consciousness, I scanned the minds of my closest friends and found them waiting for me. None were panicked, so I assumed we'd managed to avert disaster. Without bothering to pick them all up one by one, I zapped us all back to Delhi.

"I assume you managed to destroy the missiles that the North Koreans sent towards India?" Ishida said when we were all gathered together. Our troops had reached Delhi and were helping the soldiers to cut down the hybrids.

"They weren't aiming for India. They were aiming for America. I sent the missiles into outer space, like the last one," I said, to his vast relief.

"It sounds like that was a close call," Gregor said.

"Too close." My tone and expression were grim. "I just hope no one else gets it into their heads to try bombing a rival country."

Gregor shook his head reassuringly. "We have stopped the countries that have the greatest potential to destroy their enemies. The smaller nations will not attack for fear of retribution." That was comforting, but not as comforting as knowing they'd be unable to launch a missile without our say so. That would have to wait for now. We had a more immediate problem to deal with.

Not all of the mutated animals had fled from the city. Some had remained behind, either at the order of their master, or because their master had disappeared without leaving them a plan to follow. They were attacking the soldiers and were proving to be very difficult to kill. Countless birds dive-bombed the troopers. They were too fast and agile to shoot with any accuracy and the explosive rounds went off in the air like fireworks.

Out of the five hundred thousand soldiers that I'd kidnapped worldwide, three hundred thousand of them had gone in pursuit of the horde of minions that had escaped from the city. Fully one hundred thousand were dead. The remaining soldiers were attempting to finish off the beasts that were still plaguing Delhi.

"Help the soldiers," I said to my kin. "I'm going to take care of these birds."

I waited for Luc to nod and lean down to give me a quick kiss before I teleported myself onto the highest rooftop. Mutant birds in all hideous shapes and sizes soared above on their leathery wings. They made the occasional dive into the crowd of humans and came back up with a tasty treat.

Calling on my holy marks, I let the power build up then held my hands out. Imagining a wave shooting out from my palms, I unleashed the dark power and birds began to fall from the sky with cries of pain and despair. Most exploded before they hit the ground.

Shifting away from my friends, allies and servants so they wouldn't be in danger, I stayed up high and turned the holy marks on the mass of misshapen beasts below. No creature could hide from the power that washed over and through the buildings. While I couldn't sense the monsters, I heard their death cries and saw their bodies explode in a wash of guts and bright red blood. Eventually, their blood would turn as black and rancid as normal vampires. It was my desperate hope that we would be able to kill them all long before that transformation was complete.

When the sounds of gunfire and blasts of violet light from death rays petered out, I released the power and staggered. I'd never used the holy marks for more than a few seconds before and I was feeling drained. Almost too tired to teleport, I appeared amongst the human soldiers and pulled one towards me at random. He docilely allowed me to feed, as did the next three men. Full of energy once more, I returned to my small army.

Filthy and smeared with blood, Higgins trotted over to give me a report. "It appears that we've finally managed to clear the city of the hybrids, ma'am." His left arm hung at his side and blood sluggishly trickled down his skin to drop from his fingertips. His sleeve was a tattered ruin.

"Finally," Geordie muttered. "We've almost run out of bullets."

"We should return to our base and restock," Igor suggested.

"How bad is your arm?" I asked Higgins.

Moving gingerly, he lifted his sleeve and showed me the damage. His arm was dangling by a few scraps of skin and muscle. "It's pretty bad," he admitted as Geordie did his best not to gag.

"That's disgusting," one of my girls complained and I had to agree.

"Here," I said and offered Higgins my wrist. "Drink some of my blood. It might help you heal faster." It had worked well for Luc, so it should work for my number one soldier as well.

"Are you sure?" the corporal asked and took hold of my wrist uncertainly.

"Yep. Drink up."

Luc's hands settled on my shoulders as Higgins' fangs descended and he bit into my vein. I'd be lying if I said I didn't feel a slight sexual thrill at the sensation. Luc's fingers tightened, indicating that he sensed my pleasure. I turned my head to take a quick peek at his expression and was relieved when he winked. For a moment there, it had almost felt like I'd cheated on him.

Higgins swallowed a few shallow mouthfuls of my blood, then stepped back wearing a dazed expression. Holding up his left arm, he flexed his perfectly healed bicep. "Your blood is the ultimate healer," he said in wonder. He'd have healed eventually, I'd just helped him along a bit.

I pointed at the humans who stood patiently, waiting for fresh orders. Even beneath their hypnotism, they were exhausted. They were probably hungry as well. I hadn't even given a thought to their need for sustenance. "What about them? Do they need more bullets?"

Sergeant Wesley stepped in to answer that question. "We've ordered them to share their ammo, ma'am, but they're going to need to restock soon."

That would involve stealing equipment from their respective countries, since they all used different weapons. I was doubtful that there would be enough bullets and explosives to eradicate the creatures that were no doubt even now being created by the remaining demons.

For a moment, I almost wished that I'd allowed the Chinese missile to wipe out India. It would have helped to destroy the threat that had the potential to spread worldwide. The picture of the second door that showed an uninhabitable world came to mind. We'd averted that disaster, but I still had no idea how I was going to stop the mutated beasts from eating everything that had a heartbeat. Apparently, I had the power to stop them. I just wished I also had the brains to figure out how I was supposed to pull that off.

Chapter Twenty-Eight

It was easy enough to follow the path that the hungry herds of mutated animals had taken. They'd left hundreds of thousands of corpses in their wake. The bamboozled humans were doing their best to catch up to their quarry. Sprinting as fast as they could, they tried not to trip over the fallen civilians and their fellow soldiers. They weren't the indefatigable undead and didn't stand a chance of heading off the hybrids.

Driven by blood hunger, the creatures headed for the larger cities to the north and south. Only one of the silverbacks seemed to have made it into China so far and I opted to target it next. Hopefully, we would be able to destroy both it, and the minions that it had assembled before they cause too much havoc.

Leaving the bulk of the soldiers behind, I scooped up my kin and eight thousand men and women and transported them to China. This was the maximum number of people that I could shift at one time. Doing so strained my resources and left me drained.

Appearing on the outskirts of a moderately sized town in western China, we were instantly assaulted by screams of terror mixed with growls, grunts and howls of triumph. Normally, I'd evacuate the surviving civilians to safety. Unfortunately, it was long past time to worry about the loss of a few thousand souls by now. They would have to serve as bait for our hastily made trap. As long as they had something to eat, the minions would remain preoccupied. If we worked fast, we might be able to move in and start cutting them down before they even knew that we were here.

Gregor grasped the situation immediately and turned to the soldiers. "Circle the town and shoot anything that moves."

"Get moving," I said to the human soldiers and backed up Gregor's order with a nudge of hypnotism. The soldiers were predominantly Indian and Russian, with a few random foreigners mixed in. They saluted me obediently, then went into action.

As I'd hoped, there only seemed to be a couple of thousand hybrid creatures swarming through the streets in search of a meal. Screams of fright and pain echoed through the town and were soon drowned out by gunfire.

"Keep watch for the gorilla," Igor cautioned our soldiers. "It will probably try to run now that it knows it is being hunted."

"We should move to the rooftops for a better view," Ishida suggested.

It was a good idea, but I looked at the roofs doubtfully. Most were sharply angled and only a few were flat. "Try not to fall off," I cautioned everyone and took the group up high.

Renee immediately lost her footing the moment her feet touched the slick tiles. Pin wheeling her arms, she slid backwards. One of the other girls caught her before she could topple over the edge. As the youngest, not to mention the smallest of our group, the others tended to look out for her.

"I see it!" Renee shouted and pointed. The girl holding onto her glanced around and this time they both slid towards the edge.

Catching a glimpse of the fleeing horned horror, I shifted my companions back to the ground before anyone could fall off and impale themselves on anything sharp. Crossing my fingers that I wasn't about to get anyone killed, I shifted my fledglings in to surround the madly galloping beast. They boxed it in on all four sides, penning it in with their sheer numbers.

Roaring a challenge, it slashed its way through my soldiers. Charlie, the normally irrepressible redhead, let out a cry of pain when the claws raked across his face. His left eye turned to jelly and dribbled from his ruined socket. He fired his gun at the monster at point blank range. He was yanked backwards by his comrades an instant before the round exploded.

Screaming in bestial rage, the silverback tossed my people aside with both hands as it fought to free itself. The gaping hole that had been blasted in its stomach was already beginning to close. It didn't heal as fast as us, but it had the capacity to become whole again.

Standing directly in the demon's path, Simone coolly drew her sword and lunged forward. Her sword hit the tough armour on its chest and was deflected. Claws swiped at her head and Igor threw himself in front of his new love to save her from being decapitated. He grimaced in pain when his left arm was sliced off. The limb fell to the ground and Geordie snatched it up before it could be trampled.

Ignoring his sluggishly spurting stump, Igor pulled two explosives from his pocket. Everyone began to back away as he pushed the red button on the ends then tossed them into the beast's snarling mouth. Turning, he dove at Simone to carry her out of danger. Bearing her to the ground, he covered her body with his as the explosives detonated. He didn't escape from the blast entirely. His shirt and skin were stripped from his back and he became coated in the demon's guts. They turned into sludge as what was left of the demon disintegrated.

Still lying on her side, Simone grabbed Igor by his shredded shirt and pulled him to her. She kissed him until he forgot that they were surrounded by their kin and responded to her passion. Geordie pointedly cleared his throat after a few seconds, hiding his grin. Dazed by the unaccustomed public sign of affection, Igor glanced around to see us all standing in a circle, staring down at him.

"I believe this is yours," Geordie said and held out his mentor's severed arm. Igor's back had already repaired itself and his skin was now unmarked.

"Eww," Gabrielle complained. She didn't quite gag, but I sensed that she came very close to it. *They're a match made in heaven,* I thought and was hard pressed to hide my snigger.

Igor took the limb with a nod. "Thank you." Simone helped him sit up and position it to his severed stump. We waited with heavy anticipation until his arm became reattached. Flexing his fingers, he held up his hand to show everyone that he was whole again. Even as we watched, the angry red mark around his bicep where the two pieces had joined began to fade.

"If I hadn't seen that with my own eyes, I wouldn't have believed it," Sergeant Wesley murmured. Everyone had seen me doing incredible things many times. They sometimes forgot that my six closest friends were also invincible. Their abilities made me feel less freakish, but only slightly.

"I wish we could all do that," Charlie said wistfully. Being my servants, they seemed to heal more quickly than usual. The claw marks on his face had been deep and I was glad to see that they were already half healed. After a few more minutes, they'd be gone entirely. His left eye wasn't going to be as easy to repair. It had been obliterated and his eye socket would remain empty. Although my blood had the power to heal, it couldn't replace what had been destroyed.

Teleporting my team back to the town, we helped the soldiers to eradicate the mutants. Shell-shocked civilians roamed the streets once the gunfire, blasts from the death rays and tossed explosives finally ceased. While the bodies of the dead townsfolk lay where they'd fallen, only noisome blotches remained of their attackers.

Anyone who wasn't aware that vampires existed would have been highly confused about exactly what had happened here. After the events that my kin and I had been embroiled in over the past decade or so, there were very few people who weren't aware that blood suckers were indeed real and were walking amongst them.

Sending the diminished ranks of soldiers back to northern India first, I transported my army back to our base. We restocked, then headed out once more to engage the enemy. We'd killed five of the demons now, but there were still five of them left. They'd already created enough underlings to eat their way through over three million humans. The inhabitants of Delhi had fled mostly on foot and none were fast enough to outrun the pursuing creatures.

Tens of thousands of the bamboozled soldiers had banded together into several groups. They'd managed to catch up to the rampaging creatures that had stopped to the north of Delhi to feed on the fleeing civilians. I could feel them dying along with the people that they were trying to save. Although I wanted to come to their aid, my main goal was to find and kill the silverbacks to prevent them from creating more minions. The only way to narrow down the search was to head for the areas where the greatest numbers of civilians were being hunted.

Locking onto the vast number of deaths that were occurring to the north, I teleported my small band to the closest bunch of soldiers. I then sent out a mental order for the troops to move in to surround the feeding hybrids. Their master would give itself away eventually and when it did, we would pounce.

I left my friends, allies and servants on the ground and took to the highest rooftop alone. There were too many mutant birds flying overhead to risk anyone being snatched and decapitated by their razor sharp beaks. The instant that I appeared, I was dive bombed by half a dozen of the prehistoric looking monsters. A blast from my holy marks took them down and the other winged hybrids kept their distance from me. They might be hideously mutated, but they weren't completely stupid.

It was almost dawn by the time the demon in charge of the bulk of the minions finally broke from cover and attempted to flee. It barrelled its way out of a building and careened through the streets on all fours. I shifted from rooftop to rooftop to keep it in sight, then lost it when it joined the milling mass of its minions. Their greenish-brown skin blended together into one gigantic mass of constantly moving hairless flesh. Red light from their eyes bathed them all in a pretty scarlet glow.

Instinct drove the hybrids to seek shelter before the sun could rise and fry them into steaming puddles of goo. Like an optical illusion, they disappeared into the shadows minutes before dawn was about to arrive. Like the creatures we were hunting, my fledglings also needed to seek shelter. Marking the general area where the silverback had disappeared, I returned to my companions and teleported them back to our base.

Chapter Twenty-Nine

My fledglings filed to their sleeping bags and fell unconscious the instant that the sun made its appearance. Geordie tenderly tucked a stray lock of Gabrielle's hair behind her ear, then bent to plant a kiss on her forehead. Seeing me watching him, he gave me a sheepish smile that I couldn't help but return. He'd secretly yearned for someone to love and his wish had finally been granted. He never thought that he'd ever find love and he was still struggling to believe that Gabrielle was really his.

Out of my two hundred plus warriors, only eighteen of us were able to stay awake during the day. While we were few in number, we should at least be able to do some small amount of damage to our slumbering adversaries. There were hundreds of thousands, if not millions of mutants hiding in the towns to the north of Delhi. They should be easy enough to locate and kill. This wouldn't be the first time that I'd dispatched helplessly slumbering vampires. I felt absolutely no guilt at the thought of eradicating them.

Everyone gathered around and I explained my intentions. "I know the general area where the gorilla disappeared, but it might take us a while to hunt it down."

"Is it above or below ground?" Gregor asked.

My answer was a shrug. "I'm not sure. I think it's too big to head into the sewers, so it's probably hiding out in a building somewhere."

"Most of these creatures are too big for the sewers," Ishida observed with a slight shudder.

"Good," Geordie said. "At least we won't have to traipse around in poop this time." It would make a nice change. We always seemed to end up underground at some stage during our battles with our enemies and it always ended in losses on our side.

"We need some kind of covering so we won't burst into flames when we conduct our search," Igor suggested. One touch of sunlight would be instant death for most of my kin. My close friends and I would survive, but it would be a painful experience even for us.

"I'll go and find us something," I promised and zapped myself back to the department store in Italy. I was familiar with it by now and headed straight for a bedding store. It was far past closing time and I was the only shopper. I chose enough blankets for everybody and sent them on ahead of me. I didn't bother with a blanket for myself, since I could easily reduce my exposed flesh down to particles when I needed to.

My companions were donning their blankets in preparation of the search ahead when I returned.

"I feel like a nun," Kokoro grumbled as she adjusted the dark blanket to hide her face in shadow. I bit my bottom lip to stifle a laugh, but she sent me a sharp look anyway. She might not be able to read minds anymore, but she knew me well enough to know when I was amused.

Smoothing my expression to blandness, I took Luc's hand when he offered it and whisked my merry band of misfits back to the area where the gorilla had disappeared. We split up and began searching the houses, apartment buildings and stores for enemies.

I entered a five-story building and found it crammed wall to wall with monsters. They lay in a jumble, uncaring that they overlapped each other. Instinct had driven them inside where they would be safe from the killing rays of the sun. Not all had made it in time, as the dark puddles on the doorstep attested.

There were far too many places for our small number of vampires to search alone, so I reached out and teleported in several platoons of human soldiers to assist us with our task. With forty thousand humans now aiding us, I was confident that we would be able to root out the ape that had created at least some of these hybrids.

Unable to target the misshapen beasts with my senses, I had to be careful when using my holy marks. If I unleashed them at the wrong time, my friends and allies could be caught in the blast zone. Keeping my radar on full alert for friendlies, I let the dark power grow and zapped all of the unconscious creatures on the ground floor to ash.

Shifting my attention to the floors above, I quickly conducted a search and found many different types of minions, but not the one that I was searching for. I didn't think I'd be lucky enough to stumble across the silverback so early into our search. Concerned that I might accidentally kill one of my own people if I sent my dark power outwards, I zapped back down to the ground floor and directed the holy marks upwards. An invisible wave of power fluttered my clothes as it shot up towards the top floor, annihilating everything in its path.

The bamboozled soldiers used knives or makeshift stakes rather than their guns to eradicate their slumbering enemies. Their bullets wouldn't last forever and they were already running low on ammunition. I'd have to ensure that they were restocked before nightfall. That would entail many trips back to their countries of origin. I felt exhausted just thinking about all the teleporting that I'd have to do.

One of the commands that I'd given to my human underlings was to notify me if anyone found a mutant with cloven feet and horns. An excited shout rang out just after midday and I went to investigate. Materializing beside the flustered Indian soldier, I gestured for him to wait outside and entered the house that he pointed to.

My quarry had chosen a small, ramshackle house to hide in for the day. Or maybe it had simply run out of time and hadn't found anywhere else more suitable to use as its temporary lair before the sun had come up. We were in a poorer section of the city and the buildings were crammed in side by side. There was so little room between each house that shadows prevented the sunlight from entering the windows and frying the undead into true death.

The front door hung on one hinge and a split ran down the centre from the force of being kicked open. As soon as I entered the house, it seemed vaguely familiar. The living room furniture had been tossed around during the silverback's search for victims. The smell of death permeated the air and drew me towards a hallway. Three doors stood open and one was smeared with blood.

A bare foot caught my eye as I approached the first door. Pushing it open, my eyes travelled up the foot and stopped at mid-thigh. The rest of the leg, not to mention the body that it belonged to, lay on the floor nearby. Blood coated the bed where the grisly remains of another human rested. Both of the bodies were too small to belong to adults. Thick red blood stained the floor, walls and ceiling. The scene was horribly familiar, but I still couldn't quite place it.

Almost against my will, my feet carried me back into the hallway and to the last door on the right. With a feeling of intense trepidation, I entered the room of an infant and beheld my target. The silverback had fallen on its side when the sun had risen. Blood coated its horns and had formed a small red puddle beside its head. The blood had thickened, but it hadn't quite dried completely.

Incongruously, the demon clutched a headless doll in one hand. Frowning in puzzlement, I knelt beside the massive beast and examined the doll. My heart tried to lurch when I saw the bloodstains on its tiny clothes and I realized that it wasn't a doll at all. In the moments before the ape had fallen asleep, it had fed from all of the occupants of the house. It had ended its meal with the smallest and most helpless member of the family.

The body of a large black dog lying in front of the crib was the key that unlocked my memory. I remembered the dream I'd had of this exact house. A gigantic hole in the dog's chest was the cause of death. Its heart had been torn out and lay on the blood-soaked floor beside the animal. I didn't need to look inside the crib to know that the baby's head would be nestled inside.

While I'd altered the family's fate slightly, ultimately, I hadn't done enough. Grief welled that I hadn't been able to stop this terrible occurrence from happening. All I'd done was slow the horned devil down slightly and had caused it to stop hiding the bodies of its victims. After all of my efforts, I still hadn't been in time to save these people, or the others that had fallen to the mutant underlings.

My sword decapitated the ape, leaving me with a sense of cheated rage. The other demons that we'd battled had fought with every ounce of cunning that they'd possessed. I wished I could have woken the science experiment up and then torn it apart with my bare hands. My wish was futile and childish and I let my anger seep away.

Bending, I scooped up the body of the baby before the smelly ooze from the dead silverback could sink into its clothing. I didn't want to subject myself to the sight of its tiny severed head, yet forced myself to step over the corpse of the dog anyway. I picked up the small, cold head of the infant and cupped it in my palm.

I left the room and crossed the hallway to the main bedroom. Sprawled face-down on the floor beside her headless husband, the mother's hand was outstretched. She'd spent her final moments trying to claw her way to her children.

Crouching down beside her, I rolled her over onto her back and winced at the gaping ruin of her throat. Twin holes had been bored into her chest. They matched the wounds in her husband's back. His head had been kicked aside and his face was frozen in an expression of abject agony.

My lips trembled as I placed the two pieces of the baby in its dead mother's arms. *Maybe they can be together in the afterlife.* It was a poignant thought that would have brought tears to my eyes if I'd still been capable of crying.

If I didn't figure out a way to take down these monsters soon, all of humanity would eventually be joining this family on the other side.

Chapter Thirty

Now that our mission to hunt down the demon was over, I dropped my team back to our base so they could catch a few hours of rest. Just because they could stay awake all day didn't mean that they had to. The seven of us immortals could go for a long time without sleep, but the others were feeling the effects of fatigue.

My energy would quickly begin to flag once I began shifting the soldiers again, but there would be no rest for me. I went about the laborious task of teleporting the foreign soldiers back to their respective garrisons so they could stock up on ammo and food.

Out of the original five hundred thousand men and women that I'd recruited to our cause, only two thirds of them were left. While our numbers were dropping, our adversaries were rapidly increasing their armies. We were lucky that Dr Lee had only created ten of these demons.

Unfortunately, even when my blood was mixed into an unholy cocktail, it remained highly virulent. It still took only a small taste to turn the living into the undead.

While I was at each army base, I snatched up fresh soldiers and shifted them back to India. I kept the bulk of them to the north of the country. The mutant minions had moved dangerously close to Pakistan and the other bordering countries. Soon, they would spill over the borders. Once they did, they would become unstoppable.

Exhaustion plucked at me with nagging fingers by the time I'd finished transporting the new troops to where I hoped they could do some good. I fed to replenish my energy, then returned to our base. I found some of my team waiting for me on the street. The sun had set not long ago and the flesh hungers of my newest fledglings had risen with the darkness. Apparently, it had spread to my soldiers as well and they'd gone in search of both blood and sex.

I could feel their sexual bliss in the neighbouring buildings as they satiated themselves on their humans of choice. A female shriek of pleasure came from somewhere nearby and my shoulders hunched. It was bad enough overhearing my kin back home in our village when they were going at it. It seemed somehow worse when they were pleasuring complete strangers.

Luc gave me a wry smile when he accurately read my squeamishness. "It is our nature, Ladybug," he said with a shrug. I caught the mental picture of what he wanted to do to me and my mouth lifted slightly at the corners.

"Try to contain yourselves," Igor ordered us gruffly as he stalked into view. He tucked his shirt into his pants with one hand while Simone clung to his arm. She wore a self-satisfied grin that was like a banner over her head trumpeting what they'd just been up to. "It is bad enough that the girls cannot yet control themselves, you two should be able to do so by now," the Russian declared.

"Well, yeah," I agreed. "But it's nice to lose control every now and then."

Luc coughed to hide his laugh and Igor glowered at him, suspicious that he was being made fun of. Gregor and Kokoro were far better at hiding their amusement. Danton, his warriors and Gregor's guards tried to pretend that they weren't listening to the conversation at all. I appreciated their attempt at discretion.

"Stop being so grumpy, Igor," Simone scolded in her thick Scottish brogue. "You enjoyed yourself as much as I did."

Looking everywhere, but at us, Igor gave her a stiff nod. "That is true, but this is neither the time, nor the place to satisfy our needs."

"It felt like the right time and place to me," she responded sulkily.

"Me, too," Gabrielle said wickedly as she and Geordie sauntered into view.

Arm in arm, they were obviously deeply in love, even if they were still young enough to legally require adult guardianship. I'd been told on more than one occasion that creatures like us weren't capable of love. I knew with complete certainty that that was untrue. We had an enormous capacity to care for each other. I hadn't been raised amongst the selfish courtiers, so I hadn't been conditioned to think that way. Luc had, yet he'd still fallen for me anyway. His love was my own personal miracle and it was one of the only good things that had happened to me since I'd risen as the undead.

My soldiers might have been forced to feed both of their hungers, but they were well aware of their duty. They returned to our base quickly and did their best to avoid my gaze, fearing that I was angry with them.

"Is anyone missing?" I asked, knowing full well that everyone had returned.

Charlie looked around the group with his single eye. He'd covered his empty socket with a bandana. Pitch black, it had a picture of a while skull and crossbones where his eye used to be. "Everyone is here, ma'am," he said with a grin. He wasn't the slightest bit ashamed of taking the time to find a bed partner. He figured that any night could be his last and that it was only sensible to indulge his hungers for what could very well be a final time.

No one said outright that it was a pointless waste of time to dive back into battle, but I'd skimmed their thoughts and that was the prevailing sentiment. Even Geordie, usually my most stalwart supporter, was beginning to have doubts about me. I was failing to live up to my destiny on an epic scale.

To the south, I felt thousands, then tens of thousands of lives being snuffed out as the hybrids swarmed over several large towns. There were still four demons at large and I wasn't sure which one to target next. Logic told me to head north. The creatures to the south would have nowhere to go once they ran out of human treats. Not unless they could swim, which was a distinct possibility, come to think of it.

If they could swim, then Sri Lanka would be next on the list of places that would become a wasteland inhabited only by the unliving. After depleting India of life, they'd most likely head north. It would take time for them to traverse the entire country, time that we'd need to try to eradicate the forces that were attempting to cross into the neighbouring countries.

I'd lucked out and had positioned the human soldiers in the right place for once. They were stretched out in a thin line near the border of Pakistan. I sensed their alarm as several platoons sighted a massive wave of dark shapes rushing towards them. Sending out a mental order to converge on the affected areas, I zapped my small band to what I hoped would be the rear of the group of mutants.

I was in luck again and spied one of the horned demons herding its minions forward. An almost impossibly large number of misshapen monsters stretched out as far as the eye could see. *There are way too many minions for just one silverback to have created them all.* My thought was disturbed and it was shared by the others.

"The gorilla must have ordered its servants to make servants of their own," Gregor concluded. If that was true, then the ape had relinquished total control over its fledglings in order for them to rapidly make vast numbers of its kind. While it couldn't directly control the minds of its servants' underlings, it would still be able to direct the main attacks.

"This doesn't look good for the humans," Ishida said bleakly.

He was right, of course. There was no possibility that the bamboozled soldiers would be able to contain the wave of beasts and birds that were sprinting or winging their way towards Pakistan.

"Let's just focus on taking down the apes and worry about demolishing the hybrid minions later," I said.

I'm not certain there will be a 'later' for any of us, Gregor thought loudly enough for me to overhear him. He flicked a glance at me to see if I'd caught his thought and I kept my expression neutral. It hurt to have someone who I admired so much so disappointed in me.

Not waiting for a verbal response, I whisked my army after the silverback. It didn't even break its stride when I appeared right in front of it. Dropping its shoulder, it tried to barge me out of its way and stumbled when I disappeared. Shifting to just ahead of it, I used the oldest trick in the book and stuck out my foot to trip the beast.

Sprawling on its face, it left a long, wide furrow behind it as it skidded for several yards. Grunting an order to its closest servants, it stood and turned to face us. So did several hundred hideously deformed creatures. My small army began firing and throwing explosives at them. Blasts from both the explosives and our death rays tore through their ranks, drawing more of the minions towards us.

Ignoring the lesser hybrids for now, I circled the ape as my six immortal companions closed in on it from all sides. Everyone else knew to keep their distance. None of them could reattach their limbs and they opted to fire at the oncoming enemies instead. They would copy the same tactic that my human soldiers had used and would fall back to keep at a safe distance when they were in danger of being overwhelmed.

Kokoro darted forward and sliced into the gorilla's side. The thick armour-like skin protected it and she barely left a mark. It whirled around and took a swipe at her, but she gracefully danced out of its reach. Gregor took the opportunity to step forward and stab it in the back. Whirling and slashing with its claws, it bellowed in frustrated rage. The horned monstrosity spun around again and managed to backhand Ishida to the ground as he swung his sword at it. Geordie lunged at it from behind and hamstrung it before it could bite his friend's face off.

Luc dragged Ishida out of the way then his sword speared through the monster's right eye. Mine appeared beside it in the left eye and we rammed our weapons in to the hilt together. Jittering as if it had been hit with fifty-thousand volts of electricity, the ape collapsed to the ground. We pulled our swords free and it turned to watery slush. One sword in the eye just made them mad, but two was enough to kill them.

"How many of these monkeys have we killed now?" Higgins asked. He and a few of his comrades had kept their distance, watching our backs and shooting the occasional stray mutant while we'd battled our enemy.

"Seven," I replied. Not for the first time, I wished the animal underlings would die along with their master each time we took one down. Nothing was ever that easy and we would still have to eradicate them all somehow.

"That leaves just three left to kill," Wesley concluded. Eyeing the countless hordes of creatures that were making their way across the border, he shook his head. "We'd better find and destroy the last three silverbacks asap."

Igor looked even more dour than usual when he spoke. "It hardly matters if we kill their masters anymore. These things are aware that they can turn other animals into their kind now." As we watched, a former dog that was now the size of a horse, delicately pinned a writhing cat to the ground with one paw. It allowed the cat to sink its teeth into its flesh without retaliating. Releasing its captive, the mutant loped off as the cat was transformed into a huge, hairless, greyish-brown skinned atrocity.

Charlie blasted the cat apart before it could change something else into its servant. Losing an eye hadn't made him less of a warrior and his aim was still true. "We are royally screwed," he declared and I had to agree with his blunt assessment.

Chapter Thirty-One

Just because one of the demons had ordered its offspring to create minions of their own, didn't mean that the rest of them had. I desperately tried to tell myself that there might still be time to stop them from taking the final step that would lead to the worldwide decimation of all life. I wasn't sure if sea creatures would be affected by these vampires or not. So much aquatic life had been wiped out by the octosquids that it probably didn't matter.

In the off chance that the final remaining apes hadn't commanded their minions to multiply, I zeroed in on the swathe of humans that were being eradicated somewhere to the north-east. I shifted us all in time to witness them swarming across the border into an unknown country. We saw more hybrids creating their own servants and I figured the death warrant had just been signed for everyone in that country as well as in India.

"Is there any point trying to stop them?" Igor asked morosely as we watched the wave of deformed beasts take down and drain anything that had warm blood in its veins. Humans were left to die in the streets, but animals were forced to bite their attackers and become creatures from a horror story.

"We can't just give up," I replied and hoped I didn't sound as disheartened as I felt.

It took us hours to locate the leader of the spawn. When we did finally spy it amongst the flood, there was no chance that we'd be able to get close enough to it to chop it to pieces. The only hybrid able to stand on its hind legs, it turned to survey its multitude of minions. It was too far away for me to see its face, but I fancied that I could read the triumph in its scarlet eyes anyway.

If we can't get to it, maybe I can bring it to us. Latching onto the idea, I gave it some more thought. I might not be able to sense these creatures, but maybe I could still teleport one if I was looking straight at it. It had worked on the missiles that had been heading towards America and it might work on the ape as well. It was worth a try, so I slipped my swords free from their sheaths.

"Get ready to hack and stab," I told my friends and motioned my servants to stand back. "I'm going to try to teleport the silverback over here."

"I like this idea," Igor said in approval and drew his weapon.

Locking onto the horned beast with my eyes, I zapped it into our midst. I grinned, or at least bared my teeth in happiness, when it appeared right before me. *Maybe my gifts aren't quite so useless after all.*

Blinking in alarmed surprise, the demon recovered quickly and immediately went on the offensive. Ishida barely managed to dodge the claws that swiped at his head. I leapt forward to skewer it and the ape anticipated the move. Turning its back at the last instant, the barbed spikes running along its spine punched through my body and exited from my back. Now I was the one who looked like I had barbed spikes running along my vertebrae.

"*Chérie!*" Geordie shouted in distress and helpfully yanked me backwards before I could teleport myself to safety. We tumbled to the ground and my wounds healed even before our feet became entangled.

Grinning in triumph, the silverback stomped forward and lifted a hoof to squish my head to a pulp. I shifted myself and Geordie away a millisecond before the hoof slammed into the ground.

"Nice try, monkey," the teen muttered as he climbed to his feet.

Luc's sword speared the gorilla in the thigh and it spun to attack. As my beloved danced backwards, Igor and Gregor approached the beast stealthily from behind. Their swords pierced its kidneys and it roared in pain and frustrated rage.

Kokoro appeared like an angel of doom, leaping high into the air and gracefully descending. She wore a serene expression as her weapon sheared through the demon's head. Landing lightly, she watched calmly as the horned horror blinked a few times before blood began to sheet down its face. Geordie wasn't the only one to gag this time when its head split apart, exposing its brain as its face peeled open like a banana.

Unbelievably, while it was badly wounded, it still wasn't dead. Its hands feebly scrambled to push its head back together. Ishida allowed his disgust to show as he stepped forward and used both hands to decapitate it. He stepped back as it turned into a gooey stain.

"Well done," Gregor praised the teen. Ishida accepted the compliment with a composed nod.

There wasn't much that our small group of vampires could do against the tide of monsters, so I shifted us back to the Pakistan border. Exhausted from chasing after and then battling their foes, the soldiers had come close to running out of ammo again. Almost half of them had been killed during their extended battle. Their bodies were strewn around like discarded toys. The bulk of the mutants had moved on to greener pastures, presumably hunting for greater quantities of food that was less likely to shoot at them.

Not all of the atrocities were gone. A relatively small pack had been penned in by a ring of soldiers. We insinuated ourselves into their ranks and helped them to demolish the snarling, biting, clawing mob.

Dawn was nearing when the last creature was finally blasted apart. No one cheered at our victory, mainly because the soldiers were still beneath my spell and weren't currently capable of feeling much emotion. Anyone who had the ability to cheer knew that there was no reason to celebrate. After all of our struggles, we'd taken down only a tiny percentage of the undead threat. If all of the soldiers worldwide banded together, we might have stood a chance. I couldn't teleport that many people myself. By the time they arrived by road or air, it would be too late anyway.

Everyone was withdrawn and no one was in the mood to talk when we returned to our base. Almost everybody lay down on their sleeping bags and waited for the sun to rise and to sweep them into blessed oblivion. I wished I could also retreat into nothingness, but my conscience wouldn't let me. It nagged at me to do something, to come up with a plan that would save the world just one last time.

I expected my friends and allies to gather around to discuss strategy, but they also took to their makeshift beds. Only Luc stayed with me as I used Gregor's laptop to search for news of the attacks.

As I'd feared, several borders had been breached. The monsters had begun pouring through the cities, decimating entire populations. The laptop battery eventually began to fail and finally ran out. By that time, I'd already gleaned everything that I needed to know.

Turning to Luc, I found him watching me sadly. "We've lost, haven't we?" I said quietly. "I screwed up and now the entire world has to pay for my failure."

"You did everything that you could to stop them," Luc said. I sensed a slight hesitation, as if he didn't quite believe his own words. "We should rest. We are going to have a very long night ahead."

"I'll be there in a minute," I promised and watched him thread his way through the slumbering soldiers and over to our sleeping bags.

Turning my back on my team, I stared at the crumbling wall and brooded about the coming night. Luc's thought had been fleeting and he'd quickly supressed it, but I'd picked up on it anyway. He didn't think that I'd tried my hardest to stop the undead mobs. I was legend made flesh and I'd let everyone down.

I'd performed virtual miracles every time we'd been on the verge of annihilation before and I'd always come through in the end. It appeared that that wasn't going to happen this time. I'd done my best and it wasn't nearly good enough. Even Gregor couldn't come up with a solution to our problem, but he wasn't to blame. I was. I'd been given the tools that I required to stop any threat, yet I didn't see how any of them could help me now.

Chapter Thirty-Two

Instead of going to bed as I'd promised Luc, I spent the day shifting troops around. I felt a bit like a novice chess player playing against a grand master. Placing my pieces strategically on a gigantic board, I hoped that I wouldn't be check-mated when I least expected it.

Gathering more soldiers from their bases, I made sure they were loaded up with bullets and other provisions. I then shifted them to the worst affected areas and ordered them to search out and destroy the hybrids that were hiding from the sun.

Exhausted from my exertions by the end of the day, I topped up on blood before returning to our base. My team was awake and were waiting for me when I appeared. I had the distinct feeling that they'd held a meeting while I was gone and that I'd been the main topic. Normally, my telepathy tended to pick up on conversations that revolved around me. There had been so many conversations about me worldwide that I'd taken to ignoring the tingle at the back of my head.

Geordie stepped forward and I deliberately stopped myself from skimming his thoughts. His expression was a mixture of concern and something else that I couldn't define. "I just wanted you to know that, although things are looking grim right now, we all believe in you, *chérie*."

It wasn't what I'd expected to hear and I blinked in confusion. My soldiers nodded in wordless agreement and my female fledglings gave me tremulous smiles of encouragement. Geordie's emotions swelled and I knew what he was feeling; utter trust. He trusted me to come through for the humans and most of my team seemed to feel the same way.

"You'll find a way to stop the hybrids," Higgins said with quiet confidence.

"You won't let us down," Wesley added.

I came close to bursting into either tears, or hysterical laughter. Luc's hand on my elbow stopped me from letting it out. I'd tried everything that I could think of and it still wasn't enough.

"What's the plan?" Igor asked gruffly.

I took a moment to quell my morbid giggles before speaking. "We'll target the two remaining gorillas to the south, then join up with the troops to the north and try to stop the creatures from spreading further."

"It is a sound strategy," Gregor said with a show of solidarity. His eyes were bleak when they met mine briefly. He knew that it was already too late, but he was hiding his thoughts of our impending catastrophic defeat from the others.

Unless we allowed the meat sacks to deploy their nuclear weapons in the worst affected areas, there was very little chance that the mutants could be stopped. Doing so was against Fate's will and she was one entity that I didn't want to cross. She'd already caused me unimaginable pain and anguish during my existence. God only knew what she would do to me if I failed her in this instance.

The town that I'd chosen to use as our base had been untouched by the attacks so far, but the inhabitants had begun to flee anyway. Most had headed south, directly into the path of danger. The streets were eerily quiet. I heard the bleat of a goat that had been left behind and a dog barking somewhere in the distance. It was only a matter of time before they were discovered by the undead minions and would be turned into misshapen monstrosities.

Searching for the epicentre of the attacks, I zapped my small band into chaos. We appeared on the edge of a vast plague of hybrids that filled me with dismay to see. Humans fled in terror. They were either snatched into the air by gigantic birds, or were snapped up and drained by a myriad of other things that had once been domestic or wild animals.

"How are we going to find the silverbacks amongst this throng?" Ishida asked in alarm.

"They will probably be in the centre," I replied. The demons were driving the mob, after all, and they had to be somewhere nearby.

I took my group to the middle of the city and chose a high rooftop to keep watch from. My soldiers fired their death rays at a flock of birds that swooped down to pick us off. My holy marks took down the rest then we turned our attention to the streets below.

"I think I see one," Simone called after we'd been searching for over an hour and waved us over.

We lined up on the edge of the rooftop to peer downwards. Following Simone's pointing finger, I glimpsed horns and nodded. "That's one of them all right." None of the other mutants came close to the gorillas in appearance.

Our quarry turned and looked upwards, sensing that it was being watched. We all ducked back out of sight. I waited for a few moments, then edged forward and peered down in time to see the ape disappear into a long, wide building.

The windows had been boarded over and holes had been kicked in some of the walls. It had probably been a warehouse before it had been abandoned. There would easily be enough room for my whole team to fit inside, so I teleported us all to the ground. Higgins and Wesley were the first through the gaping doorway. The door itself was missing and had been carried away long ago.

Our night vision was good enough to see into even the darkest corners, but there wasn't much to see over my soldiers' shoulders. "It's empty, ma'am," Higgins whispered, then moved aside to let me enter.

Turning in a full circle, I saw no sign of the horned beast. The warehouse was devoid of furniture, equipment or goods and there was nowhere for it to hide. My eyes almost passed over a darker shadow in the corner to our right. Scuffed cloven footprints in the dust led me to what turned out to be a staircase.

I motioned for everyone to follow me, then tiptoed across the bare concrete floor. There were no humans inside and hadn't been for years. I wondered what had drawn the demon to investigate the building.

A heavy metal door hung askew at the bottom of the stairs. A large dent in the shape of a hoof told me what had broken it open. The floor down here was plain dirt and the heavy thud of footsteps came from just ahead.

Stepping through the doorway, I was surprised by the size of the underground room. It stretched out in a large square with multiple tunnels branching out from it. The walls and ceiling had been reinforced with wooden beams to stop them from caving in. The space had probably been used for storage, but I had no explanation for the tunnel system that ran below the ground. Maybe they'd used it for smuggling purposes. Whatever the reason had been, the corridors now hid our enemy.

Crossing the floor, I heard stealthy movement to the right and peered into a tunnel. Hunching down to avoid the low ceiling, the silverback glared at me balefully. Before I could break into a sprint to pursue it, movement from behind indicated that something else was down here. I saw the second demon in a tunnel directly opposite from me before it turned a corner and left my sight. It suddenly occurred to me that there were more than just two sets of animal prints in the dirt. There were dozens.

"Split up," I instructed my team. "Both of the silverbacks are down here and they aren't alone, so be careful." The apes were up to something, but I wasn't sure what it was.

Half of my team followed me into a confusing series of tunnels, while the rest of my band went in pursuit of the other demon. The gorilla stayed just ahead of us, appearing in flashes of greenish-brown skin. It ran on all fours, but it reminded me of a minotaur stalking through a confusing and complicated labyrinth. Its shoulders were almost as wide as the tunnel and it had little room to manoeuvre in.

We raced through what seemed like miles of tunnels before we emerged into another large area. Our prey wasn't alone when we halted. The room was filled from wall to wall with mutated monsters. I barely had time to realize that it was a trap before they were on us.

Drawing my swords, I sliced my way through the crush of beasts. Shots were fired and bright orange light flared when the explosive rounds went off. Igor threw some of his modified bombs and the explosions rang in my ears. Meat, brains and blood flew, then were reduced to goo with the monsters' deaths. My goal was the horned one, but there were too many minions between us for me to reach it. Standing as tall as the low ceiling would allow, it gestured with its hands and bellowed orders.

Luc appeared at my side, then Geordie popped up as well. The rest of my close friends carved their way to me. I motioned for them to stay back as I gathered the power of my holy marks. Malformed creatures instinctively flinched away from the crosses on my palms when I raised my hands. The holy power cut a swathe through them and left their leader exposed. Before the silverback could run, I willed it to us. It appeared before us and knew that death was imminent. Throwing its head back, it screamed a final order before Luc's sword pierced its heart.

Still alive, but direly wounded, the gorilla fell to its knees and almost seemed to gurgle out a chuckle. As I stepped forward to ram my sword into its chest all the way to the hilt, I felt both my servants behind me and the ones that had chased the other ape begin to die.

Frozen in horror, I didn't even try to dodge the demon's claws as they ripped through my stomach and gutted me. My intestines fell out and slithered to the floor. That pain was minor in comparison to experiencing the deaths of my offspring. One by one, my fledglings' lives were snuffed out just as easily as if they'd been humans. I watched through one of my soldier's eyes in a distant tunnel as they were overwhelmed by hundreds of hybrids.

Luc's sword flashed out, decapitating the demon before it could do any further damage to me. He shook me by the shoulder, snapping me out of my daze. "Your people are dying! Get us out of here!" he shouted.

Reaching out, I snared the survivors in my mental net and took them far away from India. I'd fallen into the trap that the demons had set and my servants had paid the price. I didn't take my vastly diminished army back to our village in Italy. Instead, I took them where they would hopefully be safe from the retribution that was going to rain down on the monsters that had decimated my kin. I didn't know what form my retribution would take yet, I just knew that it was going to be catastrophic for anything that was undead.

It was daylight in the southern hemisphere and most of the survivors instantly fell asleep. I didn't give Luc the chance to ask me any questions, because I didn't have any answers for him. I was acting on instinct alone now. Leaving my friends, allies and fledglings where they would be safe, I teleported back to the city where so many of my people had just been annihilated.

My wounds had disappeared as if by magic by the time I was standing in the grassy field of a stadium. Ranks of empty seats ringed me and I smelled old sweat and junk food. The stadium was empty of life and there was nothing to distract me from what I was about to do.

I'd been told that I had the power to stop the hordes of undead and I now realized what Fate had meant by that. The holy marks on my palms had been the first signs that had marked me as being the long awaited Mortis. They were capable of killing thousands of hybrids at a time, but that wasn't going to be enough. I needed to kill millions of enemies and I wasn't sure that I'd be able to manage it and survive the process. *You don't have a choice,* my inner voice said. *This is what you were made for. This is your destiny.*

Bowing my head for a moment, I accepted the burden that I'd been fighting since Silvius had first snatched me off the streets of Brisbane and had converted me into a monster. I let go of the last shred of my resistance and became what I'd always been meant to be: Death incarnate.

My eyes were blazing scarlet when I lifted my hands and called on the dark power that resided within me. I let it build up until the ground began to tremble and the seats ringing the stadium shook. All across the city, I felt eyes as equally red as mine turn in my direction, but they didn't converge on the stadium to attack. Sensing that annihilation was approaching, they fled with shrill shrieks of alarm. I let them run, confident that they wouldn't be able to escape from my rage, and called on more power. The air pulsed with it in nearly visible waves and still it wasn't enough. Reaching into depths that I didn't know I possessed, I wasn't just a conduit for the holy power anymore. I *was* the power.

Screaming from a combination of ecstasy and agony, I released the energy and the shockwave blasted me to the ground. Cries of pain and terror were short lived as the undead multitudes were turned to ash, incinerated by the holy fire that emanated from my very body.

Unable to sense the mutants, I strained to send the dark power out in a circle as far as it could reach in the hope that it would strike them all down. It stretched out across India and beyond. Crossing the borders, it killed everything that was undead.

When I felt the lives of the final remaining vampires who were spread throughout Europe being snuffed out, I finally released the power.

I hadn't intended to kill the unknown vamps, but perhaps it was for the best. They'd been old and crafty and would probably have been a problem for me at some stage. Now I wouldn't have to hunt them down one by one later on. The fact that they were now dead meant that that had been their fate all along. It seemed cruel to allow them to exist for thousands of years before yanking the rug out from beneath them and ending their lives so abruptly. Deep down, they probably knew that they'd been doomed. The prophecies had warned our kind of what was to come. Tonight, I'd finally fulfilled the destiny that I'd been made for, yet I sensed that it still wasn't over and that my task was not yet done.

Far beyond simple exhaustion, I lay in the deep crater that had been left when my power had been released, too tired to move. I felt hollowed out, not just from my exertions, but from the loss of my servants. How could I possibly face my friends, allies and few surviving fledglings after I'd failed them so badly? I'd had the power to stop this all along, but I hadn't used it until the last possible moment. Surely, they would despise me for being so dense that I hadn't been able to understand my full potential.

A mental slap hit me up the back of the head, making my ears ring. *Stop feeling sorry for yourself,* my subconscious snapped. *Haven't you figured it out yet?* Confused and weary to my very bones, I had no idea what it was talking about. *This was all part of Fate's plan. Your servants were meant to die to give you the incentive you needed to use your holy marks the way they were intended.* My alter ego was clearly disgusted with me for being so obtuse.

You mean Fate allowed me to create my army with the intention of killing them all along? I didn't know why I was so surprised, not to mention hurt, by that. I'd been a plaything for Fate since long before my actual creation. From the first moment that I'd been turned, I'd been dancing to destiny's tune. Every time I'd faced a challenge that had seemed unsurmountable, I'd been tortured into succeeding. This time had been no different, but instead of paying the price with my own flesh and blood, my people had been sacrificed to save the humans.

I might have won against the demons and their spawn, yet I still felt defeated. Luc had been wrong about Fate when he'd said that she wasn't entirely heartless. *She isn't,* my subconscious said in her defence. *She left some of your fledglings alive. If she was heartless, she'd have killed them all.* Very grudgingly, I conceded that my alter ego had a point. If she'd wanted to, she could have wiped us all out. *Why didn't she?* I couldn't help but wonder why she'd kept a few of us alive and how long we could hope to remain that way.

I'd snatched up my people and had carried them away from harm without any sense of who had survived the ambush. It was time to return to Australia and face my remaining kin. *Some leader I turned out to be,* I thought wretchedly. They'd trusted me and I'd managed to get most of them killed. I wouldn't blame them if they turned away from me in disgust.

Chapter Thirty-Three

Geordie ran to me when I reappeared in the underground parking lot where I'd left the survivors. He wrapped his thin arms around me and held on tightly. I steeled myself, then peered over his shoulder to take stock of the rest of our group.

Like Geordie, my other close friends had survived the hybrids' ambush. Danton and his warriors and a couple of Gregor's guards had also lived to tell the tale. The monk was already recording the events of the past few hours. He'd found a notepad and a pen and sat cross-legged on the concrete, jotting down notes.

Ishida sat beside his slumbering harem. Only four of the six had made it through the attacks. He gave me a strained smile that barely reached his eyes. He'd only known the girls for a short time, but he'd come to care for them all deeply. Renee's head rested in his lap. She wasn't just his favourite, she was mine as well. I was glad to see she was still alive.

Igor knelt beside Simone, tenderly holding her hand despite her utter lack of awareness of both him and her surroundings. Gabrielle lay beside her and I felt deep relief that Geordie hadn't lost his one true love. Corporal Higgins and Sergeant Wesley were amongst the unconscious soldiers, but Charlie's bright red hair was missing. Many of the men that I'd barely gotten to know, as well as most of my female fledglings, were gone. All up, we were now an even fifty in number. Grief for my dead servants welled and I forced it down. What right did I have to cry for the fallen when I'd been responsible for their deaths?

Geordie took a step back and inspected my face. "Are you all right, *chérie*?"

He'd sensed my misery and guilt and he'd run to comfort me rather than castigating me for my failure to keep my people safe. My answer was a wordless sob. I put my hands over my face and collapsed to my knees in exhausted grief and misery.

Luc was beside me almost before I hit the ground. Scooping me up, he cradled me against his chest. I felt his pity for my servants and sympathy for my loss. I sensed no blame or disgust in him at all. I felt his relief that I was ok and, of course, his love for me.

Assuming that I'd failed to destroy our adversaries, Gregor bleakly came up with a hasty plan. "We will have to find an isolated island somewhere that has either humans or animals that we can feed from. We will have to set up a defensive perimeter and some kind of warning system to alert us if any of the undead are approaching," he said quietly to the few who were still awake. "If we are lucky, the mutants might never find us."

I got a hold of my grief and dropped my hands. "We won't need to do that. They're all dead," I said and Luc nearly dropped me in surprise.

"What?" Geordie's astonishment was almost enough to make me smile, if my misery and guilt hadn't been so strong. "How?"

"I used these." I held my hands up to show them the crosses.

Narrowing his eyes, Gregor looked at me speculatively. "I thought you had to be able to sense your targets to be able to use the holy marks effectively."

"So did I," I replied with a weary shrug. "I guess I was wrong." I would have asked Luc to put me down, but I was so exhausted that I wasn't sure if I'd be able to stand on my own.

Danton asked a question, holding his pen poised to jot down my reply. "Exactly how did you use them to kill the hordes?"

I knew he was itching to get the details down, but I was simply too fatigued to tell him what he wanted to know right now. "I'll fill you all in on all the gory details later. I've used up pretty much all of my energy and I need to sleep."

"Before you do," Luc said, "where are we?" Being daylight, no one had been able to investigate where I'd dumped them yet. Apparently, no humans had entered the parking area while I'd been gone. The smashed window of a car that was too old and rusty to have an alarm told me where Danton had found his writing materials.

"Remember the hotel in Brisbane that you took me to when my flesh hunger rose for the first time?"

His brows rose in surprise and his lips quirked in something that was very close to being a smirk. "I remember it very well."

"We're in the underground parking lot beneath it." With that revelation, I subsided into a deep unconsciousness. I'd instinctively taken my friends to the place that I knew best, my home town.

Fate waited for me in my dream. She stood on the hill again, but this time there were only two doors hanging in mid-air when I joined her.

"You are angry with me," she said in her hollow voice.

She'd lied to me when she said we wouldn't speak again. I was sure it had all been a part of her complicated plan, but I was simply too tired to try to figure out why she'd duped me.

"You killed my servants," I responded tightly. "Of course I'm angry with you." Actually, I was beyond mere anger and was approaching a murderous rage. If it had been possible to strangle her to death, my hands would have been around her throat and squeezing tightly right now.

"They were never meant to be yours forever."

"Gee, I guess that makes it all better then."

She turned slightly at my sarcasm and I caught a glimpse of the darkness beneath her hood. Tendrils of her long black hair seemed to reach for me. They were far too reminiscent of the octosquids' hungry tentacles for my liking. For the first time, I realized we were the exact same height and build. I wondered if she'd shaped herself after me in an attempt to make me feel less intimidated. If so, it hadn't worked. *Would you rather she appeared as an eight foot tall monstrosity with purple eyes and drooling acid all over the place?* I mentally shuddered at the image that my subconscious sent me. *Not really,* I admitted.

"Answer me this, Natalie Pierce," she said almost coldly. "If anyone else had been tasked with the fate of being Mortis, do you think they could have succeeded at saving humanity time and time again?"

My automatic instinct was to reply in the affirmative. Instead, I held my tongue for once and put some thought into it. That I was different from the rest of my kin went without saying, but it wasn't just my powers that set me apart from them.

I was Australian rather than European or Japanese, so I didn't have any particular prejudices against the two vampire nations. I hadn't been raised in a culture that believed in our kind and had few preconceived notions of what I should or shouldn't have been able to do. My imagination was just quirky enough to find solutions to problems that may not have occurred to anyone else. I was unique and that was why I'd been chosen. Fate had believed all along that I would be able to save not just the humans, but a remnant of my own species as well.

"No," I said at last. "I was the right choice and I did the best I could."

"You did well," Fate responded with a hint of pride in her creation. "You were never meant to save all of humanity, just as many of them as you could. Many millions have perished, yet you have exceeded beyond all of my hopes and expectations."

We stood in silence, gazing at the twin doors. The door that had contained a planet where only the undead remained was gone. The door with the threat of nuclear holocaust remained. So did the third option of a near utopia for humanity and happiness for the remnant of my kin.

"It's not over yet, is it?" I asked Fate quietly, knowing the answer, yet asking anyway.

"No. You have one final task to perform." She hesitated, then turned to me. A gust of wind ruffled her robe, yet the hood remained firmly in place. I was very glad about that. I didn't want to look Fate directly in the face, not even in a dream. The mind could take only so much and I preferred to hold onto whatever sanity I had left. "Humanity is still in danger," she told me gravely. "You have the power to ensure that they will remain safe forever."

Studying the blasted wasteland of roiling skies and ruined cities through the door on the left, I gave a deep mental sigh. "What is this final threat?"

"That is something that you will have to discover on your own," she replied. "I must ask you one question, Mortis." Her stare became even more intent and I sensed that my answer would be crucial. "Would you sacrifice your soul to save this planet?"

Looking deep inside myself, I gave her the only answer that I could. "Yes. If I still have a soul, then I would willingly give it up to save Earth."

It wasn't just the humans or my kin she was talking about, but the very world itself. Even if it meant never seeing Luc, my friends or servants again, I would sacrifice my life to keep them all safe. If my sacrifice could save the humans as well, then it would be an added bonus.

"Once this final task is complete, you will finally find peace," she promised. Turning misty, she lost form and a puff of wind blew her faint outline apart.

The doors remained behind, floating in mid-air and taunting me with two possible futures. I'd saved the human race from the undead hybrids, yet they were still in danger. I had only a vague idea of what this final threat could be and zero idea of how to stop it.

Luc's cool mouth closing over my breast roused me from my slumber. I moaned as he teased my nipple. Lifting his head, he stared down at me and smiled, stealing the breath that I didn't have. "I thought this might wake you," he teased.

"Less talk, more sex," I demanded and pulled his face down to mine. Grappling for supremacy, we ended up on the floor, then my legs were around Luc's waist and he was plunging inside me. It was hard and fast, just the way I liked it best. I had to clamp my hand over my mouth to muffle my cries of pleasure when Luc's fangs pierced my neck and sent me over the edge.

Shuddering in his own release, Luc took a moment to recover, then rolled onto his side. "Do you know how unsettling it is to have your lover whole one moment then an inert clump of particles the next?" he asked me.

"I phased in and out, huh?" I'd done so unconsciously when I'd been mourning Luc's supposed death and I figured I must have done so again while I'd been recovering. "How long was I out for?"

"Three nights." His response was even, but I felt his anguish. "You must have used up all of your reserves when you sent out your holy bomb."

I hadn't, not quite, but it had been very close. "Where are we?" I asked, avoiding the topic, knowing it would just upset us both to discuss how close to the edge I'd been.

"Still in the hotel in Brisbane."

Now that he'd mentioned it, the room did look familiar. It had been over twelve years since we'd last been here. The décor had changed somewhat, but the room still seemed the same.

"Have you managed to verify that all of the mutants are dead?" I asked.

"I'll let Gregor answer that question," Luc said with a smile and offered me his hand to help me up.

"Is it safe to come in?" Geordie asked from right out in the hallway.

"Yes," Luc responded. If the door hadn't been locked, the teen would have barrelled inside immediately. While my beloved might be comfortable with his nakedness, I wasn't. I darted into the bathroom and snatched a fluffy white bathrobe off a hook. Luc stopped long enough to don a pair of jeans before opening the door.

Our friends piled inside and I was engulfed in a group hug. I sensed the rest of our surviving companions in the rooms around us. While they weren't in the room with us, they'd be able to hear our conversation easily enough. Danton joined us, unwilling to miss any details of my story.

Gregor held me a moment longer than the others, long enough to think something at me that I couldn't possibly miss. *I am sorry for doubting you, Natalie. Can you forgive me?* I caught his eye when he pulled back and gave him a nod. How could I be angry with him for doubting me when I'd doubted myself?

Relieved that I wasn't going to hold a grudge, Gregor twined his fingers with Kokoro's. "I've been scanning the news reports during your convalescence." Geordie sniggered nervously at his stuffy terminology, then ducked away from Igor when he raised his hand threateningly. Gregor frowned at the teen, then continued. "It appears that you were successful at destroying the undead hordes. There have been no reported sightings of mutant animals or any other deaths or disappearances anywhere else in the world."

"Thank G-G-G goodness for that," I said and ignored Ishida's silent laugh at my stutter. Even now I still sometimes forgot that I couldn't say God out loud.

"Can you describe what you did?" Danton asked.

I told them how I'd allowed the power of the holy marks to build up until I was practically glowing with it before releasing it and sending it out as far as I could reach. "I figured it had spread far enough when the last few remaining vampires in Europe were wiped out," I explained. The mutants would have had to teleport to escape from the power of my holy marks and I was the only creature with that ability.

"So, we are all that is left now?" Geordie asked. "There are no other vampires out there?"

A few of our kin had fled from Europe to Australia, but they'd been called to their doom by the First long ago. There were no strange vampires anywhere in my country and I swept my senses across the rest of the world just to be sure. "We're it," I confirmed and felt like weeping.

"Do not blame yourself," Kokoro said gently. "The deaths of the unknown vampires and your servants were preordained and unavoidable."

"Fate killed your servants to goad you into dropping the holy bomb," Geordie reminded me. "You know, I really don't like her very much." His tone was petulant and his lower lip pooched out slightly. I'd described some of my dream to them and now they couldn't help but think of Fate as female. Luc had known her gender all along, of course.

"Is it finally over?" Igor asked. "Are there any more threats left for us to destroy?"

"There's still one more," I admitted and groans of disappointment were issued from the rooms around us. "I haven't figured out what it is yet, but this is one that I apparently have to face alone."

Luc didn't like the sound of that and his concern was obvious. "You will never be alone, Natalie," he promised me. "I will always be here for you."

"So will I," Geordie declared.

"Excuse me?" Gabrielle said loudly from the room next door.

"Just as a friend, of course," Geordie clarified, then rolled his eyes at his servant's jealousy.

"Are we going back to Italy soon?" Ishida asked. "This hotel is nice enough, but I miss my computer games." He grinned to show he was kidding, but I sensed he wanted to return to the place that he already thought of as his home.

My stomach tried to cramp in hunger, reminding me that I needed to replenish my energy before I did anything else. "I'll just grab a quick snack and then we can leave," I promised.

It was late and dawn was only an hour or so away, which meant most of the humans in the hotel were asleep. Searching the rooms below us, I found a man sleeping alone and appeared beside his bed a moment later. I drank more than was healthy for him, but I left him wearing a dazed and sleepy smile. I visited four more slumbering snacks before I was fully energized again.

My troops had been busy packing their few belongings while I'd been feeding. They'd been shopping at some stage during the past three nights and all carried a backpack with several changes of clothes inside.

Luc handed me a pack of my own and I took a few moments to change in the bathroom. He'd splurged and had bought me a new black leather jacket and expensive trousers. He'd even bought me new boots. Everything was a perfect fit, which was probably due to Kokoro's help rather than my one true love knowing my size. She and I were roughly the same height and shape, after all, and she would have advised him of what sizes to purchase.

It saddened me that my entire team could now fit into one room when they gathered together, ready to be transported. We were all subdued as I teleported us from the city that had once been my home to the property where Luc had been born and raised so very long ago. It was already dark in Italy, so we were in no danger of being flash fried by the sun.

"Are we going to feel jetlagged?" Higgins asked curiously.

As a vampire, he'd never been awake for longer than one full night before. None of my fledglings would feel compelled to fall asleep until morning came again. "I have no idea," I admitted.

"I doubt you will feel any adverse effects," Gregor said. "Jetlag is a human failing and we have all moved beyond such weaknesses now." It was a gentle reminder that none of us would ever be human again.

Now that nearly three quarters of my army had perished, there were more than enough homes for everyone. I wasn't particularly surprised when most of my soldiers still paired up before heading to their houses. The men had already been a tightknit team before I'd turned them into my servants. Besides, no one wanted to be alone after the horrors that we'd been through over the past few nights.

Offering me his hand, Luc strolled towards our house. I walked beside him, feeling sad for our losses and relieved that at least some of my kin had been spared. We'd made it through the worst disaster that I could have possibly imagined, but it wasn't over yet. A sacrifice had to be made before the final threat would be over and it appeared that the sacrifice was to be my life.

Sensing the dread that filled me, Luc turned in concern, but I offered him a smile instead of an explanation. I wasn't going to ruin the little time that we had left together with the fact that I was going to die. I'd tell him when the time was right. *You mean at the last possible moment,* my inner voice said sourly.

Exactly, I responded. I might be Mortis, but deep down, I could still be a coward at times.

Chapter Thirty-Four

Several nights went by as we waited for the final catastrophe to occur. I hadn't had any more dreams to offer me a hint of what terrors were coming. The door that had depicted global nuclear annihilation was a dead giveaway, but what specific event would trigger the holocaust?

I spent as much time as I could with my close friends. I also spent a couple of hours each night going through the chronicles with Danton, making sure he had all of the details of my strange and complex unlife correct. I read through his lengthy manuscript with a mixture of amusement, embarrassment and regret that so many had died.

Geordie sensed the sadness that I couldn't quite hide. He thought it was for my lost soldiers and female

280

fledglings. I let him think that, because explaining that I might soon be gone forever would only break his heart.

The thing that saddened me the most was, while Geordie would have someone to love after I was gone, Luc would remain alone. In all of his seven centuries, he'd only ever loved me. I thought I'd lost him once, but he had been restored, thanks to my blood. I doubted anything would be able to bring me back from whatever disaster would require me to give up my life. I couldn't help but be annoyed with Fate. I'd been led to believe that I was indestructible, but that had apparently been a lie.

"A penny for your thoughts?" Luc said, snapping me out of my reverie. We were watching one of the black and white movies that he enjoyed so much. I'd zoned out after the first five minutes.

"I have a task to do," I replied, surprising myself almost as much as him.

"What is this task?" He switched off the TV and turned his full attention to me.

"I have to save the humans."

"Have we not already done so, on more than one occasion?" His eyebrow quirked in puzzlement and he began to feel a sense of unease.

"Yes, but this isn't the same." I spoke without thinking, not giving myself time to examine my thoughts in detail. "There was always a physical threat to face before."

"But, you believe that there is no physical threat this time?"

I was silent for a moment as I recalled a couple of dreams that hadn't made sense to me the first time that they'd occurred. They still didn't, but they were becoming clearer by the second. "This threat is the worst one of all and it hasn't been dealt with yet. It will be there as long as humans still exist."

Baffled and becoming increasingly wary, Luc followed me as I walked to the back of the house. I opened the door to the studio, flicked on the light and beheld the maroon chair and the backdrop of a library scene from my dream. This room was the key to the puzzle and the answer finally clicked home.

"I know what I have to do," I told my one true love softly. "We need to locate some TV cameras, a crew to man them and a talented computer hacker."

"What is your plan?"

"I'm going to send a message to everyone on the planet," I replied simply.

I wasn't sure what I was going to say, yet, but I had faith that the right words would appear when I needed them. This had been my fate all along. It seemed that I hadn't just been created to save the humans from the monsters after all. My purpose extended beyond that and I'd been tasked with a far more important role.

"I'll gather the others," Luc told me and left me to contemplate the studio alone.

As always, we assembled in the living room. Luc had brought only our close friends, Danton, Higgins and Wesley to the meeting. The rest of our team knew that something was going on, but stayed in their homes. Gabrielle and Simone chose to visit Ishida's harem. All six of the remaining torture victims squeezed onto one couch and pretended to watch TV. In reality, they were waiting to find out what was going on in the house on the hill.

Once everyone had taken a seat, I stood and addressed them. "I've figured out what I need to do," I said without preamble. Speeches had never been my thing and I wasn't particularly comfortable being the centre of attention. You'd think I would be used to it by now, but I wasn't and never really would be. "I'm going to make a speech to every human that has access to a television, radio or the internet."

"For what purpose?" Gregor asked. Even he had no idea what I had in mind.

"I'm not really sure yet," I lied. "I just know that I have to set this up soon."

"Is this about those strange dreams you had about the studio?" Geordie asked astutely.

"Yes. We have to set up cameras, find a crew and a computer hacker."

"I'll need my laptop," Ishida said and made as if to stand.

"Allow me," I said before he could move and his laptop appeared on the coffee table in front of him.

We remained silent as he fired it up and began to search for the equipment that we needed. "I've found a studio that makes independent films a couple of hours away from here. They should have the camera equipment that we need."

Returning to his search, it took him longer to find a hacker. Reading through a news article, he finally settled on a candidate. "I think I've found our man, although 'man' might be too generous a description. He's nineteen, American and his name is Chip Devondale. He was recently imprisoned for hacking into some of the most restricted computer sites in the world." Turning his computer to me, he showed me a picture of a handsome young man. He had longish bleached blond hair and periwinkle blue eyes. He looked more like a surfer than a hacker.

"Let's check out the studio first," I said. It took us less than a second to travel to what would have been a two hour car ride to the north.

The studio was actually a spacious warehouse. We stood in the middle of the gigantic space and turned in a circle, searching for what we needed.

"There," Geordie said and pointed at some equipment that was covered in protective layers of canvas. He'd spotted the legs of several large cameras.

We hurried over and Igor lifted the canvas to inspect our find. "How many do we need?" he asked as he revealed the cameras.

"Three should be enough," Ishida decided and we bowed to his expertise in all things electronic.

"Do you know how to operate these?" Gregor asked.

"No, but Natalie can kidnap some people who will be able to use them." I lifted my eyebrow in query and the teen explained further. "We can visit a television studio and 'borrow' some of their camera crew."

"Sounds like a plan," I replied. Once again, I was glad that I wasn't in this alone and that my friends were here to help me.

Now that we'd found the cameras, I zapped three of them, and us, back to the house. Next on my to-do list was to extricate Chip Devondale from prison. Picturing him in my mind, I reached out, found him in his cell in Texas and willed him to me.

Orange overalls didn't look good on even someone as young and handsome as Chip. Starting wildly at finding himself surrounded by strangers, he backed away and bumped into Igor.

"Going somewhere?" the Russian asked in a menacing tone that drained the colour from the hacker's tanned face.

"Don't scare him, Igor," Geordie chided, then giggled at the consternation on the prisoner's face.

"Who are you people?" Chip whispered.

"We're your new employers," I told him. We wouldn't actually be paying him any money for breaking the law while he helped me to accomplish my task. If my plan worked, then he wouldn't need to return to prison and he could go on his merry way.

I took control of his mind and drained any thoughts of resistance from him. Hacking was the thing that he loved to do the most and I was giving him the opportunity to wreak worldwide havoc. Not that anyone would remember it, if all went well.

"When are you going to launch your plan into action?" Gregor asked. He suspected that I knew exactly what I was going to do.

"Tomorrow night," I said.

"Then we will see you once the sun departs," Kokoro said. "Gregor and I will babysit the human." I smiled my gratitude as she linked her arm through Gregor's and guided my puppet towards the door.

Geordie picked up on the stab of sadness I felt at the thought of never seeing any of my friends again. Wide eyed, he gave me a fierce hug, then allowed Igor and Ishida to drag him away. Danton took up the rear and then Luc and I were alone.

"Why do I get the feeling that there is something you aren't telling me?" my beloved asked.

Turning to study his perfect face, I went up onto my tippy-toes and gave him a thorough kiss. "Do you want to talk, or would you prefer to get naked?"

Considering his options, he made the right decision. "Why aren't we in the bedroom already?" he asked me mockingly.

Obliging his wish, I teleported us upstairs. He reached for my jacket, but I brushed his hands away. "You first." It was his turn to oblige my wish. He didn't protest as I turned him around and pulled his jacket off his shoulders and down his arms. I trailed my fingertips down his forearms and let the jacket drop to the ground before circling him. Moving slowly, I pushed his t-shirt up, stopping to press soft kisses on his torso.

"This makes a nice change from our usual pace," he said in approval.

"I thought I might try slow and demure for once."

"Not too demure, I hope," he replied with a smile as I tugged his shirt over his head and let it drop.

"You know me better than that," I smirked. I'd keep up this slow pace for as long as I could. This would most likely be our last night together and I wanted it to live on in Luc's memory forever.

My jacket landed on the floor next to his and I teasingly worked my t-shirt up my body. Luc's stare was intense and latched onto my breasts when they were finally revealed. I wore a lacy black bra that he'd picked out and a tiny matching thong. The thong wasn't particularly comfortable, but he smiled in appreciation when I slid my jeans down my legs.

I stripped his pants off next, then led him to the bed. Pushing him down, I straddled his legs and leaned forward until my breasts were brushing against him lightly. He lasted through two long kisses before his hands rose to the clasp behind me. His eyes feasted on my bared flesh and he lowered his head to taste me. As always, passion for my one true love thundered through me. It took real effort not to push him down and ride him hard.

Appreciating my restraint, Luc put his hands on my waist and picked me up. Laying me on my back, he kissed his way down my body and divested me of my thong. It wasn't just lust on his face when he ran his eyes from my feet, along my curves and up to my face, it was adoration. He loved me with every fibre of his being and my heart swelled. "Make love to me," I said softly and emotion swept through him.

For the first time, Luc used all of the skills that he'd learned through three centuries of enforced slave-hood. He used his hands, mouth and body to bring me to the edge time and time again. Instead of his efforts being a chore, he was taking great enjoyment from my frustrated pleasure.

"Please, Luc," I begged when I couldn't take any more.

"Please what, Natalie?" he asked silkily as his tongue teased my nipple. His hand swept from my breast down my body and tormented my lower region.

"End it," I gasped, half crazed from being repeatedly denied release.

"If you insist," he said and flipped me over onto my stomach. I barely had time to brace myself before he entered me from behind. His hands covered my breasts and his face came to rest next to mine as he finally gave me what I craved and pounded himself into me.

I screamed as I came then clapped a hand over my mouth in mortification. Luc climaxed right after I did and rolled onto his side wearing a supremely pleased smile.

"What was that?" Renee asked loudly enough for everyone in the village to hear her.

"I'm not sure," Ishida lied after a short pause.

"It must have been a wildcat," Geordie called from the house next door, then burst into giggles.

"What's so funny?" Gabrielle said crankily. From all over the village, male chuckles sounded. Everyone but a few of the girls knew exactly what Luc and I had just gotten up to.

"Friggin' vampire hearing," I complained for the millionth time.

"It was worth it," Luc said, then broke into gales of laughter at the pissed look that I gave him.

As I'd hoped, the night would indeed be memorable, if not quite the way I'd intended.

Chapter Thirty-Five

Now that I'd figured out what I needed to do, I didn't waste any time when the sun went down and the new night was born. It was easy enough to locate a television studio, then bamboozle everyone and kidnap three camera people. They became my willing lackeys and busily went about setting up the cameras in our small studio.

"We need more equipment," one of the men told me. Grey haired and grizzled, he was in his fifties and had worked as a cameraman for over thirty years.

"What do we need and where can we find it?" I asked.

"We need lights, extension cords and somewhere to plug them in. Everything we need is back at the studio."

Luc nodded to indicate that he would remain behind, and I left with my helpful lackey. No one was panicking at the station from the disappearance of the two men and one female crew members. They didn't even blink when the cameraman reappeared and pointed out what we needed. My hypnotism over the station would last for some time yet. I whisked the lights, cords and other things that he'd indicated back home, then took us back as well.

In a surprisingly short amount of time, everything was ready. I zapped myself upstairs to change, then took the stairs back down to give myself a few moments to attempt to gather my poise.

We'd transferred the seldom used dining table into the studio and Chip's equipment took up most of the surface. He'd needed several of our laptops and some other assorted gear to pull off what I had in mind. He'd been busy for the past few hours. Working with dogged determination, he'd hacked into satellites that orbited all around the globe. Spying me as I entered the studio, he grinned and gave me the thumbs up. He was ready to take control of every television and digital radio station that was currently broadcasting a signal. Everything was in place and I just had to take a seat and begin.

As I'd requested, only my closest friends and Danton were present. None of the humans would remember what had happened to them in this house or that they'd ever been kidnapped at all for that matter. They would return to their lives, hopefully with the message that I was about to impart firmly ingrained on their psyche.

Geordie nervously flicked a speck of dust from the sleeve of my red leather suit that the Prime Minister of England had given me. "I am glad that you decided to wear this suit. It is very memorable," he said cheekily. It fit me like a second skin and left little to the imagination. Luc eyed me in appreciation and winked. He was doing his best to be supportive and to hide his dread. He knew that I was hiding something from him and that I wouldn't tell him what it was until I was ready.

I still wasn't ready, but it was time to confess my plan. "What I'm about to do is going to take every ounce of energy that I have," I warned them. "I'm going to hypnotize the entire population of the planet into turning on their TVs, radios or internet to listen to my message. The instructions I'm going to give them will be permanent, but new generations will need to hear the message as well. Keep a copy of the video that we're about to make and make sure you play it worldwide every few years or so."

I'd borrowed Chip and one of the workers from Luc's vineyard to run a test earlier. Chip had recorded a short message on his laptop and had shown it to the worker. The human had fallen beneath my spell as planned, which meant that I was on the right track. It was a crucial part of my plan that the meat sacks would succumb to my hypnotism merely by watching me on their TV, or listening to my voice. My bamboozlement was so strong that I was pretty sure it would still work when I was no longer around. The tape of me should be enough to keep the humans compliant if it was shown regularly.

Luc straightened in alarm. "Why will you not be able to repeat the message yourself with every new generation that is born?"

"Because…I might not be here to do it," I finally confessed.

"But, you're immortal," Geordie said in a stricken whisper. "You can't die."

"What gave you the idea that you might not survive this?" Gregor asked.

"Fate told me that I had to sacrifice myself to keep you all safe."

Stunned silence met my words, but it didn't last long.

"Fate can go to hell," Luc ground out. "I do not care what happens to humanity. Not if it means that I will lose you!"

"What do you think will happen to the world if I don't do this?" I asked him sadly.

Igor's shoulders slumped as he answered my question. "Sooner or later, there will be nuclear war. The world leaders that we have hypnotized will be replaced and new leaders will take over. One day soon, they will be free to use their bombs. The humans are their own worst enemies and they will eventually end up destroying each other."

With Igor's words, it finally hit home to everyone that I'd been created to do far more than to just annihilate the undead, clones, evil robots and rampaging aliens. My true purpose was to save the humans from the worst threat of all; themselves.

Geordie burst into tearless sobs and Ishida almost joined him. Kokoro watched me with profound sorrow. She knew all about personal sacrifice after spending thousands of years beneath the rule of several cruel emperors. Her love and respect flowed over me and it was a soothing balm to calm my fears. I wasn't sure what would happen to me once I died. *Maybe I'll just fade away,* I thought with some relief. That didn't sound so bad. It sure beat the heck out of going to hell, which I wasn't sure I even really believed in.

Luc caught me in a crushing hug that lifted me off my feet. He kissed me hard enough to have left bruises if I'd still been a fragile mortal. I kissed him back just as hard, then he put me down gently and turned and walked away. He knew that I had to do this, but he wasn't going to stand around and watch me die. It would be cruel of me to expect him to. I loved him far too much to put him through that.

Geordie's arms came around me next and then I was surrounded by the friends who had become my family. "We love you, *chérie*," Geordie whispered. "We will always love you."

"I love you, too." I met their eyes and had to fight to stop myself from sobbing at their sadness.

"It has been an honour and a privilege to have known you, Natalie," Gregor said formally.

"You are the bravest person that I have ever met," Ishida told me and bowed deeply in respect.

I bowed in return, then Kokoro stepped forward. "You may not be my sister by blood, but you will always be my sister in my heart."

"I will watch over Lucentio for you," Igor promised and some of my sadness eased slightly.

"Thank you." It was the best gift that he could have given me. "Ok, it's time to get this show on the road." If I didn't do this now, I would lose my nerve and I'd never be able to do it at all.

Stepping over the cables that snaked across the ground, I climbed onto the stage and sat down on the plush maroon chair. I blinked when the bright lights came on and shone directly on my face. Adjustments were made then the grizzled cameraman signalled that they were filming. At my nod, Chip typed in a command on his collection of laptops and gave me the ok signal. The message that was about to be broadcast was being sent all around the world and would be heard by billions of people. Anyone who didn't have access to a television, radio or the internet probably wouldn't pose much of a threat to the rest of the world anyway.

I didn't think about what I was going to say. Fate had set this up two thousand years before I'd been born and I trusted her to speak through me now. Gathering my consciousness, I spread a net of hypnotism out until it stretched all the way around the entire globe. When I let it settle, I felt a wave of faintness sweep through me as billions of people fell beneath my dark spell and my energy levels fell.

At my mental nudge, any humans who were asleep woke. Every human that was old enough to understand my command left their beds, their classes, their jobs, their showers or any other task that they were doing and headed for their closest communication device. Within minutes, all of the eyes and ears of the world were either watching or listening to me. Seeing me or hearing my voice would help to permanently cement the message that I was about to send out.

"My name is Natalie Pierce and I am the Vampire Guardian of the human race." All around the globe, recognition flared. "My friends and I have saved you many times from various dangers, but there is still one menace remaining." I waited for a few heartbeats before dropping the bomb. "The threat is you."

Shock coursed through humanity, followed by a wave of shame and remorse so strong that it would have brought me to my knees if I'd been standing. The fact that they knew that they were their own worst enemy would actually assist me to tighten my hold over them. While I was speaking in English, I used telepathy to speak the words directly into their minds as well. There could be no possibility of misunderstanding my message.

"You have the capacity and the will to reduce your own planet to an uninhabitable wasteland and I cannot let that happen. I *will not* let that happen." Staring into the lens of the nearest camera, I strengthened my hypnotism and felt my energy being drained. It was like having a million leeches all over my body sucking out my blood until eventually only a husk would remain.

"As your guardian, this is what I decree: you will destroy all nuclear devices and dispose of them in a way that will not harm the planet. You will not create any more weapons that could cause widespread destruction. You will no longer war with each other and will instead find peaceful solutions to end your conflicts." Each order that I gave sapped me of more energy.

"You will no longer rape or murder each other, or cause each other physical or mental harm. You will no longer strip your planet of its minerals and will conserve what is left of your forests. Find alternative power sources that will not cause environmental harm and create humane breeding farms for any species that are endangered."

My energy was nearly depleted, but I had a few more commands left. "Your planet is already overpopulated. Restrict the number of children that each couple can have until the population in each country is sustainable. No one is to starve or go homeless ever again. Create jobs for the underprivileged and care for the needy. Everyone is to be considered as equals from now on, no matter their colour, race or ethnicity. Be kind and tolerant to each other."

The next command was to a select few rather than the entire population, but this was the best way to ensure that

Fate's will would be done. "Any alien technology, weapons, robots, equipment, bodies, blood, flesh or any other tissue samples that were collected during and after the Viltaran invasion is to be destroyed immediately. No more experiments are to be performed on vampire or alien blood, DNA or nanobots." That should prevent another outbreak of undead monsters from rising ever again.

I had one final thing to say and then I would be done. Fate itself spoke through me, stripping the last of my strength to make her point. "If you and the generations to follow do not adhere to these instructions, humanity, and your entire planet, will perish."

Drained to the point of collapse, I signalled to the crew that I was done. Chip cut the signal that he was beaming out and normal TV, internet and radio programs recommenced. All around the world, humans snapped out of their daze. They returned to whatever they'd been doing before I'd hijacked their minds and had commanded them to reach for their communication devices. None would remember my instructions, but all would be compelled to obey me.

When I looked for my friends, I saw that Luc hadn't abandoned me after all. Standing in the doorway, his expression was a combination of pride and sorrow. He was proud that I had stepped up to do what Fate had deemed to be necessary. He also knew what it had cost me. I reached for him and he strode to my side and knelt beside me. Trembling all over, I was so drained and hollow that I felt like a puff of wind could blow me away. "I love you, Lucentio Ferrenzi," I whispered.

A profound sense of loss emanated from my one true love as he sensed that the end was near. "I love you, Ladybug."

I tried to smile at the endearment, but it took far too much effort. Luc picked up my hand and bent to kiss my knuckles, but my flesh broke apart before his lips could brush my skin. He lifted panicked eyes to mine and my trembling grew worse. My molecules had a mind of their own and I couldn't control them anymore.

I began to break down and knew that I wouldn't be able to repair myself this time. Fate had used up every scrap of my energy and there was none left inside me now. She'd asked me if I would give my very soul to save everyone. I was pretty sure she was about to claim it, and my body as well.

"I can't hold togeth-" I fell apart before I could finish the word and darkness rose up to greet me with welcoming arms.

Chapter Thirty-Six

Death wasn't as bad as I thought it would be. I floated in a calm nothingness without dreams or thought. Then I realized I was thinking and grew puzzled. I'd expected to either end up in the fiery depths of hell, or to fade away and feel nothing at all.

Instead of hell or nothingness, a thick liquid was sloshing in my ears. It seemed to have seeped into my very pores and had infiltrated every orifice of the body that I shouldn't have, since I was supposed to be dead.

"I told you it would work!" a young male voice crowed in triumph.

"She's been in there forever," another young male responded. "Is she ever going to wake up?"

"She needs to feed," an older male said. "Her body is pitifully wasted. She strongly resembles my master after two hundred years of self-imposed starvation."

Opening my eyes, I was surrounded by a dark red substance. Lifting my arm, I saw a withered stick instead of a normal healthy limb. I caught a whiff of cinnamon, but it was faint beneath the sweet, coppery substance that I floated in.

"Once Natalie regains consciousness, she will feed and then she will be restored," a very familiar male voice said. Just hearing it made warmth spread through my cold body.

Luc, I thought and touched the mind of the man that I loved above all others. I felt his overwhelming love for me and it all came crashing back. I remembered who I was and what I'd done. I'd been told by Fate itself that I had to give up my life to save humanity and vampirekind. *Why am I still alive then?*

A female voice responded deep within my mind. *The sacrifice has been offered and accepted, Natalie. It was not your life or your soul that was needed. I merely required your willingness to give your entire self. You became what humanity needed, the solution to the problem that they could not admit to.*

You have accomplished the purpose that you were created for, she went on. *You and your kind will ever be the guardians of the human race. If you continue to keep them safe from harm, you will be suitably rewarded.* By that, I was pretty sure she was talking about my kin remaining safe and happy.

Stunned that I wasn't going to die after all, I tasted the liquid that I was submerged in. I wasn't surprised at all to discover that it was fresh blood. I gulped down the unusually cool liquid until I was all but sloshing with it. Like magic, my body filled out and became young and flawless once more. The energy that had been sucked out of me from my bamboozlement of the entire human race had just been completely replenished.

Seven relieved faces surrounded me when I sat up. Only a few inches of blood were left in the bottom of the tub.

Ice cubes floated in the remaining liquid. For any normal vampire, the cold would have been too much to endure. Naturally, it didn't bother me at all.

"Are you ok, Nat?" Geordie asked me with worry written all over his young face.

"I'm a bit sticky, but other than that I feel fine."

Letting out a relieved cry, the teen pulled me out of the tub and into his arms. In days gone by, he would have ground his pelvis into mine, or tried to grab my butt. Now that he had a love of his own, he ignored my nakedness and contented himself with a hug. "We were so worried about you!" he sobbed and his narrow shoulders shook with the force of his relief.

Luc was serene on the surface, but his emotions broiled within. Our eyes met over Geordie's shoulder. "You fell apart in my arms and I thought that you were lost to me," he said. "Geordie refused to believe that you could really be dead. He said he could still feel you and he would not allow us to give up hope."

"How could you feel me?" I asked the teen.

Stepping back, he shrugged as Luc handed me a towel. "I don't know. I just knew you were still there. You were just in really, really tiny pieces." He held a finger and a thumb close together to indicate how small I'd been. My molecules must have broken down into even smaller pieces than usual after my energy had been drained.

"How did you get me into the tub if I was invisible?" It took a moment's thought to reduce myself down to particle size, then re-form and wrap the towel around me. The blood was gone and I was clean again.

Ishida fielded that one. "We used a vacuum cleaner to suck up your particles."

"Who came up with that idea?" I asked, already guessing the answer before Igor spoke.

"I did. It seemed like the most efficient way to gather all of your remains." He gave me a slightly sheepish grin and shrugged apologetically.

"It was a good idea," I said. "Very practical."

He nodded in acknowledgement of his nature.

One person amongst them might have the answer that I sought, so I turned to Gregor. "Do you have any theories about how Geordie knew that I was still alive?"

"Of course," he replied with a smile. "I believe you are inextricably linked to Geordie. You possessed him on more than one occasion, which forged a bond between you."

I'd become psychically linked to Cristov, one of the vampires who had been exiled from Earth with us, after hypnotizing him. It made sense that possessing Geordie would also have resulted in us being connected.

"Then Higgins and Wesley barged into the studio," Geordie added. "They sensed you were in some kind of danger and they also said they could still feel you." Being my servants, it made even more sense that they knew whether I was still alive or not.

"Was it your idea to put me in the blood bath?"

The teen nodded shyly. "I thought it might be able to revive you."

"We went through a lot of blood," Igor said. "The nearby hospitals were starting to run dangerously low on their supplies."

"How long was I floating in there?" I asked.

"Three weeks," Luc said and strove not to sound as bleak as he felt. "We kept the tub cold, but we had to replenish the blood every few days."

That explains the ice cubes, I thought.

"Your body slowly re-formed and began to regenerate," Kokoro said, "but it was painfully withered. It was our hope that the blood would restore you and, eventually, it did."

"Why did Fate tell you that you would die?" Ishida asked. I heard and sensed his underlying anger that we'd all been duped into thinking that I would perish.

"I think it was a test. She wanted to make sure that I would be willing to do everything necessary to ensure the survival of humanity."

"Why?" Geordie burst out. "Why are the humans so important?"

"This is their planet," I said with a shrug. "We're just their guardians." It galled me to admit it, but it was the plain truth. We'd been engineered to protect them and we needed their blood to survive. If they died, so would we. Even those of us who were supposedly immortal still required blood to function.

The others filed out and I was left alone with Luc. I stepped into his embrace and his love surrounded me. He had been there for me from the start and I now knew that he would be with me for however long we would live. Our ordeal was finally over and there were no more threats to deal with. The humans would remain beneath my spell until either the planet exploded, or time itself ceased to turn.

To test that theory, I sent out my senses and randomly touched on the minds of humans all over the globe. All signs of the urge to murder or to cause any other kind of bodily or mental harm were gone. I sensed no ill intent towards anyone else and pulled back from Luc slightly.

"What is wrong?" he asked.

"Nothing is wrong. Everything is fine," I said with a disbelieving grin. "My hypnotism worked and the humans are already obeying my orders."

"You have saved them and you have also saved us," Luc said. "I never had any doubt that you would succeed."

Delving into his mind, I realized that he was telling me the truth. Out of everyone, he was the only one who'd had absolute faith that I would come through in the end. His only doubt had been that I had done everything that I could to stop the undead invasion. He'd been right. It had taken the deaths of my servants to give me the kick in the butt that I'd needed.

"Now what do we do?" I asked him.

His eyebrow quirked and he glanced down at our bodies suggestively. "I have a few ideas about that," he replied with a small grin.

"I seem to remember you promising to build me a house where we can get naked together without anyone overhearing us," I reminded him.

His expression became serious. "There is one small detail that I would like to take care of before we take that step."

He'd locked his thoughts up too tightly for me to pry them loose and nerves made my stomach try to flutter. "What detail?"

"I want you to become my wife." Even beneath his tight control, I felt his fear that I would deny him the one thing that he wanted from me.

"I'm already your wife, Luc," I told him. "We just haven't formalized it on paper yet."

A sob came from downstairs. "That's so beautiful!" Geordie wailed and Gabrielle murmured to him comfortingly.

Fate had given me many tests and I'd passed them all, proving that she'd chosen correctly when she'd picked me for this job. Now that my trials were over, I willingly accepted the destiny that had been mine right from the start. As Mortis, I was the secret ruler of the world and all who inhabited it. I'd been wrong when I thought I would just be the Queen of the Vampires. Just as the prophet had foreseen, the whole world had unknowingly bowed down before me. Both my blanket of hypnotism and the video had only cemented their destinies.

In my dead unbeating heart, I made a pledge as my one true love leaned down to kiss me. *I am Mortis, protector of the human race and I will bring death to anyone or anything that offers a threat to this planet.*

Fate responded formally, whispering her reply in the deepest level of my subconscious where she'd been dwelling within me all along. *As has been foretold, Mortis has fulfilled the prophecies and has accepted her role as Earth's Guardian. From now until time itself ceases to be, Mortis shall reign forever.*

Printed in Great Britain
by Amazon